Copyright 2013 by Grand Mal Press. All rights reserved. Printed in the United States of America. No part of this book may be used or reproduced in any manner whatsoever without written consent except in the case of brief quotations embodied in critical articles or reviews. For information, address grandmalpress.com

Published by:
Grand Mal Press
Forestdale, MA
www.grandmalpress.com

copyright 2013, Ryan C. Thomas

Library of Congress Cataloging-in-Publication Data
Grand Mal Press/Thomas, Ryan C.

p. cm

Cover art by Grand Mal Press
www..grandmalpress.com

THIRD EDITION

THE SUMMER I DIED

by
Ryan C. Thomas

GRAND MAL
PRESS

For my friends

Acknowledgements

A lot of people helped in the making of this book. I would like to thank Jay and Lisa French for giving me a home and unbelievably comfortable couch to sleep on while I spent all my money on ink and postage; Patrick Errins for his expert knowledge of handcuffs; the focus group of many friends who gave me immeasurable feedback; Brian Keene for being kind enough to take a look at a no-name's manuscript and give advice and encouragement; Cody Goodfellow for being such a kick-ass writer it forces me to improve my game; Stephen Pastore for making sure I know the classics, my family for their continuing support no matter how stupid my ideas are; and of course my wife Tera, who is not just my favorite editor and beta reader, but the woman who teaches me the true meaning of chasing my dreams.

THE SUMMER I DIED

by
Ryan C. Thomas

INTRODUCTION: THE RITES OF SUMMER

Whether or not a writer tries—and perhaps even more if he or she doesn't—your first book is you. Into the first book goes a slice, a sliver, a core-sample of the writer's uncertain soul, of everything that has led the writer to that desk. You write your first book as if you'll never write another, giving the world both barrels, and then step back and wait to see if the world invites you back.

If I wasn't lucky enough to know Ryan C. Thomas, I would still believe that I know this guy better than most who see him every day, because the voice of his first novel—the free and easy storyteller's voice that lures readers in and leaves them helpless and naked when the shit gets real, and the deeper themes so seamlessly tucked into this grueling dark carnival ride—that voice seems like such an honest and apt self-portrait. I see Ryan in there, but readers who have never had the pleasure of meeting the man might think they're looking into a mirror.

Ryan's not a comic book artist like the hero—victim?—of this book, but he is a shit-hot guitarist who fronts a rockabilly party band and has bad-ass tats, and basically comes across like how you might've thought you'd grow up to be, when you were ten. And if you never read his book, you might come away thinking this guy rides a chopped Indian hog, battles mummies before breakfast and sleeps in a pile of hot chicks every night. It's only through his writing that Ryan Thomas can let you see that he doesn't sleep very well, at all.

Thomas's voice has a natural economy and poise to it that many writers spend their entire lives learning how to fake. As we embark with Roger and Tooth on the kind of sweetly aimless summer day that defines nostalgia, he takes the care to show us who they are and how much they love life, even as they're squandering it in dubious shenanigans and grabasstic horseplay. The looming unpleasantness might be sharpening its tools in the wings, but Ryan understands how much of the impact of horror is lost when it's deprived of its cardinal virtue. It comes out of nowhere, exacting irrevocable loss and forcing unacceptable choices. It is not what gets the characters out of bed in the morning, though it's what keeps us turning the pages. The trouble in *The Summer I Died* does not slide hand-in-glove over Roger and Tooth, as in so many bogus horror stories where hapless human sock puppets get date raped by fate. Its sudden and seemingly arbitrary detour into bedlam is a much more disturbing prospect, because it suggests that every idyllic summer scene hides an abattoir.

Layers of bone-deep meaning lurk behind the hot, runny red stuff in this novel, but don't worry about choking on it. Thomas serves the quality chops so drenched in sauce, you'll never know you're swallowing some serious themes. Sure, he could just tell us that American society has sanitized and censored all but the lamest remnants of the initiation rites that draw the line between boys and men, so that we can drift into terminal childhood if we wish, until death makes us instant adults, helpless and doomed. But questions keep us up later than even the most unacceptable answers, and the awful agony Ryan wants to share with you will leave scars like question marks on your brain.

As modern initiation rites go, first novels are tougher than most—somewhere between being left alone in the woods and circumcision by fire ants. But Ryan came through it with his inner boyhood intact, and has revisited it now to find it hardly stings at all. Because he writes like he plays guitar, and he's never stopped looking for the new hooks hidden in the old songs. He builds and drives tension like a screaming dream in broad daylight, and throws in whipsaw moments of staccato shock that'll wring a nervous laugh out of you, before they start to really hurt.

Because he *is* that guy you wanted to be when you were ten.

—Cody Goodfellow
March, 2009
Los Angeles, California

PROLOGUE

To avoid the nightmares of that summer, I take caffeine and diet pills, any type of speed to keep me up for as long as possible. As a result, I haven't slept more than a couple of hours a night in a long time. My eyes have sunken near to the hollows of my skull and I shake with malnourishment because the pills suppress my appetite. My face is bruised and my thighs are dotted with purple welts and half-moon scars from where I have punched and pinched myself to keep myself awake. I am eroding. But this is a far better alternative than the dreams of that summer. That summer of lost innocence, pain, and bloodshed beyond anything you can imagine.

The pills don't, however, prevent my daily questioning and ranting, nor do they stop me from cursing at God. They don't keep me from shaking my fist at the sky and crying with disgust, irreverence, gratitude, confusion, or any other of the myriad emotions I experience each day. Still though, I am unsure whether God played a part in it at all, or whether or not God even exists.

There are times, late at night, when the pills have worn off and I've slipped into a semiconscious state, that I wake myself yelling at the top of my lungs. I find myself back in that summer, only this time I am telling myself to leave the dice at home, or to put the gun to my head and pull the trigger. I wake up and continue to yell, until I am hoarse, until the bloody images dissipate. Then I yell some more. I don't know why I keep yelling once I realize I am at home in the present. Perhaps to feel my own rage and fear, to know I still have emotions.

Perhaps.

People have asked me—therapists, friends, even a biographer—how I felt that summer when I got home from college, before the bloodshed began. I tell them I was happy. They seem to think they can return me to that point. But, trust me, that person—the me from *then*—is dead.

For all intents and purposes, the moment I picked up the gun the first weekend I was back was the moment that started it all. Tooth was excited to have me home from school and I was eager to hang out with him. He had convinced me to go shooting with him . . .

CHAPTER 1

BOOM!
The gun jumped back in my hand like a startled cat. I winced at the shot, a screaming thunderclap that cut off my hearing as if someone had snuck up behind me and shoved cotton balls in my ears. The empty bullet shell bounced off my foot and rolled onto the ground. When I opened my eyes, I saw a puff of smoke breathing out of the tree trunk a few yards away from the trashcan I was aiming at.

Shit, I thought, not even close. If I'd been aiming at Kennedy I would have hit Oswald.

Next to me, Tooth let out a whoop and slammed his palm against my back. "Well wrap my nuts around a pole and call me Mary, looks like you just popped your cherry."

It was the first time I'd ever fired a gun. A .44 magnum to be precise, a big mother of a cannon that Tooth swore would make my dick hard. And he was right. I felt bigger, brighter; hell, I felt invincible. Holding a .44 in your hand, well, it's a bit like being deified.

"You missed the shit outta the can though," Tooth said, taking the gun and aiming at the target. He squared his feet, looked down the barrel, took a breath and squeezed the trigger.

BOOM!

With my ears still clogged, the shot sounded like I was underwater. Tooth's hands, wrapped around the grip, went flying up over his head with the recoil. He burst out laughing.

The metallic bong and firefly sparks that erupted from the metal can proved he was a much better shot than me, but then again, he'd had all winter to practice while I was down at the university.

"Did you see that? Dead on!" he shouted.

I could barely hear him through the humming in my head, but I flipped him off good-naturedly and motioned for the gun back. On the road out past the woods a car drove by. It seemed to slow a bit, like it was trying to spy on us, so I quickly hid the gun behind my leg. Tooth read my concern, shook his head in disappointment and said, "Will you relax? Ain't nobody gonna care about some gunshots out here. Besides, we're too far out to be heard."

That wasn't exactly true. The spot we were at—a dirt clearing in the woods that overlooked a small valley of evergreens—used to be a popular hangout area for teenagers, and most everyone in town knew about it. True, it was set back far enough off the road that passing motorists couldn't really see through all the trees, but no amount of dense foliage would dampen a .44's gunshot from echoing.

We'd been here many times before, whether to get high, drink beer or just shoot the shit on a Friday night. Used to be you could come here and expect to find at least someone you knew hanging around. But its popularity had waned of late

Two summers ago Mark Trieger, the prodigy running back for Lakewood High, jumped to his death here, and now the place had become associated with ghost stories and bad vibes. Nobody came up here much anymore.

"Yeah, I know," I said. "It's just—"

"Just what?"

"I dunno, people drive by here now . . . they tend to check up on things. I'm just being careful."

"Fucking Mark Trieger."

"Yeah, fucking Mark Trieger."

It happened on a Sunday afternoon after church let out. Some kids had come here to get wasted and accidentally knocked their six pack of Bud over the side of the cliff. Realizing what a bitch it would be to find another adult to buy them more, they climbed down to retrieve it.

At the bottom they discovered the beer bottles shattered from the fall. They were about to go back up when one of the boys spotted something sparkling in the fallen leaves. It was a necklace. Rumor is he was gonna hock it for more beer, so he reached down and yanked on it and up popped a blue and purple head, the mouth wide open and dripping maggots, two glazed eyes looking into oblivion.

The boy fell down screaming, his fist still clenched around the necklace. He tried to run away but because he kept gripping the necklace, the body slid after him like a zombie in a George Romero film and knocked him over. He finally let go, but he was in such shock his friends had to carry him back up.

Turns out Mark'd been down there for about two weeks, nestled among the heaps of beer cans and porno mags people had hurled over the side.

Like any small town in the New England mountains, the body had drawn a crowd as if it was the second coming of Jesus. I remember standing with Tooth when the paramedics hauled Mark up. The police kept everyone back, but you could still kind of see what was going on through the trees. They had this sort of winch thingy bringing up the body, and when it got to the top, the head bounced over the rocks and made this thwacking sound you could hear all the way back on the road. People gasped. Tooth put his Red Sox hat over his heart and said something I didn't hear. He didn't know Mark, but he'd gone to enough Lakewood games to respect him. Personally, I couldn't care less about sports, but I remember my sister Jamie being real upset. She was a freshman at Lakewood at the time, and like all freshman girls, she thought she was gonna marry the football captain someday, despite the fact that about twenty colleges were interested in recruiting Mark before he'd even graduate.

Looking back at the trashcan, I lifted the gun.

"It's easier if you pull the hammer back first." Tooth reached over and made like he was gonna do it for me. Beating him to it, I yanked it back with my thumb and found my target. I wanted to hit it this time, because if I didn't, Tooth would go telling everyone what a bad shot I was and I'd spend the summer the butt of sissy jokes. So I took a breath, and held the gun a little looser than before, a little more relaxed. The first shot had given me some idea of the compensation required in aiming. Since it had gone high and wide to the left, I aimed a little lower and to the right.

"Steady," Tooth whispered, "just relax. Once you feel it, then fire away."

I felt the weight of the gun getting heavier, like when you hold a dumbbell out to the side of your body and see how long you can keep it level. I added a little backbone to it, took another breath, and pulled the trigger.

BOOM!

The bullet careened off the lip of the barrel, sent sparks flying, and struck the branches in the trees beyond. I stood for a moment, realizing that while I'd shot a bit wide, I'd still managed to hit the target. At fifty feet away, that was a glowing accomplishment. My dick was indeed hard. Tooth threw his Red Sox hat in the air and said, "I can't believe it, you actually hit it." He ran toward the barrel. "Not bad, not bad." He poked at the indentation the bullet had made, somewhat tentatively, then turned back and yelled to me, "Hey, you gotta see this!"

I put the gun on the ground because I didn't want Tooth doing anything stupid like jumping on my back and causing it to go off. He liked to jump on people when he was drunk, and he'd downed about four beers already since lunch.

At the can, Tooth pointed out what he found so fascinating. It was a bee.

"It musta been sitting on the lip and you winged it."

The bee was still alive, but its abdomen was now fused to the barrel where the bullet struck. It was trying to crawl away but all it could manage was a feeble circular pattern.

"That's the weirdest thing I ever seen," he said. "Look at it, it's like it don't even know it's been shot." Then he got a funny look on his face and hit me in the shoulder. "You shot a bee and didn't even kill it. You fucking pussy. Man, wait till I tell everyone."

Great, that was all I needed, Tooth spreading stories. Don't get me wrong, I loved Tooth. We'd been friends since kindergarten, when he stole my cookies and I socked him in the eye—the only time I'd ever beat him in a fight, and even then I probably would have gotten a good ass-kicking had the teachers not pulled us apart and made us apologize. Then they made us play together; I guess they fancied themselves diplomats. Anyway, the next week we figured out that by working together, we could distract the teacher long enough to steal the good toys away from the other kids during playtime. You might be thinking I was the brains and he was the brawn, but actually it was the other way around. Don't get me wrong, he was definitely stronger, but he was much better at getting people's attention, and I was adept at being invisible, which made swiping Matchbox cars all the more easy. If they'd only known what they'd created.

Tooth and I had been through everything together, which was weird, because our interests began to split in junior high school. I got hooked on science fiction and became an expert on comic books, and Tooth took an interest in beer. But I guess we realized we'd always stay friends, especially after the two nights we'd spent together in jail when we were sixteen.

See, we thought it would be funny to steal the lawn ornaments off everybody's yards in town. You know, those obnoxious little ceramic gnomes and cardboard sheep that people think add flare and fun to a garden. Well, we must have stolen about a hundred of them, went over to the police station and started placing them all over the little lawn out front. I don't remember how many cops we got in our town, I think five now that Bruce Heater is one, but anyway, usually they're out driving around and only Mrs. Stefanko is in the office answering calls. But we apparently have the worst luck around, because they were having a meeting that night, and after Tooth and I finished putting the last gnome on the hood of one of the cop cars they all came waltzing out the door and caught us red-handed.

The incident made the local paper, complete with photos, and because my parents, who are both teachers at the high school, were in Boston for some teacher conference, I had to wait in the cell till they could come back and get me. Tooth's father, tired of his shenanigans, actually told the officers to keep him locked up till he thought about what he'd done. So we spent two entire days as cell-mates. It was the first time in a while that we'd really talked, not just got drunk together.

It was the first time I realized that Tooth was smarter than he let on, that his poor grades didn't mean he was dumb. He was just interested in other things besides fractions and social studies. He said he was gonna learn how to build motorcycles, that he was gonna build one and take Route 66 out to California like in a book he read. Which also surprised me, because I didn't know Tooth read. He was always making fun of me for picking up the latest Frank Miller or Todd McFarlane comic. I guess we just had different tastes in reading, but I felt maybe I had never given him credit beyond the growing alcoholic most people took him for.

He was still laughing at the bee. I punched him back. "Fuck off! I'd like to see you shoot a bee off the lip of a trash can."

"I bet I could."

"Yeah, right. It's your turn. Go back and hit it."

He gave me a shove and sprinted back to where I left the gun. Like some Hollywood detective, he rolled on the ground and came up with the gun in his hand. Standing next to the barrel, I yelled, "Wait a sec!" And threw my arms up and dove to the side. When I heard the report I nearly wet myself, went weak-kneed expecting my guts to explode out of my back. Thankfully, I heard the bong as the bullet struck its target and not me.

"Youmotherfucker!" I yelled. "Don't mess around! It's a gun!"

He just kept laughing like a toddler all hopped up on sugar. He went and picked up his hat, which had flipped away during his stunt, and put it on his head backwards. He aimed the gun again and said, "Move. I got one shot left."

I jumped up and ran out to the tree line. This time when he fired, I plugged my ears. Again, he hit the barrel. I had to hand it to him, he had good aim, a regular Billy the Kid. Together, we walked over to check on the bee. Tooth's two shots had struck about a foot below it each time. The bee was still buzzing, still fused to the trashcan.

"Yeah, all right," he said. "So I can't hit it. But it's not like you aimed for it. You hit it by accident and that still makes you a pussy."

"Bite me," I said, bending down to look at the bee.

"I'm hungry. Let's get outta here and get some fuel. Lucy Graves works over at the Wendy's now, and they got these tight uniforms, and I swear her nipples are so big you can hang your hat on 'em."

"What about the bee?"

"What do you mean 'what about the bee'?" he asked, as if I'd spoken in Martian.

"We gotta kill it. I read once they can send out distress signals to other bees. It's like a chemical scent they emit or something. Next time we come back there might be a whole swarm waiting for us."

"God, you are such a geek. Just kill it."

"With what?"

And out of nowhere, Tooth's boot flashed by my face and smashed the bee into nonexistence. Maybe I was imagining it, but I swear a bit of bee goo hit me in the nose. Disgusted, I wiped it off with my arm. "Thanks."

"What?" he said. "Better it dies quick than just stays there suffering in agony till it does. C'mon."

CHAPTER 2

When we were done eating and gawking at Lucy's huge tits, which I had to admit were as plump and firm as water balloons, we drove over to my place to catch a John Carpenter film that was scheduled to play on television later that night. Tooth insisted we pick up more beer before the movie because the food was sobering him up and he swore movies were more fun to watch when you're drunk. I doubted the movie had anything to do with it; beer for Tooth was like water for fish.

"Hand me that license in the glove compartment," he told me.

I pulled it out and read it over. "David McNulty, nineteen-seventy-one. What's that make you, thirty-two? Yeah, right. Where'd you get this? You make it?"

"Boston," he said, whipping it from my hand and stuffing it in his pocket.

We were both only twenty, but Tooth looked about thirty with his two-day-old stubble and weathered face. I guess that came from working at the Dataview warehouse where he spent his days loading electrical circuit boards onto trucks. Winter lasts thirteen months in New England; I guess you couldn't blame him for liking the booze.

As we headed to the packy store—as was customary to call it around here—the setting summer sun felt just the opposite, like a hot pair of jeans fresh from the drier. And with the humidity tapering off—which is usually so damn high you feel like you're being boiled alive all day long—I felt comfortable enough to take a nap.

The smell of pine trees baking in the residual heat and dried-up grass swirled into the car as we sped by. It was a good smell, reminding me of the times Tooth and I played war in my backyard as kids. Our little G.I. Joe figures storming over a sand hill to battle the forces of Cobra. The two of us lying in the dry grass, making machine gun sounds with our mouths.

It smelled like childhood.

We were carded at the entrance to the store by some kid with blue hair who certainly wasn't old enough to buy anything inside, probably the owner's son. That was a blessing, because the dumb shit fell for the fake ID. But the clerk behind the counter was eyeballing us from the minute we walked in, put down the magazine he was reading and leaned over the counter to watch us. Ah shit, I thought, and I knew we were toast; the bastard was just waiting to catch us.

I made like I was looking for a bag of chips and drifted down an aisle. Tooth grabbed a twelve pack of Bud and dropped it on the counter with an air of authority, playing grownup as best he could.

"Lemme see that ID," the clerk said right away.

I knew we were busted at this point.

Tooth handed it over, not saying anything. I spotted a comic book rack and started spinning it around but all it had was kiddie shit, X-men crap that wasn't written by anyone who actually knew anything about the X-men.

"Son, you better get your money back," the clerk said, tossing it back to Tooth. "I seen better fake ID's cut out the back of cereal boxes. Tell you this, too. Some kid came in the other day with the same kind. I know where you get 'em, down in Boston, buy 'em on the corner from the crackheads. Shit, you must think I'm dense."

"Actually, I think you're a chode, but that's besides the point. This ain't no fake ID, and if you don't believe me, call the police and they can verify my information."

The clerk picked up the license a second time and held it up to the fluorescent lights overhead, laughing. Tooth gave me a quick glance and pointed at me. Oh shit, I knew what that meant: he wanted me to pinch the beer. Goddamn son of a bitch, how did he expect me to get a twelve pack under my shirt? Just walk out and say

I was pregnant or something? On top of which, those nights in jail had been a wake-up call for me, and I hadn't done anything illegal to put me back there since. Well, aside from smoking some pot and drinking some beer. But shoplifting was another story. I could lose my student loans if I went to jail.

"Ok, I'm calling the cops because I've had enough of this fake ID bullshit. It's a waste of my time."

"Why, what else you got to do?" Tooth said smartly. "Hang out in the back and beat your meat to porno mags? I noticed some are missing from the stand. You're all outta the gay ones. They in the back room where you eat your lunch? Little bit of PB and J and a side of man meat?"

That poor clerk, old as he was, didn't really know how to answer that. He just started shaking a little, really pissed, like he was going to pull out that gun you know he had under the counter and blow Tooth's head off.

"Get out now or I *will* call the cops!"

"Go ahead, but I ain't leaving till I get my beer. You stupid fuck!"

Taking the bait, the clerk mumbled something and picked up the phone behind the counter. I knew there was no way I was gonna get all the beer out the door without being seen, so I moused over to a bin full of $3.99 nips. I took six and stuffed them in my socks and pulled my pant legs over them, the whole time thinking how this would look to my college advisors should I get caught.

The boy at the door was preoccupied with the scene Tooth was making, probably wondering if this was a holdup or something, so I figured I hadn't been seen.

I went back to the comic books and selected a cheesy looking *Batman* comic with Killer Croc on the cover. It looked like it had been written for six year olds. I went and put it on the counter.

You know you've got a remarkable relationship with someone when you can read each other's minds. We did that a lot, Tooth and I. Like, I would ask, "Hey, you remember that movie with the guy?" and he would answer, "Yeah, *Bloodfist 4*." And he was right. We just always knew what each other was thinking. And even if we didn't know right away, it didn't take more than one clue for either of us to catch on.

So when I put the comic on the counter, Tooth knew I had the goods and swiped his ID out of the clerk's hand and said, "You know what, fuck this. We're going to the packy on Deerfield. No sale for you, buddy."

The clerk was as red as a horny monkey's ass. "Can I buy this?" I asked him, pointing to the comic.

He leaned over and yelled, "No! Now get out!"

"C'mon," Tooth said, giving the man his customary one-fingered salute.

The poor clerk was so upset he mangled his threat as we left. "If you ever come back I'll fuck you good."

"See, you are gay," Tooth yelled back.

On the way out I picked up a bag of chips and tossed it to the door boy. It confused the hell out of him, but it also kept his eyes off my socks, which were bulging like I had elephantiasis of the ankles.

In the car Tooth slammed his head back against the headrest a few times before turning the ignition on.

"What dumbass prick went to Boston and got an ID from the same place as me. If I find him I'll kick his father's ass. What did you get anyway?"

I pulled the nips out from my socks as we drove out of the parking lot. "Just these. Two cherry flavored vodkas, two orange liqueurs, and two mint schnapps."

"Perfect, and what did you get for yourself?"

CHAPTER 3

I suppose since you've followed my story this far, I should tell you why Tooth is called Tooth. It also figures into why we were headed to my house instead of his.

When Tooth was ten, his father ran him over with his car. He didn't do it on purpose, but it wasn't exactly an accident either. See, Tooth's dad has a drinking problem. I guess that's no biggie these days; who doesn't know somebody who drinks a lot? And I guess you can make a comparison between my friend and his father, but where Tooth is what I prefer to call a functioning alcoholic—or at least he's on his way to being—-his father is a straight up drunk.

He's not a bad man, not in any way. In fact he was once a minister, back when Tooth was a toddler; probably where he first took to drinking if you ask me. He's quite the caring man when he's sober, but the last time he was sober, well, let's just say that was back when you had to get your ass up out of the recliner and turn the knob on the TV to change channels.

Tooth was in the driveway playing with some action figures, Star Wars or He-Man and whatnot, and his father got the idea he had to go to see his father—which would be Tooth's grandfather—who'd been dead over a decade. Well, you know where this is going. Drunk to the point of seeing ghosts, his father got in the car and backed down the driveway, taking Tooth under the car with him. Tooth rolled all the way underneath, missing the wheels by some divine intervention, and popped out the front where he went rolling into the bushes. When he sat up screaming bloody murder, he was missing six of his front teeth.

His mother burst through the front door like one of them snakes popping out of a novelty can, all arms flailing and hair licking about like it was made of flames, screaming incoherently and running so fast she nearly tripped. She grabbed up her little boy and rushed him away to the end of the earth—which would be Jersey. Two weeks later, she came back and got a divorce, and Tooth got his nickname because ever since then he had to wear a bridge.

And what I never understood after that was why Tooth asked to live with his father. My guess is, his father being a drunk and all, Tooth could pretty much do whatever he wanted.

Anyway, things became sort of like an after school special. You had your usual child welfare services, and AA meetings, and Tooth's parents trying to get back together and not succeeding, and you can figure the rest out.

Going to my house was just simpler than dealing with his dad, who was always trying to get us to go to church when he was drunk, even if it was three in the morning on a Wednesday. The man obviously regretted his decision to leave the ministry and take the blue-collar route, as if in the end he'd let God down. Maybe that accounted for a lot, maybe it didn't.

I told Tooth to park his beat up Camaro in the driveway. My parents were gone for the weekend to Providence, visiting my grandmother who'd been complaining of back pains. She was always scared she had the latest disease she saw on CNN, even if it was only in pumpkins or something.

Unfortunately, them being out of town didn't mean I had run of the house. Jamie was there too, and since I'd been away at college all semester, she saw fit to assume the role of homeowner. In the few days I'd been home already, she said that things had changed since I'd been away and since I didn't know how they were doing things now, I could just leave if I preferred. The only thing that had changed as far as I saw was that she'd moved into my old room and torn down my limited edition Daredevil and Gambit posters. While part of me debated shaving her hair off while she slept for ruining perfectly good collectables, the rational side of me decided it wasn't worth the fight, I'd be gone in another two months when the fall semester started.

When we came in, she was sitting on the living room couch with a bag of rice cakes, watching some stupid chick flick with sappy music and some guy talking about feelings. I wasted no time picking up the remote and changing the channel.

"Put it back, asshole," she said.

"Why don't you go up to my room and watch TV? You know this is the only one I can watch now. Tooth and I are gonna watch a movie."

"Well, in case you didn't notice, Geekmaster, I was in the middle of one."

"Yeah, I've seen it. The girl gets the guy, and somebody dies, then somebody gets married, and everybody cries and shares their feelings. It's wonderful. Now move."

"Wow, you've watched a movie that had actual adult themes and not grown men in tights rubbing their codpieces together. 'Oh, Boy Wonder, is that your gun or are you happy to see me?'"

"Robin doesn't carry a gun, Einstein."

"Who the fuck is Robin?"

Tooth, who was amusing himself with our sibling rivalry, went and plopped on the couch next to her. He put his arm around her and stared at her chest. "Hey, Jamie," he said, "ain't seen you in a few months. You're developing nicely."

She hit his hand away and stood up. "Fuck off, Mervyn. Touch me again and I'll knock out the rest of your teeth."

Mervyn. That was Tooth's real name, and also the reason he preferred to be called Tooth. He said "Mervyn" sounded too much like a verb. Jamie stormed out of the room and stomped up the stairs muttering, "Stupid geeks," under her breath.

"Nice move, Tooth."

"I figured that'd work. But I wasn't lying either. Your sis is looking fine."

Truth was my sister was very attractive, and it was starting to make me nervous. She had her driver's permit now, and I couldn't help feeling, well, almost paternal. When she took the car out to the movies the day after I got home, it was like some giant spider had dropped down from nowhere and spun me up in a web of concern. I wanted to fight it, because I couldn't stand my sister most of the time, but I also couldn't shake the feeling. I didn't need to dissect it; it came from knowing what a teenage boy thinks about—Fucking. One day you're walking down the school corridor thinking about the new *Gen 13/X-Force* crossover, the next you look up and see Lucy Graves' tits. And from that moment on, every thing you see, whether it's a chalk eraser or a folding chair, it all looks like Lucy. And you want to fuck it.

I hated to admit it, but I cared about Jamie, and I didn't want someone like Tooth—who was pretty much representative of the entire male population of our small town—getting close to her. She was all fire and spunk now, but I remember what I was like as a teenager, thinking I knew everything and nobody could teach me shit I didn't already know. Then I got to college and, well, you grow up real quick in college, learn what it means to be alone and irresponsible. You see things you only dream about—orgies, drugs, social upheaval, rape. It makes you think. It makes you realize how dumb you were in high school, and how unaware today's high schoolers are. Yeah, Jamie was all fired up, but only because she hadn't seen the downpour of the real world.

"Man, I'm hungry again." Tooth looked at me with that look that said if I didn't do his bidding he was going to keep bugging me till I did. I hated that look. "That dude at the packy got me all worked up. Feel like I could eat the world. You got any Doritos or anything?"

I went into the kitchen and found some chips and dip and we munched for a while.

CHAPTER 4

The movie we watched that night was *The Thing*, John Carpenter's classic horror film about a mutating alien that attacks an Arctic research station. With the exception of *Big Trouble In Little China*, I consider it the last good film Kurt Russell ever made. The original version, *The Thing From Another World*, directed by Christian Nyby and starring James Arness as the alien, still holds up by many standards, but does not compare to Carpenter's generous use of effects—but I'm kind of a movie elitist so take that as you will. We'd both seen it a bunch of times, but it was still as good as the first time we saw it.

Tooth asked me the same question he always asked, at the part when one of the research team is sitting in the snow looking nice and normal, with the exception of having an alien arm, and is clearly not human. Circled around him, his friends struggle with whether or not he's still their friend. "Would you kill me if it was me and you weren't sure?"

"Yup."

"Good thing, because you'd be the first one I capture. Make you toss salad in an alien prison."

We laughed.

Jamie came down once to get something out of the refrigerator and looked at us as if she were trying to shoot liquid shit from her eyes onto our heads. She was dressed in boxer shorts and a wifebeater. Tooth must have popped a rod as she passed by because he shifted around and covered his groin with his shirt like he was embarrassed. It kind of made me uncomfortable, him looking at my sister that way. I couldn't fault him for being human, I just hoped it wouldn't come to something unpleasant.

When the movie ended, it was nearly midnight. Tooth got up and said, "I gotta piss. Why don't you order some pizza or something?" And drifted into the small bathroom that ran off the kitchen. He'd finished all his liquor and let out a grunt as he released the floodgates. He pissed so long I expected to be swimming in it soon.

"Hey, Roger?" he yelled through the closed door. "Got a question for ya. If you're an American outside the bathroom—fuck, hold on, I just pissed on myself—if you're an American outside the bathroom, what are you inside the bathroom?"

"European," I answered, having heard the joke months ago.

"Shit, how'd you know that? You suck."

Never let it be said that universities are not hubs of information . . . or at least disinformation.

"Are you gonna go home or do you want to crash here?" I asked.

Tooth returned and fell on the couch, lethargic from the chips and nips.

"Where's the pizza?"

"Pizza? I thought you said anal cavity search. Hang on, I gotta call and cancel your appointment at Jim's House of Lube."

"Hey, have you declared a major yet?" he said, blazing a dialogue trail of his own. "You taking those art classes where you draw naked chicks?"

"Not yet. I'm mostly taking business courses."

"Why are those models always so fat, anyway?"

"Fills up the paper."

"Hey, don't knock big girls. They know how to get wild in bed. Ain't nothing like a monster booty to make your nuts do the mambo."

"It's called standards, look it up."

"Why are you taking business classes? You ain't gonna be no business man, you know it and I know it."

"I don't know. I told my dad I wanted to be an artist and he said I need to take business classes because art isn't a profitable profession."

"Obviously he hasn't seen a life-size rendition of a large naked woman. I'd buy one. Hell, I'd buy two, call 'em Lulu and Buffy, show 'em what it means to be abstract art."

"You get any more worked up you're gonna spunk in your shorts." I laughed.

"Don't worry, I'll use the chip bowl. Anyway, it's not like you want to become one those snooty art dudes that hang out at Java Lava dissecting paintings that are nothing but big blue splotches, going, 'The existential ramifications of this piece are subordinate at best. The artist refuses to acknowledge spatial dimensions and opts for subconscious palettes instead. Amazing, I love it, I'm going to go screw myself with a wine bottle.'"

That got me rolling. Sometimes Tooth was a funny guy, and the truth was the people at Java Lava sounded a lot like that, which was why we avoided it like it was a chick movie.

"No, probably comics. You know, *Spawn*, *Gen 13*, that stuff."

"Yeah, I remember you used to draw those comics of me in school. They were pretty good, especially the ones where I'd bang the female villain after I fought her."

"I never drew that."

"I know. Dick lover."

"Why don't you apply to city college or something? Get out of that hell you call a job. Then you can transfer to the university with me."

"City college my ass."

"You did graduate, and they do take pretty much anyone."

"Fuck, they'll take an inbred hamster with a flatulence problem, so what's that got to say about me. No way, school can blow me. Barely made it through high school as it was. Probably wouldn't have even done that without you. Besides, what do you get when you graduate from college? A thirty-thousand-dollar I-O-U note that promises to get you into the most elite social clubs in the world but in fact gets you Jack, Shit, and their cousin Fuckall."

"I guess."

"You guess nothing; you know I'm right. Why don't you drop out and move to California with me?"

"You still talking about that California crap?"

"Hell, yeah, California is where it's at. Sunny all year round, beaches littered with models in bikinis, weed growing out of the cracks in the pavement. And I'm talking about the good kind of weed, not dandelions. C'mon, it'll be great. We can rent a place on the beach, get drunk, fuck girls. You still like girls, right?"

"Hey, Tooth?"

"Yeah."

I gave him what I hoped was a serious look, one that conveyed friendship but wasn't to be taken as a joke either. "Not my sister, okay."

"Whoa there, buddy. You didn't think I meant anything by what I said about Jamie, did you? Christ, she's still that annoying pipsqueak I used to want to kick outta your room all the time. Coming in and hiding our shit and taking my keys. I screw her I might as well be screwing my own sister."

"Which you would do if you had one."

"No, I wouldn't."

"Yes, you would."

"Would there be beer involved?"

"More than likely," I said.

"Then you're probably right."

"Listen, Tooth—"

"No, seriously, about Jamie, I'm kidding. Relax, I didn't know it was gonna ruffle your panties."

Tooth had definitely meant what he said about Jamie, I'd known him long enough to know his thought process. But we were square now, he knew the deal, and him acting like this was his way of shrugging the whole thing off. As for me, after hearing myself worry about Jamie, I contemplated an exorcism.

Tooth spread out on the couch and kicked me with his feet, answering my earlier question about him staying. I moved to the recliner as he put his Red Sox hat over his eyes. He never took that damn thing off, even when he slept. He'd had it since he was twelve, when his mom gave it to him as a birthday gift. Came in the mail with a card that said "Happy Birthday" and nothing else.

He said, "You know what, Roger?"

"You're gay?"

"No, I'm being serious. Maybe I'm just drunk, maybe I'm lonely, or maybe I'm in a nostalgic mood, but I miss you. When you're not here, I don't do shit but get drunk with Tony and Derek from the warehouse, but they're married so it ain't much fun. And video games get real old when you play by yourself. So, yeah, I'm glad you're back for a bit. It's gonna be a good summer."

I've got to tell you, that kind of moved me. He was drunk, sure, but it sounded genuine and it made me feel, I don't know, wanted. As I watched him fall asleep on the couch, I kind of felt bad for him. His life had been screwed up for so long, and yet he'd pulled through okay. A drunk, religious zealot of a father, a mother who barely kept in touch, and enough alcohol to sterilize a Scottish commode. It was amazing he wasn't lying in the same heap of discarded garbage where they'd found Mark Trieger, bloated and blue from a leap off the edge of life.

"A good summer," he repeated.

Before I could respond, he was snoring.

I went upstairs and plopped down in my parents' bed. What is it about lying in your parents' bed that always makes you feel like you're intruding? Perhaps because at some age it's made clear to us that we have our own room, and there are no monsters in the closet, and crying isn't going to change anything so just go back to bed. When I was little I'd jumped in bed with them after having nightmares. It became an epidemic for a while, and my father didn't really know how to handle it. In typical male fashion he picked fights with my mom over it. Of course, I had no one to blame but myself since I would continually sneak downstairs and watch whatever monster movie was on the late show. Doesn't make a whole lot of sense in retrospect, kind of like an acrophobe choosing to live in the penthouse apartment.

I remember one time I overheard my dad arguing with my mom about it in the kitchen. I was sitting on the nearby stairs unbeknownst to them.

"I don't want him watching that shit anymore. He sleeps with his light on all night," my dad said.

"He thinks there are monsters in his room."

"I don't care. It's got to stop."

"It's normal for boys to start having bad dreams at his age. Their imagination is running wild."

"Bullshit! It's those movies, and if it doesn't stop soon I'm taking him to a shrink."

A moment later, my father rounded the corner and found me sitting there, and he knew I'd been listening. It was awkward. That was the first time I realized what shame felt like. It felt like having your insides cut up and your heart squeezed till it didn't want to beat anymore. My father just gave me this funny look, a look I would later recognize whenever I had a birthday or on Christmas. It was a mixture of love and pity.

Crying, I said, "I'm sorry, Dad. I try not to be afraid, but I get scared."

He didn't say anything, just looked at his feet for a minute and then went upstairs without a word.

The following night, as I went up to bed, Jamie crying in her room, my dad passed me on the stairs. He put a hand on my shoulder and said, "Hey, sport, you going to bed?

"Yes."

"Sit down here for a second, I want to talk to you. You know, you're getting kind of old now. What are you, eight?"

"And a half."

"Geez, you're gonna be eye-level with me in no time. But listen, this, um, this whole deal with sleeping with the lights on and coming into our room—"

"I'm sorry, I don't mean—"

"No, listen" —he put his arm around me— "I'm not mad. I mean, I think it's time we formulate a plan. We've got to get rid of these monsters once and for all. Don't you agree?"

"How?"

"Well, did you know that werewolves, and mummies, and even snakemen, they all have weaknesses that can kill them quick as you can say, 'Back to the grave with ye!'"

"Yeah, but you need silver bullets and garlic and stuff."

"Not if you know all the other ways to kill them, the secret ways. Did you know if you keep a rose petal under your pillow it'll keep vampires away?"

"Really?" I asked, stunned that my father had this knowledge. "How do you know?"

"Oh, I read it somewhere."

"Where?"

"You'll find out soon enough. But just you remember, us humans are stronger than the monsters, and once a person knows how to defeat them, knows these tricks, they can't ever hurt us again, even if we're sleeping. Do you want to learn these secrets?"

I nodded.

"Think you can handle it? I mean, eight-and-a-half is old and all, but maybe we should wait until—"

"No, no, I want to know."

"Okay, I can tell you've got the fight in you. Runs in our family that fight, that will to survive. Comes from my Grandma. I wish she were still around to see you. She'd recognize that fight in you, too."

"I've got it, Dad, I know it. Teach me the secrets."

"Okay, okay, you go on up and get some shut-eye. Everything you need to know is up there waiting for you. I love you."

Somewhat puzzled, I told my dad I loved him and went on up. When I got to my room I found a comic book lying on my bed. *Monster Slayer*, number one.

CHAPTER 5

I woke to the sound of sparring insults, pots clanging, and something sizzling in a pan downstairs in the kitchen. The smell of coffee was like an uppercut to my brain, thick as mud even with the covers over my head. There was some laughter, then an angry harrumph, then what sounded like a plastic cup bouncing on the tiled floor.

"Don't you have a home?" I heard Jamie say.

"Yeah, but I ran away because I didn't want to be king anymore," came Tooth's reply. "Too many responsibilities. I beg of you, poor farmer, let me live with you and understand the people."

"Roger! Come get your loser friend away from me!"

Ah shit, didn't she ever shut up? Throwing back the covers, I forced myself out of bed and looked out the window, attempting to stretch but not finding the strength. The windowpane was warm already, promising another humid day.

Throwing on a robe, I shuffled down the stairs as if none of the bones inside me were actually connected to anything, and slumped into one of the chairs at the table. My vertebrae cracked like someone walking on dry twigs. Tooth was eating some eggs with little pieces of something purple in it and I didn't want to know what it was. Actually, yes, I did.

"What the hell is that?" I asked, poking at it with my fingers.

"Fruit Roll Up. I found it in the pantry."

"You're kidding, right?"

"Nope, I can't eat eggs unless they have something in them. It's like eating a hamburger without any ketchup, which you don't have any of by the way."

"I found him down here rooting through our food like a shit-covered rat," Jamie said as she sat down with her bacon and eggs. "There's fucking Fruit Roll Up goo all over the pan and I am not cleaning it."

"I take back what I said about you developing." Tooth sneered with purple teeth. "You're still as annoying as ever."

Jamie flung a piece of egg at him. "Shut up, scavenger."

I left them to bicker and trade more insults, which was plainly enjoyable for both of them. Scraping some purple goo out of the pan, I cracked a couple eggs open and poured myself a glass of milk while they cooked. There was a small basket on the counter near the refrigerator, filled with little bits of this and that, the kind of stuff that should go in the junk drawer but somehow managed to make a deal with the warden for better accommodations. I rummaged around in it while the eggs sizzled in the purple bacon grease, which spat and popped onto the burners. A key from some unknown lock, a pin from St. Patrick's Day, a couple nails, some paperclips, rubber bands, a Formula 409 magnet that had come with a free sample in the mail. I decided on a pair of dice my folks had bought on their trip to Vegas last year. They were red with white dots and said SNAKE EYES CASINO on them over the ones.

They had gone on that vacation alone, the first time without Jamie and me. Jamie had relished it because she was in that stage where parents are worse than homework. But me, I sort of missed the family vacations we'd had. The fighting, Dad's manic need to make good time, Jamie and me dividing the backseat with an imaginary line. Instead, I'd had to stay home and watch Jamie, who'd spent the week at her friend's house, no doubt fawning over magazines with some Hollywood pretty boys on them.

I tossed the dice up against where the counter met the wall and wagered on how long I could stand these two squabbling before I lost my temper. Finally, Jamie stood up and dropped her dishes in the sink, noisily.

"Mom said I can have the other car while they're gone so you're shit out of luck."

"Fine with me," I said, happy to be getting rid of her. "But I thought you had to have an adult in the car when you go driving."

"I will. Tracey's cousin is twenty-three and he's coming with us to the mall."

"What mall? Only mall near here is down in Manchester and that's over an hour away."

"Yeah, and if you tell Mom, I'll tell her about the time I caught you and Mervyn trying on her underwear."

I smiled. She was trying to play hardball but she wasn't very good at it. Fact was, despite my run-in with the law, my parents trusted me more than they trusted her. Stealing lawn ornaments was one thing, but getting caught smoking dope in the attic with your friend was another. And she was, naturally, the offender of the second.

"That never happened," I replied, juggling the dice now, "and even if you make up some stupid shit to get me in trouble, it'll never work. Mom doesn't trust you anymore."

"Oh, yeah—"

"Why don't you go pop that huge zit on your nose?" I knew that would piss her off. She had perfect skin, but her crazy teenage vanity turned every tiny bump into Mount Olympus.

"Fuck you," she screamed, and with that, stormed out.

I sat at the table with my eggs and rolled the dice as I ate. Outside, the sun was high and the air coming through the window smelled of cut grass and pine needles and baking dirt. A murder of crows flew from a tree in the woods out back and sat on the power lines over the driveway.

"I want to go shoot my 9mm today," Tooth said.

"Jesus, how many guns do you have?"

"Just two. I would have got them long ago if it wasn't for you always worrying what your mom would say. But you looked pretty happy shooting that .44. Gave you a hard on, didn't it? I told you it would."

I didn't want to let on how much firing the gun had affected me, but it had certainly turned my nuts into giant Epcot Centers of steel. The sense of power was unfathomable; suddenly I was the mightiest thing in existence, all men bowing before me. With the squeeze of a finger I could undo all of God's creations. Truthfully, I couldn't wait to try the 9mm.

I rolled the dice; they came up seven, a lucky number if ever there was one.

"Okay," I said. "But let's go somewhere different. I didn't like being so close to the road at that other spot. And besides, you and I still go there so maybe other people do too and I don't want to shoot some fucking dude traipsing through the woods on his way to down some suds."

"Fair enough."

Just then the phone rang. Tooth leapt up and grabbed it, said, "Starlet Productions, you swallow the cream, we give you the green. Oh, hi, Mrs. Huntington. Yeah, Roger's right here."

I took the phone from Tooth, and waved him away. "Hi, Mom."

"How much green we talking here?" she laughed

My mom was pretty cool, all things considered. "Only thing Tooth has that's green are the skid marks in his panties. How's Grandma?"

"Oh, great. She thinks she has Psittacosis."

"Sounds bad."

"It is, if you're an owl. I don't know where she gets this stuff from."

"She's not an owl, is she?"

"An old bird, yes, but there's nothing wise in that addled brain."

"Be nice. She gives me money for Christmas."

"I'm glad I taught you not to be superficial."

"I'm just kidding. I love the old bird."

"Hey, you can't call her that until you've lived with her for eighteen years."

"Eighteen years with an owl?"

"Well, she can't get her head all the way around yet but I doubt it's for lack of trying. You and Jamie haven't killed each other yet, have you?"

"Why, would that be bad?"

"It would if you got blood stains on my rug. Blood doesn't come out without professional cleaning equipment."

"I'll lay down some tarp."

"Good. But try to do it outside, if you could."

"Agreed."

"Is she up yet? I want to talk to her."

"Yeah," I replied, "I'll get her."

"And, Roger?"

"What, Mom?"

"I love you. Sorry we had to take off so quickly after you got back."

"No sweat. I'll see you in a couple days."

I didn't realize I didn't say I love you back, and I don't think she thought too hard on it—she knew I did—but I regret it now.

I put the phone down and hollered for Jamie to pick it up upstairs, then went to take a shower.

CHAPTER 6

We had to go to Tooth's house, which was on the other side of town, to get the other gun. It was a small yellow house with a couple of bedrooms, a wrap around porch held up by some four-by-fours, and lots of empty, forgotten beer bottles still standing where'd they'd been placed when finished. The crispy yellow front lawn looked like uncooked spaghetti, and a basketball net stood tilted in the dirt driveway like a giant metronome that had stopped to slightly left of center. The net had been ripped long ago but a few remnants of tattered rope hung from it and blew in the slight breeze.

Tooth's father was sitting on the porch with a beer in his hand, reading a magazine about cars or airplanes or something. I couldn't really tell because it was old and faded, like the kind you always see in patches of weeds by abandoned parks. He looked up when we pulled in and wiped the beer can across his forehead in an attempt to cool down.

"Get the gun outta the back," Tooth told me. "We gotta clean it before we put it away."

I grabbed the gun, which was in a black plastic carrying case, and followed Tooth up to the porch. He mumbled an apathetic hello to his father, and disappeared inside. Sometimes I didn't know if they were really family or just roommates. I nodded to the ex-preacher, hoping to pass by without any conversation, but luck was not on my side.

"How you been, Roger?" he asked with the gait of a doped-up turtle.

"I've been good, Mr. Elliott. How are you?"

"Well, can't complain. Other'n the heat it's been quiet. How you doing at school? Merv don't tell me much about what he hears from you."

"School is good," I said, trying to end the conversation quickly. When he didn't say any more, I figured that satisfied him so I headed for the door.

"That's good, got to stay in school. I told that to Merv, but he don't listen. Says he's through with that shit ... his words exactly."

I stopped at this, hoping it was the last bit of afterbirth to come out of his ethanol-soaked mind, but he continued with words that almost made me pray for mercy.

"I've been thinking, Roger."

Shit. In my book, listening to a drunk get philosophical is on par with rolling down a hill in a barrel full of nails. You get dizzy, your insides shriek with stabbing pain, and you end up someplace lower than where you started. I stopped and resolved to excuse myself politely at the first possible opportunity.

He ran his hand through the few remaining hairs on his head. "I ever tell you about the time I saw Jesus in the gymnasium when I was at seminary?"

Oh, Lord, only six hundred and four times. "Yeah, actually you did. You saw him drinking from the water fountain."

"Well, let me tell you again. I know you think I'm just a crazy drunk, but I got methods to my madness. He was getting a drink," he continued, his eyes glazing over as he looked into the past, voice slower than ice trying to melt in Siberia, "and when he bent over and turned on the water, it wasn't water at all that come out, but wine. Took a long swig, He did, and then He turned to me and a tear fell from His eye and landed in the wine. When it struck, little blue bolts of lightning stitched themselves across the purple liquid and formed a cross." He stopped and looked at me to make sure I was still listening, then went back to the past. "I put down my basketball and walked over to ask Him what it meant, but He turned and walked out of the room. I followed Him outside but when I got there, there wasn't anybody in sight except a student I didn't know. 'You see anyone come out here?' I asked. 'No.' I searched high and low and never found Him. By the time I got back the wine was water again, and no evidence of Him having been there remained. Until today, I didn't know what He was trying to tell me."

That you're insane, I wanted to say. Instead, I just smiled and said, "I gotta help Too—I mean Merv."

He looked at me, eyes back from their holiday at the seminary, and took a sip of his beer. "Now wait, I'm getting to my point. I've been sitting out here all morning thinking on that, and I came up with a theory. What if every person has a purpose in life, but not one they can necessarily see or are even aware of. Like me for instance. Sure I drink, I don't deny it. I got my problems—hell, we all got our problems—but suppose that's my purpose, suppose my drinking causes a reaction somewhere else. And suppose that reaction is doing some good. Why else would He have drawn a cross in wine? See, Jesus was born to die on that cross, saved humanity by giving His life on it. That cross was His purpose for being. I think He was telling me my purpose in life was to drink—my cross, if you will, is to drink wine . . . or beer anyway."

He looked down at his beer can, kind of chuckled; this was fucking torture. I could feel time stopping, the hair growing on my legs.

He continued: "I mean, beer, wine, same thing really. I just wish I knew how it was helping."

If ever there was a man trying to justify his vices, Tooth's dad was him. I don't believe in God; I guess because my parents never made me go to church, but I do like to think there are things out there, out beyond space and time, that have a better understanding of life. Not in a religious way; I don't think we should worship them, but it's nice to think we're not alone. And perhaps someday we'll meet up with them, whatever they are, and learn from them. But I sure as shit didn't think Jesus, even if He did exist, would make an appearance just to get a man drinking. First time I heard this story, I figured someone in their bathrobe must have stopped to get a drink from the fountain, saw that it was flowing with rust, and walked away. The blue cross? Who knows? Reflection from overhead lights most likely. I just figured the old man's brain was pickled.

"Could be, Mr. Elliott. But I gotta help Merv."

"Help him with what?"

Tooth's father didn't complain much about what Tooth did, but guns were something else. He might be a drunk, but he was still a good man.

"We're gonna grab some tools and go work on my mom's car," I lied.

He took another swig of his beer and looked out toward the road. "Want me to help?" he asked. "I'm good with cars."

Like the cavalry, Tooth popped his head out the door and said, "Roger, c'mon, before the Second Coming. We got shit to do."

I left Mr. Elliot on the porch with his beer and followed Tooth to his room. It was as messy as it had been the last time I was there. A mattress on the floor covered with a sleeping bag, a small television on an old footlocker with a Playstation beside it. The floor seemed to be made of used clothes so rank with stink they'd fused together like a giant quilt. Several beer bottles sat atop the furniture, reeking of week-old Budweiser. Not to mention it was so hot inside you could spit and it would evaporate before it hit the floor.

In the corner was a dresser with every drawer pulled out so that it looked like poorly-constructed steps. Tooth slid it out from the wall and pulled out another black case like the one we'd just brought in. He opened it up. Inside, a black 9mm lay like a sleeping adder. He took it out and handed it to me.

"Feel how light it is."

I hefted it and aimed it at the wall. It was far lighter than the .44, maybe about two pounds tops, and smaller as well. It fit in my hand like it had been built only for me.

"Make sure you check the chamber before you go pulling the trigger," he told me. "Never too sure when I'm drunk whether I clear it out or not. More than once I found a bullet in there."

I used both hands and cocked it like I'd seen in so many movies, sliding the chamber back and letting it snap forward again.

"It's empty," I told him.

He was smiling at me, like Dr. Frankenstein marveling at his monster. I must have looked hypnotized because he poked me. "Go ahead, pull the trigger, see how little tension there is."

I pulled the trigger with ease and the gun went *click*. A wave of anticipation washed over me and left me feeling a little disturbed. I'd never been a gun freak before and didn't know how to handle this new sense of power the weapon carried. I felt almost guilty for wanting to shoot it, see what type of destruction it could do. There was a wrongness to it all, so I handed it back and watched him put it in the case.

"How much did these cost you?" I asked.

"Got 'em both used, which is why the targeting is slightly off. Four hundred for the 9mm and six hundred for the .44."

"That's a lot of dough. If you're making that kind of money why don't you move out and get an apartment or something?"

He took two small bags out from behind the dresser. The first was a bag of marijuana, which he squeezed and then stuck in his back pocket. The second was small and black, and from it he removed some cleaning materials, including a little wire brush, some oil and a few rags, and began cleaning the .44. "Remember when I said I was gonna go to California?"

"Yeah, you say it all the time."

"No, you remember when we were in jail and I said it?"

I remembered. That was the first time he told me he wanted to get away from everything.

"Well, that was the night I told myself I was really going to do it," he said. "I started putting some money away every week since then. Nickels and dimes at first, then about twenty dollars a week since I got the job at Dataview. I've got myself a nice little stash. Three grand right now, and I still got some bills to pay, and I owe Dad a few months rent, but as soon as I hit five I'm leaving."

"If you hadn't bought the guns you'd have four grand."

"And if I hadn't fixed up that Camaro I could have left long ago, but I'd have had to walk there. These guns, they're a bit of insurance. Besides, it's not like it's a bad thing to know how to shoot straight." He stopped cleaning the gun, took off his hat and wiped the sweat from above his eyes. He looked at me with one of those looks that make people feel uncomfortable, like he was going to tell me how I'd die. "Quit that college shit and come out with me."

"I can't quit college, you know that."

"No, I don't. And yes, you can. You said you want to draw comics. Having a degree isn't going to accomplish that. All it's gonna do is get you nice little cubicle next to someone else's nice little cubicle, where the two of you will swap family photos and talk about how cute your kids' poopie is. You don't need to study economics to get a job drawing Batman. You just need a pencil and paper and the know-how to draw a fucking cape and horns and—*voila!*—you're living your dream."

The sad thing was, he had a point. I wasn't sure why I was going to college, other than it was what you were supposed to do, and my dad would rip my asshole out through my mouth if I quit. Also, I'd been conditioned to believe that a college diploma was like a skeleton key to the world. I was banking on that somewhat.

California would be great. I could see us now, surfing, drinking, just soaking in the sun. Probably be the only two idiots rooting for the Red Sox when they came to town. But, for now, it wasn't in the cards for me. Would Tooth wait? No, he'd go, and he'd move on without me. I could feel it happening already, the slow separation of our lives. We'd survived this first year of college, but we hadn't seen each other much. Adulthood was coming in like a wedge to our friendship. Was this summer our last one together, the final hoorah for the road?

I heard Mr. Elliot come in the house and open the refrigerator, clank beer bottles together, and saw Tooth scrub a little bit harder at the .44's barrel. The fridge door closing was followed by some serious coughs and a loogie being hacked up from so far down it probably had "Made in China" stamped on it.

"Is he all right?" I asked.

"Who knows. I ain't seen him sober in a while but he don't bug me either so.... He says God will take care of him, and then he starts preaching to me about faith and I have to run out of the house. He quit working at the mill a few months ago and filed for workman's comp when a log fell on his leg. You don't need to be Kreskin to know he was drunk and caused the thing to fall on himself."

I couldn't imagine what it must be like to live with his father, watching the man seep down through the floorboards of degradation before your eyes. But that was the life Tooth chose and, thus far, he hadn't seemed to mind it let alone try to fix the problem. I guess some problems were too big to fix and you just hoped they would take care of themselves. I felt uncomfortable for having brought it up so I changed the subject. "Batman doesn't have horns, he has ears."

"What?"

"Batman has ears, not horns. You said I had to know how to draw horns."

"God, you're a geek sometimes. C'mon, this is clean enough. Grab the 9mm and let's go."

Tooth put the case with the .44 in it back behind the dresser, slid the dresser back in place, then went into the kitchen and grabbed some beers. We walked out of the stifling house into equally stifling afternoon dust. A cloud of gnats trying to fly through the screen door turned their attention to our eyes and mouths and Tooth swatted them with his cap. Mr. Elliot was back sitting in his place on the porch. As we walked by, I kept my head down, pretending to be wrapped up in my sneakers so he wouldn't talk to me.

"Got to have a purpose in life," he said as I opened the car door. I was still pretending to be interested in my feet when Tooth started the car and we sped away.

CHAPTER 7

The Camaro rumbled down the road like a metallic fart with a purpose. Heat wave rose off the baking blacktop as I searched for a radio station worth listening to. In the part of the county we were in, I knew we wouldn't get much but country music—which explained all the goth kids and wannabe punks who infested the shops along main street, just begging for an alternative. Only way we'd get any good radio would be to head north toward Canada or a few hours south toward Boston.

I kept flipping stations, hoping something would come up I could hum along to, but the best I could find was some song about a man whose woman left him and took the dog when she did. I looked at the CD player and sighed. If it weren't for online CD distributors I'd have gone Charlie Manson a long time ago. But we couldn't use CDs in the Camaro because Tooth had fucked up the player trying to fix it.

I finally just turned it off and stuck my hand out the window instead, let it catch the wind and swim up and down like a dolphin. We took a lesser-traveled back route that ran under the trees and offered sporadic shade. Crooked limbs criss-crossed overhead like giant arthritic fingers. The blazing sun stabbed through them here and there creating a kind of flicker effect as we drove.

"Where to?" Tooth asked.

"I don't know. Let's go up toward Bobcat and see what we find. Should be pretty secluded and we can shoot all we want."

He reached into his pocket and brought out the bag of weed

and tossed it in my lap.

"I bought you a coming home present. Roll a nice fatty for us."

Shaking the bag in front of my eyes, I thought, fuck yeah, this is the shit that makes coming home worth it. I opened the bag and took a whiff and holy Christ was it bad. "This stinks like a hobo's asshole. Is it even good?"

"Probably not, but it's weed, ain't it? Who cares what it smells like long as it gets us fucked up, right?"

I took a bud out and crunched it up in my lap. The wind whipped some of it up and stuck it to my Silver Surfer T-shirt. The papers were in the bag as well and I took one out and rolled it as best I could despite the wind. It looked rather pathetic when I finished, but I agreed with Tooth's philosophy.

"How's that?" I asked, holding it up like a prize catfish.

"Looks like a piece of bird shit, but it'll do."

Bobcat Mountain was farther north than we liked to travel, about an hour and fifteen minutes, but it was as desolate as volunteer day at the old folks home. A few years ago there was an attempt to turn it into a ski resort, but a bunch of tree-hugging hippies rallied against it, arguing it would drive the mountain's animals out of their natural habitat and into people's bedrooms. I hate hippies.

I lit the joint and sucked in the rancid-smelling weed, then passed it to Tooth, who took a big toke. I hadn't smoked pot in over a month because I was afraid it would affect my finals. I got okay grades, but they weren't going to get me into Harvard Law or anything. The drug wasted no time climbing into the recesses of my mind and convincing my brain cells they could run the place with minimal staff. I slumped back in the seat and watched my dolphin-hand dive for food. When I got bored with that I took the dice out of my pocket and we played an imaginative game of craps.

"What odds you give me I roll a seven?" I asked, shaking the dice in my hand.

"I bet you an ass-kicking."

"For you or for me?"

"For your mother, who do you think? Just roll 'em so I can get started. I been waiting to give you a good ass kicking for a while now."

I rolled them on the floor and they came up seven. Scooping them up, I showed Tooth. He blew smoke in my face and punched me in the arm like a prize pugilist and I almost went through the door.

"Ow! Youfuckingbitchthathurt!"

He erupted in laughter and flicked the spent roach out the window. I rubbed my arm and felt it bubble up. My fist already balled, I went to hit him back, but he caught me with another blow in the other bicep. My arms went flaccid and hung down like a basset hound's ears.

"Sonofabitch!" I yelled.

Tooth was high and just kept laughing. I was pissed at him, but pot giggles are a pox that spreads fast, and soon we were both cackling like a couple of idiots.

"That weed tastes like shit," he said.

"I told you."

"I think I know a good spot around the backside of the mountain. It has some trails that were supposed to be ski paths. They go up into a nice clearing on the side; you can see out over the whole forest."

"We should have packed a lunch," I said, suddenly aware that our inevitable hunger would have to wait a considerable amount of time to be satiated. The nearest town from Bobcat Mountain was Bobtail, so named because it was at the back end of the mountain, and it was a good half hour away.

I put the dice back in my pocket. We drove in silence for a bit until we arrived, then sat a bit longer until we convinced ourselves to make the hike. Tooth took the 9mm out of the case, tucked it in his waistband and pulled his shirt over it.

"What are you doing that for?"

"Park police patrol here sometimes. They see some strange case they might get nosy and ask me to open it up. This way, I just tell 'em I got a gargantuan cock."

Unlike most mountains in New Hampshire, this one didn't have a little man in a booth asking for parking money, so we just drove up a dirt road that dead-ended about two hundred feet up, and parked off to the side. We took the six pack Tooth had grabbed from his house and started trudging up the nearest trail like two dwarves high on ore fumes. Tooth even whistled, the gap in his bridge making him sound like a hot teakettle. It wasn't long before mosquitoes and gnats considered us fine dining. At one point, in the shadows of the trees, the bugs got so bad that I put my head in my shirt and jogged a bit. Through the fabric I could smell pine sap bubbling out of the surrounding tree trunks. The firecracker snapping of twigs behind me told me Tooth had followed my lead.

We came out into a clearing about a third of the way up the mountain. The sun was out in full force and I could feel it working its claws into my face. Tooth was smart to wear a hat; unfortunately, my head was small and I looked kind of ridiculous in them. Looking out you could see for a distance, though there wasn't much to see but trees, the road we'd arrived on winding through them, and summer haze.

"Motherfucker those mosquitoes are hungry," Tooth said, swatting at a few brave ones that followed us into the open air.

He stared at the mountains in the distance and narrowed his eyes. "You see that?" he asked.

"What?"

"That. That interesting thing over there." He pointed out at the mountains and I tried to follow his trajectory. I squinted but all I saw was trees.

"I don't see anything interesting," I told him.

"Neither do I. I have to get out of this place. And soon."

He was "California dreaming" again and I'd walked right into it. I'd kind of figured by now that Tooth's summer mission was to get me to move to the west coast with him, and since I had no intention of going, it was going be a long summer. He popped the tab on one of the beers and handed it to me, took another himself and chugged it down in one gulp. When he was done he looked me in the eye and I could see he wanted to say something. I figured he was going to ask me to move again, but instead he punched me in the arm again and yelled, "Let's shoot something, you pantywaist!"

Any pain that had dissipated from my arm was now back in full force. I'd have returned the punch but quickly realized the futility of it. Tooth always got this way when he drank; I was used to it. Hitting him back would only encourage him and fuel his energy.

He walked to the tree line, put the empty beer can on a low tree limb and backed up to where I stood. "Bet you an ass kicking I make this shot," he said. Aiming the gun, he squared his feet and fired.

Bang!

The report wasn't nearly as loud as the .44 had been, and the recoil was mild at best. The beer can flipped up in the air like a gold medal gymnast and landed on its side a little ways in the woods. He looked at me and smiled. I flinched.

"Here," he said, handing me the gun. "I'll have to owe you that ass-kicking. I hurt my hand last time I hit you. You're a bony little fucker."

I hefted the gun while he went and put the can back on the limb. When he was walking back he pretended to dodge bullets. And that was the first moment in my life I scared myself, because I felt how easy it would be to shoot someone in the head, dump the body in the woods, and walk away scot-free. The simplicity of it shook me.

Or maybe I'd just read too many comics and seen too many movies where the only time someone had a gun was when they were blowing another person's head off. Because, somehow, despite knowing the feeling was wrong, it felt like that's what I was supposed to do.

I handed the gun back to Tooth.

"I can't shoot. My arm hurts from when you punched me," I said.

"You pussy. Suck it up and squeeze the trigger. This gun is so light a baby could shoot it."

Forcefully, he pushed the gun back in my hand, placed his own hand over mine and made me grip it firmly. He didn't back away until I faked an air of confidence, though what I really did was clear my mind of any thoughts that would land me in the loony bin. Across the field, the beer can reflected the sun so it appeared a train was coming out of the woods. I relaxed my grip, sighted down the barrel, and pulled the trigger.

Bang!

The noise was more like a firecracker than a cannon, and perhaps because of this I felt less nervous. My shot landed square and sent the can cartwheeling backwards to the ground. Tooth ran over and picked it up and brought it back.

"Damn, you're a natural," he said.

The bullet had gone through dead center, a bit below Tooth's hole. I didn't tell him I had pictured the can as a man's head when I shot, though I doubt he would have given a shit. Then again, maybe I didn't tell him because I didn't want to hear myself admit it.

CHAPTER 8

By midday we'd shot so many holes in the cans they were unusable even as targets. At twenty yards my aim had gotten so I could hit my mark about seventy percent of the time. Tooth's accuracy was much better. Even drunk he could shoot the ass hairs off a gnat. After we'd grown bored, he wobbled around picking up the empty shells.

"I can reuse these," he told me.

I wasn't so sure homemade bullets were a good idea, but for all I knew the ones we'd shot hadn't come from a store anyway.

We rolled another joint and sat and looked out over the forest. Not much had changed in the past couple hours, except maybe some clouds had reshaped themselves. Off in the distance, a bleak gray was spreading over the blue sky and I figured by supper time we'd be in for rain.

Tooth passed me the joint and said, "Want to go to O'Conner's tonight?"

I sucked in the stale smoke and coughed, then drummed my fist on my chest, apelike. "I'd just as soon not go back there."

"Yeah, but they're the only ones that don't check IDs."

Getting carded was the least of my worries. The last time we'd ventured into O'Conner's was on Christmas break and I'd ended up with a fat lip and piss-drenched pants and Tooth had ended up with a broken nose. O'Conner's was a local hangout for some bored skinheads who had nothing to do and no one to take it out on, these parts being primarily white. As a result, an unsuspecting soul who happened to remark about a film starring a black man was like a gift from the gods.

No sooner had I mentioned the Wesley Snipe film *Blade* to Tooth than a fist the size of the moon hauled me out of my chair and brought me face to face with a suspender-wearing gorilla with two lightning bolts tattooed on his skull.

"We don't discuss eggplants in here," he breathed. "You want to proliferate the spreading disease that is the black man, you do it somewhere else."

Had I been alone, I would have thanked the man for leaving my neck in one piece and slinked out the door like a frightened mouse. Unfortunately, I was with Tooth, who never passes up an opportunity to land me in jail or a hospital bed. He came around the back of the skinhead and put his arm around the guy like they were best buddies.

"I say we lynch this little fucker," he said.

Naturally, my eyes went wide and I hoped Lightning Bolt Head understood the joke. He gave Tooth a hard stare, as if he might pick him up and use him as a toothpick. The owner of the bar came over, carrying a golf club, and told us to knock it off or he was calling the cops. But like hyenas trapping two lion cubs, the other skinheads gathered around to support their friend—who could have easily taken both Tooth and me with one finger.

"We're just talking movies," Lightning Bolt Head said.

The other patrons in the bar, mostly drunks and a few college students home on break, stopped all conversation and started salivating for blood. Normally, I'd have been just as eager for some violence, but my heart just wasn't in it this time, what with my face likely to be the first target and all.

As the owner walked back to his bar, Tooth gave me his famous glance, the same one he'd shot me in the liquor store, the one that always made my scrotum shrivel, and I suddenly knew I was very likely leaving the bar with missing teeth. It was kindergarten all over again. Tooth was setting up for a distraction and I was going to do something on the sly. But what? There was nothing to swipe from these guys and I sure as hell wasn't going to blindside one of them.

"So what do you say?" Tooth continued. "Let's take this liberal trash out back and show him what it means to live in the white man's world. Maybe we can get points on our community service, eh?"

"I know you," Lightning Bolt Head said. "You're that guy who got run over by his daddy. What do they call you, Mouth or something?"

"Tooth."

"Yeah, Tooth, nice name. Well, listen here, Tooth, why don't you fuck off before I stamp my name on your forehead."

He raised his other fist and proudly displayed a three-fingered silver ring that was more brass knuckles than jewelry. Beveled in reverse were the words BRODY WAS HERE. I almost laughed. Almost.

"Nice ring," Tooth replied, "I got one, too. It says 'Once you go black you never go back.' Put it right where I had that epiphany. Want to see it?" He pretended to unzip his fly, and it was at this moment I realized Tooth had stepped over the line of safety. We were in for it now. As the skins stood in stunned silence, waiting to see if Tooth had a cock ring on, I slowly put my foot against the back of Lightning Bolt Head's knee—and prayed.

"That's it," the skinhead yelled as he adjusted the ring on his hand for optimal stamping, "we're all going outside."

Tooth snapped his arm back, fist balled into a battering ram, and I shoved my foot forward. Lightning Bolt Head stumbled as his leg gave out, and in that instant Tooth hit him square in the face. The force of the blow slammed his head back into mine and split my lip. A flash of white erupted under my eyelids and I felt myself falling. Then everything kind of exploded, as if a pack of wolves had been released into a hen house. Fists came from every direction, combat boots flashed at eye level. Yelling and screaming and bottles breaking. Grunts and gouts of blood spitting through the air. Taking advantage of my new position on the ground, I began crawling toward the door over shards of green and brown bottle. I was inches away from salvation when a dozen hands reached down and yanked me up and I knew, without a doubt, that I was a dead man. I pissed myself.

The next thing I saw was a golf club slicing the air and bodies flying this way and that. *Whoosh!* I ducked a swing that would have made a hole-in-one in my cheek and came up to find Tooth in front of me. His face was awash in blood and his bridge had been punched out.

"Let's get the fuck outta here!" I yelled.

"Holdth on, I woft my tees."

We bent down as skinheads careened around us, bleeding and moaning. Cheers went up from the other patrons, whose expectations had been generously fulfilled. I found his bridge under a barstool, covered in a glob of ichor that reminded me of a stewed tomato. I thrust it in his hand and nearly wretched as he shoved it in his mouth. He yanked me up and we bolted out the front door and sped away.

And that was how my last trip to O'Conner's had ended.

As I looked at the encroaching grayness crawling toward us over the mountains, I passed the joint back to Tooth and thought, no, I'm not particularly interested in going to O'Conner's tonight. I told this to Tooth.

"You're afraid those skinhead jerkoffs will be there," he said. "Man, when are you gonna get a backbone?"

"I have a backbone, and it's straight and in one piece. I kind of like it that way."

"You kind of make me sick sometimes."

I wasn't expecting that. But then again, he was drunk and he was unpredictable when drunk. I didn't take his bait though; if he wanted to give me shit about not wanting to fight he could work it into the conversation on his own.

Man, he was pissing me off.

"You never take any chances," he continued. "How long are you gonna stay in this hick town, doing nothing but reading comic books? When was the last time you got laid?"

"I get laid."

"No, you don't. Shit, you must pull your dick as often as I take a drink."

"I'd have my dick in my hand right now if that were the case."

"Christ, don't you feel suffocated here?"

"The university isn't like that, there's opportunity, cool people. You'd know that if you came to visit."

"There's no point. All college girls want to do is talk about how they're going to be lawyers and doctors. None of them want to rape me like a bitch in heat, like the Internet says."

"It's not like that. Mostly they're all hippies, listen to reggae music, hang out and let their leg hair grow. And they're so sheltered, like they all grew up in communes. These girls came in my dorm room one night while I was watching *Evil Dead* and they asked what it was. Can you believe that? They'd never seen *Evil Dead*. I just laughed."

"You elitist jackass. You should have fucked them."

"Who said I didn't?" I replied, annoyed at his lack of faith in me. Though the truth was they had walked into my room by mistake and asked the one question and left. I didn't know too many girls, at least ones I could relate to. There was one girl living in a room down the hall who was very cute, small nose, short brown hair, had a picture of Ewen MacGregor on her door in his Obi Wan Kenobi costume. I liked her, and we'd talked briefly, but I learned she had a boyfriend and not a very nice one at that. She left soon after anyway. Tooth was right—I pulled my dick a lot.

"Fuck, I need to get laid," he said. "It's been over two weeks."

"Who did you get with?" I asked.

He took another pull on the joint and handed it to me. His eyes were red and clouded, and I doubted he could drive anymore, which meant I had better start sobering up or we'd be camping in the mountains like a couple of cro-mags.

"Michelle Murphy."

"Bullshit," I yelled. I handed the joint back to him and blew smoke in his face. Michelle Murphy had been every boy's dream back in high school, the kind of girl you would have given all your paper route money for, the kind of girl you jerked off to on a nightly basis. She was also the kind that made a big deal about her faith and her virginity, which made her all the more desirable.

"Yup. I was at O'Conner's and she came in with some dude. I hadn't seen her since high school so I asked what she'd been up to. I don't remember what she said but her breath could have sterilized the bottom of my shoe. That girl can drink. She starts rubbing on me and telling me she always thought I was a cool guy, which is horseshit, but I didn't care. Anyway, she grabs my dick and says to follow her home. I said, 'Who's this yahoo?' pointing to the guy she was with. She said, 'Boston, meet New Hampshire.' Then she leaned in real close, put her lips on my ear and said, 'He was round one, you're round two.' So I went home with her and damn, that little girl is all grown up I tell you. I thought it was a little weird how the guy sat in the corner and watched, but hey, it didn't affect my performance none."

I pitched a rock into the abyss of trees and stood up. "You're a fucking liar," I said. "I'm starving, let's go to Bobtail and grab a burger."

"I'm not lying."

"Yeah, right."

"You think what you want, all I know is the devil's gonna high five me when we meet. Aw, fuck it, a burger sounds good."

We walked back down the path, which was now so thick with mosquitoes it was like walking through a stinging fog. Tooth put the gun back in the car.

And that was when we heard the scream.

CHAPTER 9

It was a woman. It was desperate. And it came from all around. We stopped moving and scanned the treetops like a couple of dogs sniffing out a trashcan. It sounded as if it came from everywhere at once, and even shifting our focus about we still couldn't place the location. Then it stopped, the echo died away and all was silent again. Tentatively, the cicadas took up their buzzing once more; the ancient tree limbs went back to creaking like haunted house doors. A few mosquitoes tried to nest in my ear and I batted them away.

"Okay then," Tooth said, and started to get in the car.

The scream came again, its urgency plain as day, and I knew somebody was hurt or at least needed some big time assistance. The hairs on my forearms stood on end, something that hadn't happened to me in a while.

"What the fuck is that?" Tooth asked. A sudden fear wrinkled into his brow.

"I don't know," I replied, my heart beginning to race. "Sounds like it's coming from over there but I can't be sure. Wait, did you hear that?"

But before he could answer, the scream came again, and this time there was an unmistakable plea for help. But it was all run together so it sounded like "helpmepleasehelpme!" Then it stopped and we stood still, not knowing what to do, Tooth with his hand on the car door, me looking into the woods, my stoned brain replaying scenes from slasher films. The forest was on mute, every creature silent in the face of the unknown.

"Sounds like she's hurt," Tooth said.

"Probably hiking through the forest and fell or something," I offered, "whoever she is. You don't think there are any bears or anything in there?"

"Wolves maybe, but I don't think they're brave enough to attack a person."

"What if she's trapped under a rock or something?"

"I suppose they'd attack her if that were the case."

"That's not what I meant. I mean maybe she needs help. Maybe her leg's broken or something."

Tooth's mocking stare told me how dumb my last statement was so I shut up. He cocked his head to listen for any further noises but there were none. He shuffled his foot in the dirt and took out his keys, jingled them in his hand like he was using them to think. He put them back in his pocket and looked at me but I already knew what he was going to say.

"Let's go look."

Son of a bitch. I should have walked away, should have taken the keys and driven us right out of there. But I didn't. Instead, here we were, in the middle of frigging nowhere, surrounded by nothing but woods, with someone screaming for help, and we were about to go investigate. Every bad horror movie I'd ever seen rushed back to me.

"I don't think that's a good idea. I've seen this movie before," I told Tooth. "We'll walk in there and the psycho with the ax will split my head in half."

"Movies aren't real. She is. We can't just leave her if she needs help."

Tooth was right, what else could we do? It was a half-hour ride to Bobtail, and even farther the other way. By the time we reached anyone who could help, whoever was screaming might be dead.

There was also another reason—aside from playing good Samaritan—that I felt compelled to find this person: simple curiosity. Somebody screaming from the woods could only turn out interesting. Perhaps a camper who'd fallen off a cliff, maybe a hiker who'd twisted their ankle, or maybe even someone fending off a wolf, though I hoped it wasn't the latter.

I was apprehensive and mesmerized all at once. Or to put it another way, I was just stoned.

When I saw Tooth take the gun and reload it I felt a little better.

"C'mon," he said, and started walking into the trees.

I ran around the car and got beside him, followed him like a puppy following its mother. We ducked under some low branches and stopped short a little ways in.

"Which way?" Tooth asked.

"Not sure. Thought it came from over there," I said, pointing off to my left. The woods went on forever. Tooth broke some branches blocking our way and began blazing a trail in the direction I'd suggested. We went another hundred feet before Tooth stopped abruptly and I walked right into him. He turned around, gun pointing directly at my belly.

"I must be high," he said, and stormed past me back the way we'd come. Utterly confused, I ran after him, snapping twigs and running through a spider web that had me wiping my face like I was on fire. When I emerged from the trees I found Tooth reaching into the car. He pulled out a cell phone.

God, we really were stoned.

He made a face as if he was the village idiot and started dialing. Three numbers could only mean 9-1-1. With the phone to his ear, he waited for a minute then said, "Shit," and started pacing back and forth. The trees crossing over us formed a big tunnel and offered little in the way of clear reception so Tooth walked all the way down to the main road. I watched him shrink into a dot, spinning around in an effort to connect to a satellite. Ironically, I prayed someone would drive by and see him holding the gun and report it, if not stop and ask if we needed help.

While he spun and swore, I leaned against the car, wondering if our mystery woman was okay, who she was and would she be hot and, please God, naked.

After a few three-sixties, Tooth came back up and slammed his palm on the trunk. "There's no reception here," he said.

I was about to suggest driving a little ways down the road and trying the phone there when she screamed again and I nearly jumped out of my pants. Just three little words but they scared the living shit out of me: "Oh, God, no!"

Then there was nothing.

"She's in trouble," Tooth said, running back toward the tree line. I stood where I was, paralyzed, as if my body and brain were at odds. Tooth looked back at me and yelled, "Don't wuss out on me. Move!"

I sprinted forward and crashed through the trees with him, smashing my knee on a low limb and grabbing his shoulder for support. We dodged more limbs and stumbled over boulders as we pushed further into the woods. The sun began to fade away to shadow the further we went, and the moist underbelly of the forest gave rise to slithering insects and small rodents that dashed out of our way in a frenzy. In front of me, Tooth used the gun to hack through some thick foliage. I took a look around me and realized I wasn't sure which way led back to the car anymore, since we'd been twisting and skirting around so many obstacles. A few minutes later, we emerged into a little clearing where a couple small trees had been knocked over, probably by a storm. Up to my left I could see the mountain clearing we'd been up on earlier when we'd shot the beer cans.

"Why don't we go back up there and look out and see if we see anything?" I said.

"We already looked out all afternoon."

"Not really, just shot the shit over the scenery."

"We won't be able to see through the tree canopy."

"But we can't see two feet in front of us now."

He seemed to consider this but I could tell he wanted to keep going the way we were headed. Reluctantly, he said, "Okay. Maybe I can get reception up there."

We trekked over to where the mountain began to slope upward and climbed up by grabbing tree limbs and hauling ourselves forward, almost like doing chin-ups. Probably it would have been easier to go around the base of the slope and find a path but I didn't think of it until we were a ways up. The mosquitoes came back in full force, and since we couldn't cover our faces they attacked like hungry vampires. They bit through my shirt and into my neck, my cheek, my elbows, all over. I made an attempt to swat at them at one point and nearly fell down the mountain.

Tooth was first to reach the lip and get on top. He covered his face with his shirt, put the gun in his waistband, and pulled me up.

From there it was about twenty feet to the clearing. I stepped over one of the beer cans we'd murdered earlier and recognized my own work. Tooth started dialing but again got no service. "Motherfucker!" he yelled. "See, this is why we need to move. Nothing here works."

I walked back to the edge we'd just come up from and looked out over the valley. I couldn't see anything but treetops—a vast sea of green. Tooth had been right and I felt like sitting down and giving up. The whole Mighty Mouse routine was a bad idea from the start. I don't know what we thought we were going to accomplish tramping through a mountain stoned out of our gourd. Hell, Tooth looked high enough to see God. We were going about this all wrong. I started to say this to Tooth but when I turned around he was gone.

I found him on the other side of the clearing, looking toward the direction of Bobtail. He was squinting. "You see that?" he asked.

"I'm not going to California," I said.

"No, dipshit, over there. You see that rock cliff?"

In the distance, across a small valley of pines, was a sheer rock face.

"Yeah."

"Okay, now see that?" He pointed off to his left, toward Bobtail. I followed his finger and squinted, clueless as to what he wanted me to see. Then the trees swayed and I saw what he was looking at. I was stunned. It was sort of the way you feel when you find Waldo in one of those cartoons. Once you see him you can't believe you didn't notice him earlier. What I mean was, there was a house. I could see it through the treetops as they blew side to side, could make out its log cabin walls and a beat up blue pickup truck parked on the side. There was also something moving under the canopy near the house, but I couldn't tell what it was. Shadowy and large, it swam beneath the trees. A bear, I wondered.

As if in answer, we heard a dog bark. Only it didn't come from the house, it came from the rock wall.

"It's bouncing off the cliff," Tooth said. "That's why we're having a hard time pinpointing it. It's echoing off everything."

"Jesus," was all I could reply. Then, "What the hell is a house doing in the mountains? Aren't there zoning laws and shit?"

"Probably it's further toward the road than we think. Look, the road goes around the mountain toward the house. With a long enough driveway, that would put the house back toward the edge of the woods but not necessarily in them. We're not really that far in ourselves."

"Okay, so if that's where the woman is she must have a phone."

"Maybe you were right, maybe something fell on her. Maybe she was working on her truck and the jack broke."

"She'd be nothing but mush by now."

"Well, we can't leave her if she's still alive."

"Yes, we can. Tooth, I don't feel good about this. Nobody even knows we're out here."

"Chill out, Wolverine. When we get there the first thing we'll do is call the cops from her phone."

"But what if she's dead by then?"

"Then call Japan and ask for sucky fucky. They like that."

I looked at the house and listened to the barking coming at me from the other direction. There was a pang of shame in my gut because I knew I was being a wimp about the whole situation. I was like a squirrel who couldn't decide whether or not to cross the road when traffic was coming, while Tooth was already on the other side safe and sound. I must have looked worried because he pulled up his shirt and showed me the gun.

"Besides, we've got a little backup of our own," he said. As I spun around to go back down the mountain trail, he grabbed my shirt and added, "Let's go down over here. It'll be faster than having to walk back around."

"We should get the car."

"It'll be there when we get back."

"But what if we need it to get help, to rush her to the hospital or something."

"We'll take her truck. C'mon."

"But what if it broke when the jack broke?"

"What if I punch you in the boys for being a pussy? Look, it's gonna take us twice as long to go down and get the car and then drive around than if we just run down right here."

Shit. He was right.

We started climbing down the mountain again, breaking limbs

and sending rocks rolling down the slope. Going down a mountain is always harder than going up because your body naturally leans forward. That coupled with gravity makes downhill hiking a bitch. The damn dog wasn't helping my nerves either, and when a moment later I heard the first rumble of thunder in the distance, I knew this was going to be a stressful night.

If I'd only known what was going to happen next I would have taken the gun from Tooth and put bullets in both our brains.

CHAPTER 10

Pushing through the woods was harder than I'd expected. The branches interwove like latticework and we couldn't break them all with our hands, so we circled wide and came back around. As we neared the house, the overgrowth gave way to rotting logs stacked here and there. Some of them were split into cubes and small triangles, possibly leftover firewood. Then again, maybe not, because after the logs we had to scale a makeshift fence created from old tree limbs. Log cabin, split rail fence—maybe she was a lumberjack? I'd seen female lumberjacks before; they gave logging demonstrations at summer camps. They also scared the shit out of your average womanizer.

The damn dog was still barking and I started to think we'd get bit before we could even find our damsel in distress.

On the other side of the fence, we could see the back of the house clearly through the remaining trees. It was a small two-story deal, with cream curtains in the windows, and dead flowers in the window boxes. Between us and the house was a small back yard with a broken swing set, some car parts, and a big gas tank of some sort. The ground was all dug up like some big dog had been burying things, which reminded me . . .

I grabbed Tooth before he left the cover of the trees. "Watch out for Cujo."

He put a finger to his lips to shush me and followed the woods around to the left, where the driveway came up beside the house. We were keeping just within the tree line.

Treading softly, I followed under the noise of the barking dogs, which were still out of sight. Seconds later, the barking stopped and I heard panting heading our way. I froze, praying Tooth had heard it as well. He did. We both stood like statues as two big rottweilers the size of bulls came trotting around from the front yard. They stopped next to a door set in a little windowless alcove that jutted out from the side of the house. From the look of it, it probably went down to a storage cellar under the house.

Man, those two dogs were beasts; they wouldn't break a sweat taking down a wolf. Together they could probably make a rug out of a bear. They pawed at the door, whimpering, while we maintained our best tree impersonations.

"Ten bucks says those are cellar stairs and she fell down them," Tooth whispered.

"How the fuck do we get past those dogs? If we move at all now, we're dead."

"I don't know. They look pretty concerned. Maybe they're nice. Rottweilers are pretty nice animals, you know."

"We're in the middle of fucking nowhere. They're not nice. They're protection."

Slowly, he began to slide the gun out of his waistband. Was he going to shoot them? I may not have been a member of PETA but I didn't see the sense in killing animals that were only doing their job. He said, "Just in case," and moved toward the yard.

As we tiptoed through the trees, we heard a voice coming from behind the door. It was muffled but it was still as hysterical as when we'd first heard it. Sure enough, it was our woman and she was still alive. I was studying the dogs, trying to figure a way to distract them, when I got this sudden rush that something wasn't right. I couldn't place it at first; it just made me nervous, like my spider sense was tingling. Then it hit me: the paw prints. The dogs had left bright red paw prints all over the door. Was it . . . was it blood? Tooth had seen it, too, and glanced back at me over his shoulder like he was going to say something, but before he could utter a word, everything went to hell.

Two bodies exploded out of the door, running full speed directly toward us.

One was a woman, bound, gagged, covered in blood. The other

was a thin shirtless man waving a hand ax in one fist and a saw in the other. My stomach lurched and I went rigid. I couldn't move. My brain sort of refused to accept what it was seeing. Up was down, black was white.

Instantly, both the woman and the man saw Tooth and me, and both went wide-eyed. The woman kept screaming, kept racing our way. The man went ape shit, his face twisting into furious determination.

The gag on the woman's mouth slid to the side and she wailed with all the energy of someone whose last attempt to live depended on it. It was deafening.

She was almost to the edge of the yard, maybe ten feet from where we stood, when the man swung the ax down on her, wedged it into her skull with a loud crunch. Blood spit out like a fountain. Her body went into spasms but she kept running, bolting into the trees beside us.

There was a loud bang.

The gunshot shook me out of my trance and I pissed myself, screamed, and ran into the woods. I didn't know where Tooth was, or who or what he'd shot at, and I didn't care. I was pure adrenaline. I ducked low limbs and hopped boulders and ran right into the makeshift fence, which I'd forgotten about. I jumped up and grabbed the top of it when something plowed into me like a battering ram.

It was the woman.

Together, we fell to the ground, and I landed on top of her. She was out of her mind, mouth wide open, blood spurting from the ax in her head. Her eyes spun about like a robot's with broken servos. She wailed, I screamed, she grabbed for me—I lost it. This wasn't happening. I jumped off her. Screaming like a lunatic, I went for the fence again.

Out of nowhere, one of the rottweilers clamped down on my leg and sank his fangs into my flesh, piercing my shinbone. I screamed for God to save me, to pull me from this blizzard of mayhem. I saw the trees go whizzing by my face, felt flesh tearing off my leg, saw the woman flip-flopping on the ground like a fish out of water, felt my head smack against the fence, saw the dog's fangs snap near my throat, saw more trees whiz by, the dog again, the woman.

A searing fire raced up my leg.

The dog was thrashing me like a rag doll.

I punched it as hard as I could in the face. I punched it again and again until I heard something crack. With a yelp it let go and dashed back toward the house. I reached down to my leg and ran my hand through the wetness running out of it, struggling to see anything through my own blinding tears. It didn't matter; there was no way in hell I was going to look at it until I was safely away. If I saw my bones sticking out I'd have to stop to throw up.

Thump thump went the woman on the ground. I stood up, scared so fucking senseless I couldn't make a noise, white-hot pain blazing in my calf muscle. I wiped the tears away and looked around so fast I could barely make out anything. I kept expecting a hand saw to slice across my throat at any moment. Back toward the house, I spotted Tooth and the shirtless man swinging at each other, rolling on the ground. Next to them one of the rottweilers lay on the brown grass as still as a statue, a river of red running out of its neck.

Like a jack in the box, the woman sprang upright in front of me and I fell down screaming nothingness. She had one hand on the ax and was trying to pull it out of her skull but it was stuck fast. I had this crazy image of her lifting herself off the ground with it, like in a cartoon. Her hair was coated in blood and little white bits that were either bone or brain. I kicked her in the stomach, sent her tumbling to the ground away from me. I never realized how fast I could run when I was scared to death, but I leapt up and scaled the fence so quick I doubt my hands even touched it.

When I landed on the other side, my leg gave out and pitched me to the ground. Back from the yard, I heard a sickening thwack, followed by a grunt, and I knew Tooth had gone down for the count. I peered through the split logs that formed the fence and saw him on the ground, rolling ever so slightly. He put a hand to his head and moaned. The skinny guy was holding the gun, triumphantly, and I could tell he'd just beat Tooth with it. I lay still, watching, not believing this was happening. The man went and picked up his hand saw and gave Tooth a once over.

I didn't know what to do. I was lame, scared shitless, and I was about to watch my best friend get hacked to pieces by some sick fuck. And worst of all, I knew if I made a noise I'd be next. There was nothing I could do. I wanted to scream, to run, to take that saw and cut that fucker's head off and slice him into tiny bits. I wanted to kill him, his family, his dogs, everything in this world that was even remotely related to him. Instead, I closed my eyes.

I would not watch my friend get hacked up. That would not be the last image I had of Tooth. And yet, I had to know. Swallowing my fear, I opened my eyes and looked again.

The skinny man didn't shoot Tooth. Instead, he kicked him in the gut and once more in the head until Tooth went still. Then he kicked him again just to be sure. Satisfied with his work, he bent over the dog that was lying on the ground nearby and put a hand on its head.

"Motherfucker," he said, looking back at Tooth, "I'll kill you so slowly it'll feel like an eternity. Shoot my dog. You fucking piece of shit." He kicked Tooth again, whose unresponsive body took the blow with a dull thud.

He pulled the clip out of the gun, and seeing it still had bullets, slid it back in and started walking into the trees, straight toward me. I lay down as flat as I could, pushed some leaves over my legs and in front of my face. I had on dark brown shorts and my black Silver Surfer shirt, enough to camouflage me, but certainly not enough to save me. On top of that, I could smell the piss on myself, and it was making me want to puke. I was a dead man and I knew it. As he walked toward me, I didn't see my life flash before my eyes, I didn't think of my parents or the comics I'd never draw. I just thought, please let it be fast, please let me not feel it. Then I started crying some more.

He stopped a few feet from the fence, bent down, and picked up the woman he'd tried to behead. She was still alive, though I doubted she knew her name or what day of the week it was. She reached up to grab the ax and he swatted her hand away.

"No no, my dear," he said with a grin, "if you pull that out you're likely to lose all your brains. You'd probably die pretty quick and we wouldn't want that. We haven't even started having fun with you yet."

I don't know if she understood his words or not, but she frantically reached for the ax again, got hold of it and started to yank it out. He grabbed her hand, and in two swift motions, ran the hand saw across her wrist and lopped it off. It fell to the ground with a light thump.

She wailed. All I could do was bury my face against the fence rung. When she stopped, I risked a look back up and could tell she was in another place. Not dead, just far away, farther than she'd been before, somewhere out past Mars. The man picked up the hand and waved it around. "Here, Butch, here boy."

Through the woods, the remaining rottweiler, the one with my blood smeared all over its mouth like clown makeup, trotted over and took the hand from its master. Carrying it in its mouth, it went back to the yard and lay on its belly, put the hand between its two front paws, and began eating it. Vomit raced up my throat but I forced myself to swallow it. Oh, God, please, I pleaded, I don't want to die like this. Please. Please.

Through the fence I saw the man's feet move toward me, slowly, and my heart went wild. Did he see me? Did he know where I was? Would he pass by me and go looking for me? I gave in to tiny convulsions, shaking the leaves off me, my teeth chattering like a rattlesnake.

A foot slid into the open space in the fence near my face and I realized he was climbing over. If I didn't move he would land right on top of me, put his heels through my teeth.

Breathe slower, Roger. For fuck's sake breathe slower.

I felt the fence move from his body weight, expecting a foot in my face any second. But nothing fell on me. Instead, he said, "What the hell are you two doing on my property? Don't you know it's against the law to trespass? I got the legal right to shoot you, you know. Hey, I'm talking to you. Least you could do is look at me."

It was as if my body was under some magical spell; I couldn't *not* respond. I rolled over and looked up. His upper body was bent over the fence so that his face was only a foot away from mine. His breath was acrid, hot. His unshaven black beard was peppered with bits of gray, and his dirty face was cracked and spotted with blood that I doubted was his own.

The gun was pointed at my eye.

"You should have kept running," he continued. "Lot of places to hide in these woods. Probably could have hidden from me. Then again, that leg looks pretty bad. Butch would have sniffed you out in no time. He's good with tracking, and better at catching. I trained him myself. Yer friend back there, I'm gonna make him pay for shooting my dog. And seeing as how I got his gun, too, you can either come back over here quietly, or I can just shoot you now. Don't make a whole bit of difference to me."

For the first time I looked at my leg. The muscle was ripped open and I could see the striations inside. A small chunk of flesh was torn off and the blood was starting to coagulate just a little. It was so dark it looked like oil.

"Well, what you gonna do, boy?"

His eyes were wild in his gaunt face, his teeth dark yellow, the prison tattoo on his neck was faded but looked like Jesus on the cross pissing on a woman. Mary, it was Mary. And it wasn't piss. He was insane, sick, and two seconds away from splattering my brains all over the ground. What's worse, he was enjoying himself.

"Please . . . please . . ." was all I could manage.

"Please nothing. You should have minded yer own business and stayed away. No one to blame but yerself now."

I was a piss-drenched child looking at the boogey man. "I won't tell. I swear to fucking God I won't tell."

"Boy, if you don't shut up and get over this fence you won't be able to tell because yer mouth will be hanging from that tree over there. Now get up! And stop crying!"

I stood up, sobbing like a girl. I should have let him shoot me, should have taken it fast and clean. But it's not that easy. You don't just concede defeat in these circumstances. You take every second you can find and use it to pray for another few seconds. Hope is a cruel bitch.

I climbed over the fence, smearing my blood all over it, and trembled as I stood next to this demon with a gun. On the ground, the now handless woman with the ax in her skull lay staring into oblivion. I envied her.

"Turn around," he said.

I turned around, half expecting a bullet in the back.

"Now march."

Struggling against my shock, I put one foot in front of the other and started walking toward the house, dimly aware of the

crunching sounds coming from the dog as it gnawed on the hand and bit through the small finger bones. The last thing I remember was feeling a slight sting on the back of my head.
    Blackness.

CHAPTER 11

As I swam into existence, I smelled wet cement and mold, heard rain falling outside. My leg was throbbing and my head hurt like Nomar had used it for batting practice. I went to put my hand against it to feel for a lump, but my arm wouldn't move. I flexed my fingers to make sure it hadn't fallen asleep and it was working just fine. Slowly, my vision cleared and I took in my surroundings, which consisted mainly of shadows and cement walls. Something cold and hard ringed my neck and I shook my head to free myself from whatever it was.

Excruciating pain exploded inside my skull, so intense I didn't dare scream. I stayed still until my eyes stopped watering, and the pain ebbed, and then I glanced down to see what the hell I'd tried to shake off and noticed the chains.

Chains?

Have you ever played dodgeball, and had someone hurl the ball at you at mach 5, knowing no matter how fast you move you're still going to take it head on? That's how I felt as the very recent past came back to me like a line drive to the nose. When it hit me, and I realized where I was, my body went into a frantic, yet restrained, dance—restrained because the chains that were binding me offered little in the way of movement.

I also noticed I was biting down on something soft that smelled and tasted like oil and ancient piss. I tried to push it out of my mouth with my tongue but it was tied tight around my head, probably the only thing holding my brains in.

"Roger, relax, it's no use."

I knew that voice. It was Tooth. Tooth was here with me somewhere. I turned to my left and saw him standing a few feet away. Looking at him, I suddenly knew what my own situation was like. Around his waist, a chain was wrapped tight and fastened to a metal plate in the wall behind him. His hands were handcuffed to the waist chain on either side. A metal collar, like something from an S and M whorehouse, was padlocked around his neck and connected by a chain to the metal plate as well. Two leg irons, again chained to the wall, kept his legs from moving. A brown stained rag was wrapped around his chin, as if he'd not been able to shake it all the way off.

"The chains are too tight and the cuffs are sharp," he said. "Don't bother fighting it or you'll hurt yourself."

His face looked like roadkill. Dried, crusted blood flaked around every orifice. A small rivulet of crimson meandered down his cheek and disappeared under his chin before it dripped onto his shoulder. Jesus. What was happening to us? One thing was certain: I was no longer high.

My eyes were adjusting to the gloom and I could see the room somewhat clearly now. Four concrete walls, a dirty concrete floor, cross beams above us with a single light bulb in the middle. A basement. On the right wall, a rusty black boiler chugged quietly, its pipes extending into the ceiling like antennae. Directly across from us stood a door with a cheap gold knob. Pinned to it was a poster of something I couldn't make out. Against the left wall, at the base, a pair of dog dishes sat surrounded by bits of food. Now that I saw it, I could smell the food as well. It smelled like rancid garbage, and I figured for a man who claimed to love his dogs, he sure didn't care about them enough to buy some high quality Iams. Next to the dog dishes was an old wood burning stove, the kind used to heat up kettles in the 1800s, its pipe extending up through the ceiling. A tiny wooden table sat next to that with some tools—pliers, box cutters, nails, hammers, wrenches, screwdrivers, etcetera—hanging on the pegboard above it.

I looked at Tooth again and tried to speak through the rag but was so scared I couldn't find any words to say.

"Listen to me," he said, "this is no joke. We're in real trouble here. This guy is fucking crazy and I think he killed that woman. I don't know what to do, but I sure as fuck know if we don't do it fast we're going to die. Do you understand?"

I nodded, the surrealism of the moment numbing me. I was scared. Too scared to even care about the absurd number of mosquito bites that were itching like mad.

"I'm scared, too," he said, as if reading my mind, "and if you need to cry, go for it, but I'm going to need you to be awake and aware when he comes back. I need to get him to release us somehow. As soon as he does I'm going to jump him. You run for that door and don't stop until you get the cops. My cell phone is in my back pocket. I'll try and flip it to you, but if I can't get to it, grab it and run. You understand?"

I nodded again and felt my brain slosh about in my cracked skull. I didn't remember being hit but I must have been cold-cocked with the gun.

"He left a few minutes ago, after he chained you up. I pretended I was asleep so I could think. I'm betting he went back for the woman's body."

Last time I had seen the woman she'd been alive, at least physically. I wondered if he would finish her off, but suddenly remembered him saying something about playing with her first. Oh no, I thought, oh shit. My breathing raced and my blood pumped rapidly. He wasn't going to kill her; he was going to torture her.

Was he going to torture *us*? Or was she an ex-girlfriend or something, someone who in his twisted mind deserved to be tortured? I knew the answer to that one instantly. We were chained up, in a basement, in a madman's house. I started sobbing. I didn't want to die.

"Shh," snapped Tooth. "I hear something. I think he's coming back."

Shuffling footsteps grew louder from behind the door, each one followed immediately by a thumping sound. When they got just outside the door they stopped. Keys jingled briefly, began working the lock, and the door flew open.

Covered in a mess of blood, the man—Skinny Man—stood in the doorway like an angry demon late for an appointment. Sweat and blood glistened on his bare chest, which pumped with fury. He put the keys back in his pocket and picked up a bundle of something near his feet. As he dragged it into the room, I saw it was our mystery woman. Her eyes were glazed, her body limp, and I couldn't tell if she was alive or not. The ax was still sticking out of her head.

He dragged her over to the dog dishes and slumped her on the ground. *Clink* went the ax as her head hit the ground. I started dry heaving at the sight of it.

After he was sure she wouldn't move, he came over to me and stuck his face in mine, our noses touching. The collar kept my head from turning too far away, and every time I moved he moved with me, laughing like I was the funniest thing in the world. He grabbed my nose and squeezed it hard. My sinuses felt like they were being crushed and my eyes teared up. Struggling did nothing; he held fast and kept laughing. With the rag in my mouth I couldn't breathe and I knew this was it, this was how I'd die. Spots jumped before my eyes.

"Let him go, you fucking pussy!" Tooth yelled.

No, let me die. Just let it end peacefully.

"You fucking coward! Unchain me so I can kick your pussy fucking ass!"

The man pushed his forehead against mine, his breath hot on my lips. Then he slammed my head back into the wall and let go. My knees buckled and I sagged, but the chain caught my throat and started to choke me so I struggled upright again, my head searing with pain so intense my vision wobbled.

Still laughing, he went and stood in front of Tooth. "You killed my dog" he said, and slapped Tooth in the face. Tooth took the blow without a sound, but I could see he was on the verge of tears.

"Unchain us, and show us what you're made of," Tooth said. "Unchain us and fight us fair. You coward. You fucking mama's boy. C'mon, we'll let you use the gun even. What have you got to lose? C'mon!"

Skinny Man ignored him and went back to the woman on the ground. He lifted her body and sat her up against the stove. Then he disappeared into a door on the other side of Tooth. I hadn't noticed it before because Tooth's body was in the way, but it must have gone back under the rest of the house. He came back out a minute later carrying some more chains. He draped them around the woman and began chaining her to the stove. She didn't move the whole time, as if she was a doll or something. When he was done he took a step back, folded his arms, and looked at her.

"What are you doing, you pussy?" Tooth was still trying to goad him into a fight.

The man continued to ignore Tooth. He was unhappy with something, his face scrunched with annoyance. "What's wrong with this picture?" he asked.

"My foot's not up your ass yet?" offered Tooth.

"Nope." Then as if struck by inspiration he grabbed the ax handle and lifted the woman's head off her chest so she was looking right at us. He rested it against the stove, the handle of the ax sitting atop the surface. Her clouded eyes bore through us. "Much better," he said.

Satisfied with his work, he left the room and shut the door, leaving the three of us to get acquainted.

Slowly, like a glob of pudding, the woman's head sagged forward and fell on her chest again. Was she defying him, or was the ax blade to too heavy for her neck?

"I've got to get my phone out," Tooth said, straining to get a hand around toward his back pocket. The handcuff prevented him from reaching it, only the tips of his fingers brushed the pocket. He held his breath as he stretched, as if this might help, then exhaled, defeated. "Shit, I can't get it. Are you okay?"

Blinking away tears, I nodded yes. Working the rag out of my mouth with my jaw and tongue unleashed another wave of searing pain in my head, but I ignored it. I was having trouble breathing through my nose now, so there wasn't much choice in the matter; I needed air. Tooth took another stab at reaching his back pocket. He was getting closer, I think.

"I can . . . just about . . . get it . . . "

A heartbeat later, the door crashed open and slammed against the wall. Skinny Man was back and he had an armload of firewood. He carried it over to the stove and shoved the logs inside, moving them about so he could stuff in as many as possible.

"Why don't you just kill us and get it over with?" Tooth asked, no longer going for his pocket.

Again, Tooth's remark went ignored. From his back pocket, Skinny Man took out a newspaper and tore it into sections. He twisted them up like he was wringing someone's neck and placed them under the logs. Then he took out some matches and lit the contents of the stove. Immediately, my eyes darted to the woman chained to it. If he didn't move her she would fry.

Like a bolt of lightning the man rushed at Tooth and punched him in the face. Hard. The smack of fist on jawbone was horrific. I closed my eyes and turned away, struggling against my chains, thrashing like a swordfish on a hook. Again, the smack of knuckle on jaw resounded. Again and again and again!

With each blow, Tooth's grunts and gurgle-choking filled the basement. The sweet aroma of burning wood began to mingle with the stench of fear-induced sweat and blood. I cried. I prayed. But the beating wouldn't end. Why was this happening to us? What had we done to deserve this? Why wouldn't he just leave us alone? Just leave us alone! Stop, stop, stop! I jammed my tongue forward, pushed the rag out of my mouth.

"Hit me, you fuck!" I screamed.

He stopped.

I quivered.

Sluggishly, my best friend's head lolled to the side—a mass of contusions. The man faked like he was going to punch me and I winced, but no blow came, and I guess that's what he wanted because he just laughed. When I opened my eyes, I saw him stuffing the rag back in Tooth's mouth, keeping his eyes on me the whole time. When the rag was tight, Tooth's blood had nowhere to go but out his nose.

Skinny Man sneered at me for another half minute before coming over and running his hand through my hair. "I'll hit you, little boy. Oh, man, I'll hit you. But not yet, not like that. I'm gonna come at you with something special, something unreal." He put my rag back in my mouth, tied it in back. "I'm going out to bury my friend, and I when I get back, maybe we'll discuss your punishment a little more."

He stopped to look at the woman, gave her a nudge with his boot, saw she was still in her coma-like state, and left.

Next to me, Tooth was mumbling incoherently and trying to open his swollen, puffy eyelids. Something started to smell like smoked ham and together we realized that, against the stove, the woman was starting to burn.

CHAPTER 12

She sat in a pool of blood that flowed from the stump at the end of her arm. Her hair, face and neck were stained with dirt and gore; fresh leaves stuck to her like reptile scales. She wore a pair of jeans and a button down flannel shirt. Her feet were bare.

As soon as I smelled her flesh cooking, I knew it was going to be bad. She was going to die horribly right in front of us. Considering her wounds, especially that ax in her head, she had little chance of surviving even if she escaped anyway, but to watch her burn to death was something I couldn't stomach. Seeing her head get cleaved and her hand chopped off seemed far less cruel in comparison. Don't ask me why, perhaps because those acts were quick and I didn't anticipate them. This was different. We knew what was coming, and it was the waiting that was making us crazy. I could already feel the heat of the stove from where I was, a good ten feet away.

If only she would stay comatose, stay half asleep like she was, maybe it wouldn't be so bad. Maybe she would just melt away without a sound, peaceful, quiet. But she woke up. And the show began.

She blinked her eyes, as if pulled from a restful *siesta* by a strange noise, then lifted her head, trying to figure out where she was and what the hell was going on. It took a few tries to get her head level because the ax was throwing off her equilibrium. A snaky tendril of smoke rose from her back as her shirt started melting away. Then something sizzled and popped, and as if on cue, she went wild. Her scream was deafening, worse than any gunshot, like being slammed sideways in a high speed, metal-crunching car wreck. Tooth snapped to attention, worked his rag a little out of his mouth, enough to form words, and called to me. "Roger!"

"I'm fine!" I managed to yell around my gag. "But she's burning to death. He lit the stove. We've got to stop it."

We both struggled against our chains but to no avail. She was starting to bleed from her back, frantically trying to scoot away from the heat. The chains were just loose enough that she managed to open a small gap about a centimeter wide between her and the hot iron wall of the stove, but unfortunately, it wasn't enough. The heat melted away her skin like candle wax. Desperately she kicked and rocked, but still her flesh singed. Blood fizzled as it ran down the stove and pooled beneath her. A gooey cream-colored substance joined the mix; either skin or fat, I didn't know which.

The screaming was unlike anything I'd ever heard. It was guttural. It raked my bones. She spasmed, shook, saw us watching her die; she shrieked at us. The ax swung about as she flailed, and the handle banged against the wall, keeping time to this hellish nightmare. A nightmare so unreal I couldn't look away.

Neither could Tooth. He was watching with tears streaming down his cheeks, his puffy eyes beginning to slit open just a little. The smell of charred flesh was so awful it made me want to stop breathing, but the rag was so full in my mouth that if I didn't try to use my nose I would die. Which meant I was forced to smell her body cooking. Tooth started screaming. I started screaming.

We all screamed. We all flailed. We were in Hell.

Then one of the chains gave. I couldn't believe it. It just went slack. Skinny Man must have left a kink in it which she pulled loose. Not missing a beat, Tooth was yelling at her to move, quickly, to pull at the chain. I doubt she heard him but her gyrating, twisting body instinctively tugged away and pulled free from the slack. She slithered out from her binds, leaving a sickening trail of melted flesh and blood on the floor like snail mucus. Tooth was screaming at her, "Get up! Get up and untie us!"

But she wasn't listening; she was out of her mind in pain. She flopped on the ground like a wind-up toy that had fallen over, her feet kicking slowly, and lay with her back against the wall so I couldn't see what damage had been done. Tooth kept yelling through his swollen, purple face. I couldn't stand it. She wasn't getting up, and I fucking hated her for it.

"C'mon! Bitch, move!" I screamed.

Jesus Christ, this was our chance to escape and it wasn't going to happen because this poor woman, who by all rights should have been dead by now, who was suffering beyond all human endurance, wouldn't listen to us. Still, I pleaded because what option did we have? "Get up! Please get up! Please, please, please!"

I kept chanting the "get up" mantra for several minutes before I heard Tooth's voice. "Enough, Roger. Enough." He must have been saying it for a while because he was very calm, and the room was hot as a car engine fresh from a circuit race. I got the feeling I'd been yelling for longer than I realized. "Enough. She's dead."

She was motionless, that was for sure. Her eyes were closed. Blood coated the entire floor; I looked down and saw I was standing in it. "She's not dead," I replied. "Look, her chest is moving."

Like a light breeze, her chest moved up and down. You had to look hard to see it but it was happening.

"Holy shit. How can she take that much abuse and not die?"

"I want to go home," I said, my adrenaline finally seeping away.

"I think my jaw is broken. Oh, man, it fucking hurts."

"He's going to kill us. We're going to die and he's going to torture us and kill us. Oh God, I don't want to die."

"Listen, my car is still parked out there. Someone will see it and call the cops if we can just last—"

"Lot of good that'll do. We'll be dead by then or at least wish we were."

He hung his head down and sighed.

"We should have gone shooting at the other place."

That pissed me off. Was he blaming me for this? I never expected this to happen. Hell, he was the freak with the arsenal. We'd never have been out here if he hadn't gone Rambo while I was at college. "Fuck you, Tooth. Why did you have to be a hero? Why did you need to find this woman? What did you have to go and shoot the dog for?"

"Because it was trying to eat me. Fuck, Roger, I'm not blaming you."

On the floor, our burnt cellmate started groaning. She actually sat up and rubbed her head.

"Easy," I said. "Can you hear us?"

She looked up at me and I felt a renewed sense of hope. Maybe she could get us out of here after all. Maybe I'd shit gold bricks and marry Nicole Kidman, but still . . . maybe. She looked like a giant slab of half-cooked bacon covered in ketchup, and I couldn't believe I was even looking at her without puking. With a bewildered expression on her blood-soaked face, she put a hand in the gooey skin-fat-blood mixture around her ass and sat still. Her shirt, now burned away in back, hung loose around her.

"What's your name?" Tooth asked her.

Her eyes drifted over to him and her mouth muscles attempted to form words but nothing came out.

"You need medical attention," he said.

Medical attention? Shit, she needed a priest.

"If you can unchain us we can get you to a hospital," Tooth continued. "Can you move?"

Her answer consisted of spit dribbling down her chin and some feeble rocking. It was hard to tell if she was trying to stand up or if she was just having a breakdown. It was an infuriating moment and I kept thinking she was trying to help us but somehow I knew she wasn't going to do jack shit but sit and die slowly.

Then, like an infant, she struggled to her feet and stood, teetering. My heart leapt. Was she going to free us? Were we saved after all? Wonder Woman had nothing on this lady. This was the strongest female I had ever seen. She took a step toward us and wobbled.

"That's it," Tooth cooed. "You can do it."

That's when the door flew open and Skinny Man stepped into the room waving a shovel in his hand. It was a satanic stage entrance, our screams providing the background music. He ran in and kicked her in the stomach, shattering our hopes, and from the sound of it, some of her ribs as well. She landed in the goo and lay still. Then he hefted the shovel and turned his attention to us.

"This is for Sundance," he sneered, and swung the shovel into Tooth's thigh.

The blade slipped right through the flesh and bit into the bone, sticking there with a clunk. Tooth let loose with a scream that was pure blood and hatred. Dizziness washed over me, steering me toward a fainting spell, but I remained conscious somehow. Skinny Man left the shovel protruding from Tooth's thigh and went and dragged the woman to the center of the floor in front of us.

"Now," he said. "We're gonna play a little game. It's called—" And he started to sing. "The arm bone's connected to the shoulder bone. The leg bone's connected to the hip bone." He flipped her onto her stomach and exposed a back so grotesque, so extensively burned, I couldn't tell where the muscle ended and the skin began. Her entire lower-middle half glistened with third degree burns, and there was a small glint of white bone visible through it all. And the blood: so much of it I felt like I was looking through rose-tinted glasses.

"The hip bone's connected to the—will you stop screaming?" he said to Tooth.

But Tooth had gone from screaming to blathering. It was an angry, cursing nonsense filled with a lot of "kill you" and "fucking die" phrases. Blood trickled from the shovel blade and ran down his leg and soaked into his white sock. I prayed it hadn't hit the artery, but until it was pulled out we wouldn't know for sure. Now neither of us could run.

Skinny Man gave me an I'm-not-playing-around kind of look and pointed at Tooth. "If he don't shut up, I'm gonna put that shovel in your neck."

I knew he was serious; hell, he was hoping for it to happen. I wanted to purge my tear ducts of everything inside but was too afraid of the consequences. "Tooth, please," I mouthed around my gag, "I don't want to die."

I don't know how, but he stopped making noise and composed himself. Tooth wasn't so much tough as he was just crazy, a lost soul with nothing at stake. Right now, the look in his eyes would send Hannibal Lecter running. But he was also in tremendous pain and the fact he was able to calm down said a lot about his will power. He was going to live through this. I, on the other hand, was going to die like a bitch.

"That's better," Skinny Man said. "Noise makes me crazy, hurts my head. And stop calling me names! Acting like you didn't have that coming, killing my dog and all. Lucky I didn't shove it up yer ass. I done a girl that way once, split her right up the middle. Oh yeah, the asshole is a pretty flimsy invention, rips like tissue paper."

"I'm gonna kill you," Tooth said.

"I don't think so. You've got a penance to pay. You shouldn't have hurt my Sundance! He didn't do nothing but try to protect me."

"You're a half wit." Tooth's mouth was full of phlegm and spit.

"No, I'm not. I'm an animal lover is all. I had that dog since he was a pup. Watched him grow up, him and his brother both. He didn't deserve to die like that."

"Why don't you untie me and I'll kill the other mutt, too, make everything even-Steven."

Skinny Man didn't like that. He gleefully wrenched the shovel from Tooth's thigh and put it in the fire, the handle sticking out the little iron door. Not a peep came from Tooth.

"Boy," Skinny Man said, "you in a lot of trouble."

"We won't tell," I pleaded. "Just let us go and we—"

"Shut up, you twit, you're not going anywhere."

I glanced at Tooth's thigh and saw blood gush out like a fountain. The artery had definitely been sliced, and without aid he would drift off into sleep and never wake up. Tooth knew it too; he was looking at his leg with panicked eyes.

Skinny Man cracked his knuckles and looked down at the woman. "Now, where was I?" There was renewed pleasure in his voice. "Oh yeah, our game."

He went back out the door, up the stairs, and came back a moment later with the saw in his hand and his dog at his heels. The dog came over and sniffed at Tooth's leg then started licking the blood from the open wound. His dog collar jingled as his tongue flicked up and down.

"Butch, leave him alone and come lay down."

The dog looked back and forth from his master to the wound a few times, as if deciding which was of greater importance, and finally went and lay down near his bowls. Skinny Man took the saw and cut into the woman's arm at the shoulder.

"Jesus!" I screamed.

"You son of a bitch!" Tooth said.

With a shit-eating grin, the man hacked through her bone, the sickening *zzz zzz* echo of the saw filling the sweltering room. I closed my eyes and muttered some kind of prayer even though I wasn't sure I was even speaking English. Butch started barking, and through all the noise I heard the dog get up and start padding about. I heard Tooth screaming profanities. I heard Skinny Man grunt like he was having trouble getting through the bone. And when I opened my eyes, I saw the arm separate from the body.

I choked back bile. A numbness floated into my mind, a drunk co-pilot taking the helm. My brain just couldn't wrap around what it was seeing. It just wasn't real; I would wake up soon. I knew I would because this stuff only happened in dreams.

Skinny Man took the arm and licked the blood flowing from the hacked shoulder. It dribbled down his chin and he laughed like a goblin. He rushed at me and grabbed my face and kissed me, smearing blood all over my mouth. His slick tongue lapped thick, bloody saliva on my eyes. Every bump on his tongue, every whisker on his chin, scratched itself across my face.

Butch was going wild, running and jumping up to get a taste of the arm. He tried to snatch it out of the man's hands and got a smack for his troubles. "Hold on two secs, will ya?"

Taking the saw again, the madman cut the arm in two and put the pieces in Butch's dishes. The dog tore at the flesh, shaking his head back and forth until the chunks of flesh pulled away. Then, like a vacuum, he inhaled the meat.

"That is a nasty wound you got there," Skinny Man said to Tooth. "Lucky for you, I fancy myself a bit of a doctor. Got my first aid badge in the Cub Scouts."

He bent down and yanked the ax from the woman's head. It came loose with a gurgling fart as the pressure from the internal bleeding escaped.

And that was enough for me, my brain pulled the plug.

The last thing I saw before I passed out was Skinny Man taking the glowing shovel out of the stove and placing it flat against Tooth's wound. I heard a sizzling pop of flesh, Tooth's bloodcurdling scream, and then all was black.

CHAPTER 13

When I came to all was quiet. The rag was in my mouth again, swollen from my drool, or my tears, or both. I sucked it out and swallowed it. The smell hit me next, an eye-watering stench of decomposition, worse than the time I found a dead raccoon in the garbage out back of my house. That raccoon had been in that trashcan for weeks and when I lifted the lid the rot had hit me hard as a punch and almost knocked me over. Fucking-A if this wasn't a hundred times worse.

My neck ached like I'd been kicked in the esophagus, and my chest felt constricted. When I'd fainted my body had fallen forward and been caught by the collar. It's a wonder I didn't snap my neck or choke myself to death. As I stood up, I could feel fresh cuts under my chin from where the collar had cut in.

The macabre realization that I could have died somewhat peacefully washed over me and I didn't know if I was happy or sad.

The jingle of chains next to me meant Tooth was moving around. Slowly, my eyes adjusted to the faint glow coming from the stove door. The wood had burned down to embers but their light was enough to make out the shadow of my best friend.

"Tooth?"

At my voice, the chains stopped. "You awake?" he asked.

Our words were muffled by the rags, but Tooth and I had that connection, that ability to understand each other.

"Yeah," I replied. "What happened?"

"Oh God, Roger, he cauterized my leg. He burned it shut. This guy is crazy. We have to do something."

"Jesus fucking Christ. He sealed your wound? Why? So he can torture us some more?"

Tooth was quiet for a moment and I thought maybe I'd said something he hadn't thought of. In a funny way, that made me feel bad. Both because I'd just scared him, and because, so far, he'd taken the most damage. But I knew that was just a momentary thing, I was going to get mine, too.

"The girl?" I asked

"He took the body upstairs. I think she was dead. I'm pretty sure she wasn't moving or breathing or anything, and she'd lost a hell of a lot of blood. The dog ate her arm."

There was another pause; neither of us knew what to do or say. I used the moment to begin working the rag out of my mouth. The good thing about the rags was that even though they cut off our ability to speak clearly when they were tight, with some tongue and jaw work the material would begin to stretch. They were a poor choice for gags—unless he was hoping the bacteria on them would give us e-coli or something and send us into a fit of poisoning that would have us *wishing* for death.

"Roger?"

"Yeah?" The gag was loosening a bit.

"Promise me if we get out of here, you'll come to California with me."

The moment was so unreal I started laughing. Right there in the middle of all this death and torture I just lost it. Imagine it, Tooth and I on the beach, smoking weed and riding the surf, talking to hot women in bikinis, laughing about the time we were chained up in some madman's basement. I wanted that more than anything. I wanted to be so far away from reality I started to smell the sea and feel the breeze in my hair.

"Sure, I'll go with you. You're right, there's nothing here for me," I said.

"Except Lucy Graves' tits."

"Yeah," I laughed, "those are pretty nice."

He winced as he shifted his leg. "Someone's bound to see the car. Rangers patrol there daily, right? All we got to do is make it through tomorrow and hope a ranger notices the car sitting there for two days and comes looking for us. I figure it's got to be around midnight now. That psycho ain't been back in a while and my guess is he's sleeping. Let's just make it through the day. We can do that."

"But a ranger won't hear us down here," I said. The walls were concrete and even though the ceiling was made of cheap, rotting wood, with enough rugs and furniture over us our yells would go unheard. "Plus," I added, "if he doesn't have a warrant he can't come in anyway."

"He will if we're loud enough. We just have to listen carefully, make as much noise as possible. Scream like crazy. I've made some calculations while you were blacked out. That door there in front of us is a stairwell, most likely the one we saw from outside. That means the driveway is out that door and if someone were out there . . . . Remember when we heard the woman? The sound *does* carry. We can be heard if we yell loud enough. This door over to our left must go under the main part of the house. Under the living room and stuff. So if he lets anyone in the front door, they won't hear us because he's probably sound proofed it somehow. But if someone comes up the driveway, we'll hear the car and can yell our asses off."

"Have you heard any cars?"

"Not yet. I heard the door at the top of the stairs when he left. The hinge squeaks a little. And the ceiling above us connects to the whole house. Sometimes the dust shakes off it and I figure that's him walking around."

"But what does all that mean? How does that help us?"

"Not sure. But it gives us a heads up when he's coming anyway."

I watched the glowing stove in the corner of the room. The wan light from the slats in the door illuminated the nearby dog dishes. Something was in the dish though I couldn't make out what it was. Then again, I didn't need to. I knew it was the woman's arm, or what was left of it.

"How's your leg?" I asked.

"Hurts like a bitch. I think the bone is broken."

"We're going to die, aren't we?"

"I don't know. I can't really wrap my head around all this. I keep waiting to wake up."

Good ol' Tooth; as usual he was on the same page as me.

The human brain has a difficult time rationalizing the absurd.

It's like watching aliens land in your backyard and take a dip in your pool. You think, "This is a dream, any moment now I'll wake up." And then you do wake up. And you laugh about it and go back to sleep.

Only we weren't waking up.

"But did you see what he did to that woman?" I asked. "What kind of sick fucking maniac is this guy? Why did he do that? He's not human. Do you hear him when he speaks? We or us or they. Is he talking about the dog or the voices in his head?"

Out of nowhere, I started crying again. My emotions were bubbling like a tar pit. Tooth had cried some, too, but mostly he was just mad. Somehow I knew that without him I would have broken down and given up long ago. He wasn't optimistic, but he wasn't giving up yet either.

"Don't worry," he said, "when I get loose I'm gonna kill him. I'll feed him to his own damn dog."

"My parents are in Providence and Jamie thinks I'm at your house. What are we going to do? We can't just sit and wait for a park ranger. You need to get to a hospital."

"I know, I know. But these chains . . . I can barely move."

"So we're done."

"Maybe not. Can't think like that anyway. Look, they lock into these steel plates in the wall, and maybe if we pull hard enough we can start to loosen the mortar around them. But be careful, I cut my wrist already." He started writhing again, yanking the chains from the wall. He rocked back and forth with all of his body, careful not to let his neck take too much of the weight. We both did this for several minutes until we grew tired. Then we stopped and leaned back against the wall.

My eyes had adjusted enough I could finally see the poster on the door. A sunset, a fucking joke. Something to get his victims thinking about life, I suppose. But I didn't think about life, I thought about pain, and how we'd stand up to it, and how long I'd go before giving in to it, and how long before I accepted my inevitable death.

I could also see the swelling of Tooth's face, which had blown up like a bunch of grapes.

"It's no use," I said. "I'm tired."

"Okay, let's take a rest, conserve our strength."

I knew he said that for me; I knew he'd go all night if he could.

Some time went by and we didn't say anything. We tried to break the chains again and when that failed I resorted to sniveling. Tooth calmed me down and started talking to me about comics. "You know, I never read Silver Surfer. What does he do?"

I knew he was trying to get my mind off the present, and although it didn't work, I appreciated the effort. "He rides a silver surfboard and saves people."

"Yeah? That'd be nice about now. How come people are always saying Batman is the shit? I don't get it. I mean, I like Batman and all, but he's not like Spider-man or Ghost Rider or anything, he's just a guy with gadgets."

"But that's why he's so cool. He's just a normal guy with guts and skill. A regular Joe who doesn't take shit from nobody, minds his own business, makes some bad choices once in a while, but ultimately does the right thing. A true hero."

I thought about Batman, the Dark Knight, and how easy it would be for him to escape these chains. He'd have some gadget on his belt or up his sleeve that would melt these cuffs and then he'd torment his captor and make him pay. I had nothing in my pockets, and Skinny Man had our gun. Tooth had his cell phone but neither of us could reach it. What a cruel joke.

"Hey," Tooth said as he rocked against his chains, "let's work on the chains a bit longer. We gotta keep it up if we plan on getting out of here."

"Yeah," I agreed, but before I could start he spoke.

"I'm sorry, Roger."

"For what?"

"For this. For getting us captured by a bloodthirsty lunatic."

Wasn't much to say to that so I just nodded like an idiot.

We worked at the chains again but it was the same old song and dance—they weren't budging. I quit pulling and put my head against the wall and tried to find a comfortable position to rest in. Normally I would have found leaning against a cold stone wall on par with getting kicked in the back, but I was sapped of morale and energy. I barely remember shutting my eyes before I was out.

I saw my parents. They were standing outside of a jail cell, shaking their heads at me. Their look of disappointment ate away at me like acid and I felt ashamed and embarrassed, though I wasn't sure why. My mother pointed an accusatory finger at me and frowned. My father put his arm around my mother and looked away. Why was I in jail? What had I done? Nobody spoke to me or tried to offer any assistance. I was alone.

Tooth came into the room and sidled up next to my parents like they were his own. He was beaten black and blue, his sunken eyes glaring at me with malice. There was a large purple scar wound around his neck, as if he'd been strangled. Like a magician, he pulled a barking rottweiler out of thin air and began to open the door to my cell. The dog, wild and enraged, started drooling and snapping at me in anticipation of a meal. But before the door opened wide enough for the dog to pass through, Tooth reconsidered his action. He stopped and said, "If you can hear me, just pretend you're asleep."

My parents puffed away in a cloud of dust, as did the jail cell and Tooth, and in their place a naked man covered in tattoos danced in the glow of a candle. The dog appeared behind him, its head following his movements.

The man looked like an enchanted stick bug as he floated across the ground, his lanky legs bending like straws. He held something ovoid in his hand, something he repeatedly tossed in the air and cooed to each time he caught it. As the vision became clearer, I saw it was a human head covered in dirt. It was Tooth's head!

No, it wasn't.

It was the woman's head.

And I suddenly realized I was no longer asleep.

I went rigid, my breath caught in my throat. He was here, in the dark with us, with her head. There wasn't any candle; it was the stove's embers casting the light. Tooth was whispering so softly I could hardly hear him: "Don't move, Jesus Christ, don't move."

Naked, the man rolled the severed head over his body, down to his balls and stuck his dick in its mouth. I shuddered; I was at a loss as to what to do. So I followed Tooth's advice and pretended I was asleep, even though I was pretty sure he had seen me wake up. Through slitted eyelids, I continued to watch the freak show before me, horrified and mesmerized.

I could see the head's lifeless eyes, its gaping mouth caked with dried blood. Just hours ago it had been alive, attached to a woman with a *real life*. Maybe a mother, maybe a wife, someone with dreams and childhood memories. Now it was just an object, a sickening prop that could no more scream than tell you its name.

"I like it when you do that to me," Skinny Man said to the head, still fucking its lifeless mouth. Then, placing the head on the ground, he began fondling himself. Faster and faster he went at it. Butch snuck up behind him and took the head in his teeth and ran back up the stairs. Still jerking off, Skinny Man came up to me and looked right at me, his hands still stroking his erection. I shut my eyes completely, but even with my eyes closed, I could see him looking into my face. The whiskers of his beard brushed against my lips, tiny needles poking their way into my mouth. A tongue flashed out and licked my lips and I lost it.

I screamed.

That just made him laugh. He laughed and laughed and danced around some more with his dick in his hand.

Our game of opossum now exposed, Tooth shouted at him, "I'm gonna kill you, you dumb fucker!"

But Skinny Man didn't seem to heed the threat. He grabbed Tooth's gag and tied it so tight I thought it would cut Tooth's head in two. "Boy," he sneered, "you yell at me one more time I will show you your insides."

Tooth mumbled but couldn't form any words.

Holding himself and moaning, Skinny Man came on the floor. When he was done, he gave a little shiver and pushed his hair out of his eyes. "Now," he said, "Let's see what we got here."

He reached up and turned on the light. The room looked like a slaughterhouse. The walls were stained red, blood saturated the floor, a mutilated arm lay near the dog dishes. Skinny Man was covered in prison tattoos, most of them faded. A couple of them showed demonic orgy scenes of animals raping women, or at least that's what they looked like. He slithered over and stuck his hands in my pockets and pulled out my wallet. Opening it in front of me, he took out my driver's license and licked it. "Roger," he said and laughed. "143 Union Avenue. Let me guess, white picket fence, two-car garage. Does Mommy know what a bad boy you've been?

Maybe I should stop in and let her know where you are."

"No!" I screamed. "Stay away from her, you fucking maniac. If you touch her I'll kill you."

"Enough with the yelling already! You make too much noise. I hate noise." With that, he put the gag back in my mouth, tying it tight until it felt like my cheeks were tearing. "If I find these rags out again, I'm gonna wrap you with barbed wire."

Tooth was frantically trying to kick at Skinny Man, but the leg irons barely let him get his feet up.

He reached into my front pocket and played his fingers around near my balls. "What do we have here," he said. He pulled out the pair of dice I had taken from my kitchen that morning. "Snake eyes," he read, and rolled them around in his hand. Next, he fished around in Tooth's pockets and took the cell phone. He threw it at the wall and it exploded like a firework. My heart sank. Tooth stopped struggling and hung his head. We'd been counting on the phone.

Sensing our defeat, Skinny Man did a little dance back toward the center of the room and stopped. He spun around and muttered something under his breath, looked back at us. "Any of you all see a head, about yay big, with white teeth, long brown hair, pretty mouth? It was here a minute ago." Then he started laughing again, occasionally flicking his tongue at us.

He searched Tooth's pockets once more, looking for anything he may have missed, and wound up with Tooth's driver's license. "David McNulty," he said, reading it. "Thirty-two. Shit, you ain't thirty-two. Where'd you get this, Boston?"

Tooth mumbled.

Skinny Man punched him in the face. "You liar! I don't like liars." He went and opened the door to the stove, bent down and reached inside. When he stood up, a pile of glowing embers sat on the fake ID, orange heat pulsating on the surface. They looked like little magic gemstones. In his other hand he rolled the dice about. "Oh boy, oh boy," he said, "been a while since I made a wager of any kind. You hear that rattle, huh, that's luck being shook up like juice. You gotta mix it all together and get it just right or else you get too much bad luck and that's no fun. Or you could get too much good luck, which might seem a good thing, but it just leads you on until it runs out and then you got nothing. Nope, gotta shake it up just right for this game. Roger, you want high or low?"

I didn't know what he was talking about.

"Okay, I'll decide. You're low, and yer buddy here is high. Place your bets."

He bent down and tossed the dice on the ground and I suddenly knew where this was going. He was betting on our fates. Any combination of two through six would represent me—low—and combinations of seven through twelve would represent Tooth—high. The dice came up a five and a three. High.

"That's too bad," he said looking at Tooth, whose dazed head was already hanging to the side from the punch. He undid the gag and forced open Tooth's mouth. I started screaming but my gag was so tight I barely made a noise. He shoved the fiery embers in Tooth's mouth.

Tooth went crazy, flailing his head, spitting out the embers as well as fresh blood. Skinny Man punched him again and I nearly vomited when I heard the crack of bone. More blood shot from Tooth's nose and sprayed on Skinny Man's face like a Pollock painting. The man went back to the stove and collected more of the hot orange gems, came back and punched Tooth in the stomach, knocking the wind out of him. He thrust the embers in Tooth's mouth and then, using both hands, he forced Tooth's mouth to stay shut and tied the gag up again.

I looked away. I kept looking away, listening to Tooth' groans of pain, hearing them from someplace else. A place from our past, from our future. Block it out, I thought, just block it out, go somewhere else. You're not here, you're wherever you want to be but you're not here. And before long, there was Tooth and me stealing lawn ornaments, there was California with the waves crashing on the beach, there was us driving on Route 66 on our way out West, the purple sunset blanketing the dusty buttes. At some point, through my closed lids, I saw the light turn off. I heard the door open and the man go back upstairs, his cackling dying away into the night.

I kept my eyes closed and listened to Tooth cry for a long time, not knowing what to do, just feeling like a kid again, yearning for my parents' bed. And always asking, like a skipping CD in Tooth's Camaro, the same stupid question that wouldn't go away: Why was this happening? Why wouldn't I wake up?

Stress and fatigue finally took over, shut me down into a semiconscious state. It wasn't exactly sleep, because I could still hear the choking sobs of my friend, but it removed me from the larger picture. I didn't know it then, but those moments before the ember attack would be the last time Tooth would look like the friend I had grown up with.

CHAPTER 14

Morning, or at least I thought it was because I could swear I heard birds chirping somewhere. I was leaning against the wall, the gag still tight in my mouth. My whole body ached like it had been steam rolled. On top of that, the bite on my leg was beginning to itch, a possible sign of infection. The room was pitch black, which meant the embers in the stove had burned out. Tooth was snoring. The rain had stopped.

I said a little prayer to God, feeling like a fair-weather fan, slinking back for acceptance from an establishment I'd eschewed. But still, it's funny how you find God in such moments, almost instinctively, like a caterpillar on a strand of silk stretching for the first branch it sees, even if the tree is dead. Yeah, it may seem pointless, but at least it's something. I even swore that if I survived I would go to church.

Church. Would I really? All those nights listening to Tooth's dad preach about God and faith and Heaven. I thought he was just a sad old drunk, but the truth was that he was home tossing back a cold one and we were chained in some psycho's basement. He was watching television; we were watching human dismemberment. Perhaps he wasn't so crazy.

I wondered if he'd be smart enough to come look for us. In all the years I'd known Tooth his father had never seemed too concerned about his whereabouts. He'd let Tooth spend that weekend in jail, and Tooth's mom rarely visited or called. She had a new life in New Jersey, or so Tooth said.

I remembered being at Tooth's one night when his mother had come back for a brief stint, back when we were in junior high. We all had dinner in the living room while we watched sitcoms. Tooth's dad had ordered a pizza. A commercial came on urging parents to get to know their kids better, you know, talk to your kids about drugs and sex and shit. Tooth's parents kind of looked at us like they knew we'd started experimenting with drugs, but they didn't say anything.

Tooth got this funny look on his face and he asked, "Hey, do you remember our password?"

At first I thought he was talking to me, but I didn't know what password he meant. We had so many passwords for so many things they were hard to remember. Like, we had a fort in the woods behind his house and the password was pussylicker. (As with most kids, curse words were taboo to us and therefore used *ad naseam* in the absence of adults.) I thought maybe he was trying to get me to swear in front of his parents, who probably wouldn't have minded, but I wasn't going to test it.

His father answered, "Wasn't it macaroni and cheese?"

"That's it," his mother said.

I thought, what the hell are they talking about? Macaroni and cheese? What fort did that get you into?

Tooth said, "Yeah, that's a stupid password."

After that, we all went back to watching sitcoms. I found out later what the password meant. It was in case anyone had tried to kidnap Tooth. If anyone had approached him when he was younger, he would have asked for the password that only his parents knew, and if the person didn't know it, he'd have run away. It dawned on me that despite the dysfunction that overshadowed their family the majority of the time, there was still a modicum of love under it all.

My family never had a password.

I was thinking about this when the basement door opened and Skinny Man came in carrying something large in his arms. The sunlight from upstairs drifted down and backlit his frame. He was dressed in jeans and a button down and was wearing a baseball cap that said MACK TRUCKS on it. Butch was at his heels, running in circles as if he was about to get a juicy steak.

"Morning," he said. "Roger, I want you to know you have a lovely house."

My heart stopped and I couldn't even swallow much less gasp. He'd been to my house.

That's when I realized the thing in his arms was a body. When he reached up and turned the bulb on I nearly fainted, because in his arms, slumped over like she was dead, was my sister Jamie.

Oh my God. There are no words. Breathing, focus, rational thought: they all locked.

What welled up inside me came from a deep place in my heart, a place so sacred I didn't know it existed until that moment.

I wailed. I pleaded. I begged. Though none of it made much sense through the gag. He just laughed like the Joker and carried her to the door beside Tooth. He took out some keys and, still holding her, undid the lock and disappeared inside.

My desperate cries woke Tooth, who looked around as if he'd forgotten where he was. His entire mouth and cheeks were blistered red and black. The rag in his mouth was caked in crimson goo and pus. When he saw me, he remembered where he was and swiveled his head looking for our attacker. I motioned with my head toward the door on his other side and he looked over, but when he looked back at me he just shook his head. I think he was trying to tell me he couldn't see anything.

It wasn't long before Skinny Man came out and shut the door. In his hand he fooled with the dice he'd taken from me. "She's nice," he said, "just ripe enough for me. We'll have to play with her a little later." He gave Tooth a stinging smack in the mouth, pulled his hand away and wiped off the fresh blood. "Guess you won't be talking for a bit, my friend."

Butch was sniffing the wound on my leg, whimpering like he was waiting for an okay to take a bite. I hated that dog. I wanted to kill it just as slowly as I wanted to kill Skinny Man.

"I searched your car and found this," he said to Tooth. He held up a pay stub. "Mervyn. What the fuck kind of name is that?" He balled it up and tossed it on the floor. Butch ran to it and sniffed it but sensing it wasn't a fresh kill went and sat by his bowls.

It hit me that he must have moved the car. No park ranger would come looking for us now.

From the room behind us came a plea for help. Jamie was awake. Tooth recognized her voice and looked at me with bulging eyes. I wanted to call to her, to tell her to be quiet, but the gag filled my mouth and I didn't want to piss off Skinny Man. Now more than ever I needed to get out of here before anything happened to Jamie.

He went up the stairs and returned with an armload of wood which he lit up in the stove. Like a Pavlovian dog, I started sweating, because the last time he did that he tried to cook the mystery woman, and now he had Jamie, and would he cook her right in front of me? After the logs were cracking and popping with flames, he took the shovel off the tool table and placed it back in the fire.

"Don't know where you live yet," he said, waltzing back over to Tooth, "but I've got other ways of amusing myself." He pulled the gun out from the back of his waistband, cocked it, and put it to Tooth's head. I cringed, expecting my friend's brains to explode onto the side of my face, but the bastard didn't pull the trigger. He was just trying to drive us crazy. Instead, he put it in his pocket and held up the dice.

Tooth was breathing hard, his charred lips singed and gooey like marshmallows that had fallen in a campfire.

"Oh boy, what to do, what to do. This is always the hard part, deciding where to begin. Never had three fresh ones at the same time before. I kind of feel like a kid in a candy shop. I don't want to go too fast, though, an opportunity like this should be savored. Had me two before. Had me one and half, too. Fuck, I had me halves scattered all about like the earth was bearing babies. Babies, oh yeah, had me one of them once, too. Pretty little girl with bright blue eyes. So trusting when they're young, will follow you anywhere you call 'em sweetie and precious. Yeah, that one, I hung her face on my wall to remind me of how precious our time together was. And now I got me three. What to do, what to do. Best to let fate decide for me. You're one through four," he said pointing at me. "You're five through eight," he said to Tooth, "and the bitch in the back is the rest." Butch barked a couple times to which Skinny Man replied, "I'll handle it my way! You stay outta this!"

He tossed the dice on the ground and they came up a three and a six. Who was nine again? Then my stomach bubbled, my head swam. What was he going to do to Jamie? He was going to rape her, I just knew it. Jesus Christ he was going to rape her and beat her and cook her alive. Tooth was thinking the same thing, I could tell. He was yanking his chains away from the wall to no avail.

Butch barked. Skinny Man screamed, "Just hold on! I only got two hands!"

My God, he was insane. He was the devil, arguing with his hellhound.

A shoe flew at my head and missed by an inch. The crazy fuck was getting undressed in front of us. I shook my head, bit the rag to try and rip it in half. The dog kept barking while the maniac tore his pants off. Faster and faster he ripped his wardrobe off and then flung it about the room. Once he was fully naked he squeezed himself and lurched about as if he had no control over his body, as if he was Satan's marionette.

As he moved, his tattoos undulated like underwater scenes of hell. I could see them clear as day now: dogs raping women, wolves eating babies. The muscles in his arms and back tightened and flexed, and even though he was skinny, he had a tautness to him. One look and you knew he could lash out at you with rattlesnake reflexes. He took up moaning as he danced, like an engine revving up for take off. When his dancing reached its frenetic peak, his arms and legs snapping this way and that, his moaning a full on siren, he took a pair of hedge-cutting shears off the table, spun around wildly, ran into the room with Jamie and slammed the door.

Then for a few moments everything went silent. Tooth and I stopped fighting the chains, just listened. The raspy wheezing of Butch's breath was all we heard, a scratchy sound like someone raking leaves.

Then faintly, Jamie spoke. "Please don't. Oh God, please don't." I could hear her hyperventilating. "No. No, please!"

Then she screamed.

I went wild. Tooth struggled with all his might but the chains held. Over the dog's breathing, and our frantic attempt to free ourselves, Jamie's high-pitched wail cut into my heart, stopped my breath like someone was stamping on my chest.

She just kept screaming and screaming. Butch was up and pawing at the door, licking his chops. I fought so hard my wrists began to bleed. Maybe thirty seconds went by before the door opened again and Skinny Man came out carrying the hedge-cutting shears and a mound of gore. I felt faint. I had no idea what part of my sister the bloody flesh belonged to, but I knew it was part of her. Tooth was trying to scream around the gag but he wasn't making any sense. The sores around his mouth split, dribbling more snot-colored pus down the corners of his lips.

Skinny Man dropped the goop in the dog dish and removed the shovel from the stove. I felt like I was watching it all through the large end of binoculars. It seemed so far away. The glowing shovel, bright red from the fire, left an afterimage in my retina when he went back in the other room.

I waited with baited breath and it wasn't long before we heard the faint singe of skin followed by Jamie's horrific cry. Then he returned, with that sedated look people get after eating a big meal, and put the shovel back in the stove. He scooped up his clothes and went up the stairs. Before he did though, he set the clippers against the wall near the door, as if to remind us of our nightmare.

Despite the gag, I screamed for Jamie, annunciating as best I could. "Jamie? Jamie, please, talk to me, say something." I sounded like a drunk with a swollen tongue.

We waited and listened. There was no response. Was she dead? Did that psycho just kill her? The moment was too much to bear and I threw up. The puke shot around the gag and ran down my shirt. I hadn't eaten anything in a long time, so most of what came up was bile. The combination of piss and blood and puke collecting on the floor was so foul I figured the stench of the house alone might bring the police.

The boiler rumbled, the fire crackled, Tooth panted. I stared at the dry puddle of skin that had melted off Mystery Woman and tried not to think of anything.

I could tell you that time passed, but it didn't so much pass as jump ahead to another point, everything in between just a black spot in my memory.

Until, finally, she spoke.

"Mom," she said. He words were strained. "Mom. Dad. Please, somebody help me. Oh God, it hurts. It hurts."

"Jamie." Whispering her name in the dark . . . I'd never whispered like that before. You know, that kind of whisper where the words become an emotion. The kind of whisper that wakes something inside of you.

I threw my head back and let my body shake; I don't know why. I was just so happy she was alive it was more than I could bear.

Tooth and I exchanged determined looks and I knew what he was thinking, same as he knew what I was thinking. We had always shared the same brain more or less. We were thinking, there's always a way out, you just have to find it. Neither Batman nor the Silver Surfer was going to save us. This was real life, and if we wanted out we had to do it ourselves. At that point, with myself covered in regurgitated food, and Tooth swollen and burnt, a silent vow passed between us. No more waiting to die. We were going to escape. And if we died trying, then so be it.

As I leaned back listening to my sister cry, I realized for the first time how much she meant to me. All our fighting and name-calling meant nothing anymore. She was my sister, and I loved her, and if I had to die to save her I was prepared.

Near the stove, Butch chomped up the last of her flesh and licked his lips. He pawed the door open, slipped through, and with a grunt he went upstairs.

I turned back to Tooth and nodded a few times to let him know I was ready and able. I imagined myself with him, in California on the beach, watching the waves roll in. It was serene, and suddenly I felt okay about dying—not the pain part, just the part about not existing. Probably we would never see California, or the outside of this cellar ever again, but I felt okay.

I caught Tooth's eyes and followed the motion of his nodding head. It was his way of telling me we had to talk so I started working at the gag. Barbed wire or no, we had to formulate a plan.

CHAPTER 15

We worked tirelessly to get the gags out of our mouths, until our jaws were damn near swollen. It was worse for Tooth, because every time he moved his jaw his burnt lips split and bled like squashed cockroaches. And the gags were tight; Skinny Man hadn't been playing when he tied them. It took about a half hour of mandible work before we loosened them enough to converse coherently. We left them wrapped around our bottom lips so we could put them back in our mouths if we sensed trouble.

First thing I did was call out to Jamie, to see if she was okay. Her faint response was disheartening. She couldn't tell it was me; I guess she thought I was Skinny Man because she kept begging me to let her go, saying she wouldn't tell anyone. It was a familiar plea, and I realized how crazy it sounded when I put myself in our maniac's shoes.

I shouted, "Jamie, it's me, Roger. I'm in the next room. Can you move?"

She just babbled and cried and told God she hurt. She was alive, but no help to us. I could only imagine what had been done to her. Every time I blinked I saw Butch licking his lips—it made me ill.

"She doesn't know it's you. You're just scaring her," Tooth said.

"Exactly why I want her to know it's me."

"She's in shock, it won't register. Worry about the chains first and then we'll get Jamie."

"These chains are welded tight," I said as I yanked on them. "I can't break 'em. You make any progress?"

"No. Plus I can't feel my leg anymore, feels like I'm floating on air."

"Can you move your foot?"

He shifted his foot just a little. "I guess, but I don't feel myself doing it. We have to stop this guy."

"I'm way ahead of you. But how, when he's got us bound like this?"

"I think we're going about this all wrong. The chains can't be broken, and he ain't going to let us out. He wants us tightly wrapped so he can pick at us like leftover turkeys in a fridge. So let's think about this in a different way. How can we get him while we're chained up?"

We looked about the room, reevaluating what we had noticed earlier. Nothing had changed; it was the same dank cellar with a couple of future murder victims chained to the wall. The shovel was in the stove, the hedge shears were against the wall near the table. The boiler still droned its incessant hum. The arm that had been on the ground near the dog dish was stripped bare and covered in dirt. But those few items made little difference toward escaping.

"This is useless," I said, "there's nothing here to help us. He's crazy but he's not stupid. Look, he left those shears there to remind us of what he did to my sister. He knows these chains are foolproof and we can't get out of them."

"There's got to be something. You read a lot of comics, what would someone in our position do to escape?"

"Fuck, Tooth, this is real. Nobody in a comic would be in this position unless it involved kryptonite chains or laser beams or some piece of science fiction. But this ain't fiction. Not even the best writers could get a regular hero out of this." I thought about Batman using his utility belt again. What would he do without it? He'd probably have to rely on Robin to save him or tricking his captor into setting him free. When it came to real life situations, comic writers weren't all that imaginative. "They'd just write a rusty link into the chains and break it. But these fucking chains are like new. And the cuffs are sharp enough to cut us open."

"What about the wall?"

I looked at the concrete behind me, leaned back against it. It was thick. I couldn't be certain just how thick, but it was part of the foundation, and based on other foundations I'd seen, it had to be at least twelve inches. We weren't going to break it, which is what I told Tooth.

He ignored me and tried to pull his hands through his handcuffs. He did it until it cut into his wrists and blood trickled down the chain. Finally, resignation settled across his face and he gave up and leaned back. "God, I'm tired," he said.

So was I. The few minutes I'd been able to sleep had done nothing to revitalize me. And I ached as well. The chains were rubbing away the skin around my wrists, and I could feel blisters forming. My cut wrist stung every time it scraped my bindings. At least I wasn't alone in that club. It happened to Tooth as well.

We thought silently for a bit, desperately inventing methods of escape that couldn't come true without Hollywood special effects or an act of God. If only the chains would break. If only the plates could be pulled from the wall. If only someone would come by so we could yell to them. Anything.

Jamie was still crying. Mostly it was a low murmur, but at times it was worse. She would call for my mother or father, and that's when I felt hopeless. I gave up thinking about escape and sort of floated out of my body, thinking about other things like how no one would ever know what happened to us. How the dog would eat us and shit us out in a small hole in the yard. How my parents would spend the rest of their lives hoping some day we'd walk in the front door saying, "Hi, sorry we were gone so long, just went sightseeing for a while, but we're back now, what's for dinner?" Then Jamie's voice brought me back, because she said my name.

"I'm here!" I shouted.

But she didn't respond. She was just going out of her mind, calling out any name that was lodged in her subconscious. Tooth met my eyes and then looked away, unsure how to console me. If we got out of this, the therapy we would undergo would be unearthly.

"I lied to you, Roger," Tooth said.

I didn't know what he was talking about. "What do you mean? About what?"

"I kind of dig your sister. I was going to try and fuck her when you went back to school. I'm sorry. I'm only human, and your sister is hot."

I was mad. I couldn't believe he would do that to me. I couldn't believe he was even bringing it up right now. "You sonofabitch. Why do you have to screw every girl you see? She's my sister."

"It's funny, you guys have been at each other's throats for years, now all of a sudden you come back from school and you're all Mr. Protective. Why the change? You really care about her, huh?"

"Yeah, I know, I never thought I'd see the day. I guess it's because I've been at school. College guys only think of one thing."

"Was it any different in high school?" he asked.

"No, but the difference is college girls give it up. And sometimes assholes think that because a girl has sex it means she'll do it with anyone. A girl in my dorm was raped last semester. She didn't come back this year."

I didn't tell him it was the one I had a crush on, with the *Star Wars* poster, or that it was her own boyfriend who raped her. I didn't want to talk about it. When I came home and saw Jamie, saw how much she'd changed in those few months, with her tight clothes and low cut jeans, it made me think of what went on at college campuses all over the world. Tooth was right—Jamie was good looking, and he was exactly the kind of guy that would hurt her.

"If it means anything, I wouldn't have fucked her and chucked her, I would have . . . I mean . . ."

But I think her cries got to him, because he suddenly jerked on the chains until he was almost out of breath.

"Shit! We can't give up," he said. "This can't be our fate. No way, motherfucker, no way. We're going to get out of here and go out West, sit under some palm trees and watch the waves."

I thought about that, not the waves and palm trees, but fate. Like I said before, I wasn't religious, although I was turning fast. I didn't believe there was a cosmic plan, I just felt that shit happened and you dealt with it. But if fate existed, why was it our fate to become dog food? What end would it serve?

I thought about what Tooth's father had said, about everyone having a purpose, but I couldn't figure out how it applied to us. What was Skinny Man's purpose? He'd already killed one person we knew of, bragged about some others and most likely was going to finish us off, too. What possible purpose was there for him on our planet?

"You're not giving up on me, are you, Roger? That better not be defeat I sense in you."

I almost said yes. "No."

Still struggling, Tooth tried to pull his hand through his cuffs again, and this time he pulled so hard a spout of blood arced into the air. There was no way for me to duck out of its way so it landed on my shoulder. "Nhhhnn!" He ground his teeth and kept pulling and pulling until a flap of skin hung around his palm like a piece of luncheon meat. He was in tremendous pain but he was smiling.

"Are you okay?" I asked like a fucking idiot. "What are you doing, committing suicide?"

"No, but I think I know a way out."

"What, skin yourself? The cuffs are too tight. Even if you flayed your flesh, you wouldn't get your bone through it."

The cut looked bad, but luckily it was on the back of his wrist, away from the artery.

"These cuffs are really sharp, like he purposefully sharpened them."

"No shit. What's your point?"

He just kept staring at me like he'd won the lottery. I thought maybe he was starting to go a little insane. They say you do in situations like ours. Or maybe all that beer in his system had dulled his nervous system and he couldn't feel pain anymore. If alcohol consumption was a power Tooth was a superhero all right. Then again, maybe he had figured something out. I was about to ask him when he shushed me and motioned toward the ceiling. Dust was falling in time with footsteps. Skinny Man was walking to the stairs.

Quickly, we worked the rags back into our mouths and pretended they were still tight even though they hung a little loose at the back of our necks. A second later the door swung open and our captor sauntered in, rolling my dice in his hand. He carried a black duffel bag in the other. He was clothed in the shirt and pants he'd had on earlier, but the cap was gone. Butch was at his heels, like a piece of shit-stained toilet paper stuck to his shoe.

"Hi, boys. Butch and me were just discussing something upstairs," he said. "He's real upset about Sundance and I'm not sure how to console him. Not like I'm a fucking grief counselor or something. I tried to tell him that Sundance is playing in Heaven, having a grand ol' time, but he don't believe me. When he gets this way there's no talking to him. So I asked what I could do to make him feel better and he said he wanted to come play with you, maybe get his mind off things. Personally, I think it'd be kind of therapeutic for him, don't you agree? Hell, what could I do?"

Skinny Man had this sort of dazed look in his eyes, the kind of look you see on people who don't sleep much. He probably stayed up all night talking to the mice in the walls. While it wasn't funny the way he talked to Butch, I thought it was funny that he had named both animals after two outlaws that arguably died at the end of the movie. Was that fate working for us?

Skinny Man played with the dice like he was rubbing his own balls, rolling them over one another. He put the duffel bag on the ground and stared at my chest for a moment, mulling something over.

"Silver Surfer," he said. "I know that. Used to read that when I was younger. Metal man from outer space imprisoned on Earth, helping mankind fight against the evil of the universe. Boy, that was the kind of hero I loved when I was a kid. That was the kind of thing made you want to do good in school, and bring flowers home to your mama. You ever bring flowers home to your mama?"

I didn't respond. He grabbed my throat and squeezed hard until it felt like the front on my neck was touching the back. Tears fell from my eyes and through them I could see Tooth watching intently.

"Politeness is a virtue. Answer the question or I'll go get your mama and bring her back here and we can have a family discussion."

I cried, "No!"

Skinny Man liked that; he smiled and let go of my throat. Air rushed into my lungs and I immediately started coughing. "Answer the question. Did you ever bring your mama flowers?"

I faked a muffled yes because I didn't want him to know we'd loosened our gags.

"Son, I'm not stupid. I know that gag has been out of your mouth. You think I was born yesterday? Normally, I got some duct tape lying about but *somebody* thought it would be funny to bury it, and all I had left was these old rags I used to clean up *somebody's* piss."

Each time he said "somebody" he looked at Butch.

"Anyway, you don't need to answer. I can tell you were a good boy. You were never in trouble. Must have been a straight-A student, apple of your mama's eye."

I didn't like the way he used the past tense when referring to me. It was not a good sign. He ripped the gag clean off of me and threw it on the floor.

"But you did break one law: trespassing. Why did you trespass on my property?

"Because we heard a woman screaming." My voice was shaky and unsure.

"Because you wanted to be a hero like Silver Surfer here. But there are no heroes in this world, my friend, only winners and losers, the strong and weak, the chosen and unchosen. Trust me, I know. Ain't that right, Butch, we know all about that kind of thing. And we know what happens to little boys that break the rules, don't we? They become the property of the demolition crew. You ever see a building get torn down? They smash that big ol' wrecking ball into it and *kapow!* the wall crumbles and falls to the ground. Too brutish, I tell ya. Some poor soul took the time to make that building, took care to place each brick just right, gave a piece of himself in the process. Yet every time, they just bash that ball into it. We're not like that though, are we? No sir, we're a different kind of demolition crew. Someone took the time to make you, and we're gonna take the same kind of care and passion in unmaking you . . . my little rule breakers. But this is neither here nor there. Butch wants to play, so we're gonna play."

He put the dice in his pocket, opened the duffel bag and reached inside. He pulled out a length of razor wire and two heavy work gloves. I went flaccid, as if my bones had been turned into wet noodles. Tooth thrust his gag out and yelled, "Fight me, fight me man to man!"

Skinny Man put the gloves on, took hold of the wire, and whipped Tooth across the face with it. It made a sound like someone undoing their zipper. Little pearls of blood splashed against the side of my head, some of it flying into my ear and lodging in the ear canal. No sooner had he hit Tooth than Tooth picked his head back up and looked right at him, stubborn as ever. His right cheek was slashed open in three places. The bruises inflicted yesterday, which had since filled with puss, were pumping out all sorts of blackish fluids.

That's when Skinny Man thrust the razor wire into Tooth's mouth and tied it around the back of his head. The razors sliced off part of Tooth's bottom lip, which fell to the floor. Butch ran over and snatched it up, bobbing his head up and down as he ate it. Tooth screamed. But he stopped quickly, realizing that any movement of his jaw would cut him. It was too late though, the razors cut into the corners of his mouth, and within seconds had sliced them open to his cheeks. The blood ran in rivulets.

I realized I was trying to scream but wasn't making any noise. It's funny how they say your voice can be a weapon, but when you're dead fucking scared, and could probably use it, it takes a hike. Didn't matter how horrified I was—my throat wouldn't respond to the image in front of me.

"That'll shut you up," Skinny Man said. "I warned you, didn't I!" He stepped back and admired his handiwork, nodding acceptance. "Okay, enough bullshit. It's time to play." He took the dice out of his pockets and held them down to Butch, who sniffed them eagerly. "Blow on 'em for me, honey." He thought that was something awful funny and broke into that cackling laugh again. He rolled a six.

"This just ain't your day is it, Mervyn."

Tooth was beside himself, his slashed face swollen, his charred, cut lips transforming him into something entirely alien. This was not the Tooth I knew. This was biology at its basest, and lacerated skin was only the beginning. All around where his cheek was slashed, bone and sinew peeked out.

Skinny Man took up the duffel bag again and pulled out a butcher's knife.

"No," I begged. "Please. Please, leave us alone. We didn't mean to trespass, we didn't know. We never meant to do anything wrong."

"It's a little late for apologies, don't you think?"

He reached out and undid Tooth pants.

"Wait," I said. "Wait. I've got money, I've got lots of money."

Skinny Man spun to me and put the knife to my eye, pushed the point into my flesh just under my lower eyelashes, but not enough to pierce anything. "You speak again, I cut your sister's throat. You all wanted to interrupt my last game, be superheroes, so now you got to take her spot. Fair is fair. Now where was I?"

He pulled down Tooth's pants and tore off his boxer shorts. Tooth's dick had shrunk in fear and his scrotum was as tight against his groin as a walnut.

Skinny Man went dazed again, started touching himself as he looked at Tooth's genitals. He started to dance a bit, rubbing himself harder and harder. Then he licked his lips and looked at Butch, who was licking his own chops.

"Who's hungry?" he asked. Butch barked.

Skinny Man lunged, grabbed Tooth's dick, and sliced it off.

Tooth screamed, the razors opening his cheeks back to his ears. His bowels let loose and evacuated all over the floor, piss spraying out like it was coming from a showerhead.

From the back room Jamie screamed and I followed her lead.

Skinny Man took the wormish body part and tossed it into Butch's dog dish. The dog walked over and sniffed it and sank his teeth into it, bit it in half and swallowed the pieces. Once again, this was followed by a quick repair job from the blazing shovel, which Skinny Man pressed against Tooth's stumped, bloody groin. Smoke rose as the hair and flesh fused shut.

Tooth passed out.

Skinny Man put the shovel back in the stove and shot me a smile. "Back in a bit," he said.

CHAPTER 16

The collar around Tooth's neck caught him as he fainted and swung him side to side, slowly. I thought for sure his neck would break, but his chin was taking most of his weight. He was alive, though I wasn't sure how long that would last. His naked lower half was bubbled with third degree burns, and fluids were leaking out like lava from a cracked volcano wall.

Upstairs, Skinny Man was stomping around and talking loudly to someone, no doubt Butch. It sounded like they were arguing about something: a day of the week, laundry, other nonsense that meant nothing—or everything—depending on how you looked at it. This went on for several minutes and then I heard the door to the driveway open and Skinny Man go out, slamming it behind him. Faintly, I heard a car motor start and fade into the distance.

We were alone.

If we didn't get out now we might not ever. "Help! Anyone! Help us!" I yelled. I didn't know how long he'd be gone for and I had to try the obvious. "Please, somebody, help me!" I waited and tried again, but still got no response.

"Tooth," I said, "You've got to stand up. The chain is going to choke you."

He didn't respond, just hung there with his eyes closed, his feet dragging through his own feces. He looked like a monster, an unrecognizable mass of contusions. The razor wire had done its job and I imagined you could flip his head open and use his skull as a bowl.

I pulled on the chains again, hoping they might have loosened in the past few hours, but my wishful thinking was squashed like a bug; the chains were fortified links of imprisonment. Tooth was onto something before, about figuring out how to get Skinny Man while still in our binds, and right before he came downstairs, Tooth had that proverbial lightbulb over his head. Unfortunately, I hadn't the faintest idea what he had thought of.

I had to think, and I had to do it outside the box. Tooth had tried to yank his wrist through the cuffs, ripped a chunk of skin off, and beamed. But I knew he'd never get his hand through in one piece. What was his plan?

I was wracking my brain when I heard the car return, tires crunching on the gravel driveway. Shit, that was fast. Or was it? Time didn't measure the same to me anymore; the seconds lasted hours and the hours blurred into a single frozen moment. The driveway door opened and keys jingled down the stairs, stopped behind the sunset photo. For a brief moment Skinny Man just stood there, listening. There was nothing to hear though—Tooth was out, Jamie was crying softly and incoherently, and I was quietly listening. What was he hoping to hear? Us making plans? Then it dawned on me: he was just playing around. Coming down the stairs as loud as he did, he knew I must have heard him. Like the incident with the gun, he was just messing with my head.

Sure enough, the door unlocked and Skinny Man came back into the room carrying a brand new roll of duct tape in his hands. Butch followed him in and went and sat by his dishes.

"Should have done this first I guess," he said. "Some people just love to say 'I told you so.'"

He tore off a piece and slammed it over Tooth's mouth, covering the razor wire. The blood, saliva and pus made the tape slick and he had to put a few pieces on, wrapping it around the entire head before it would stick. He did me next, pressing it against my face so tight I thought my head would cave in. Having to breathe solely through my nose accentuated the stench of the room, which was beyond anything I'd ever dreamt possible. Dead fish in a hot trunk would have smelled better. Next, he disappeared into the back room and muffled Jamie's cries. When he came out he put his hands on his hips and stared at Butch.

"Are you satisfied now?"

The dog sat like a bump on a log, obviously aware that his master's brains were made of diarrhea. But Skinny Man gave a little chuckle, and for the first time I thought maybe he was just messing with us. Maybe the whole talking-to-the-dog thing was a ruse in case we escaped. I tried to remember if Son of Sam had pleaded insanity, but I couldn't recall.

He came over and picked Tooth's Red Sox cap off the floor, brushed it off and put it back on Tooth's head. "Should've known you was a Red Sox fan. Never met an asshole that wasn't. Hear tell that Red Sox fans are the most loyal fans around, but if you ask me, anyone who roots for these losers year after year after year, that ain't loyalty, that's just plain ignorance."

Tooth made a little snuffle and blinked his eyes. I prayed for him to wake up, at least so he wouldn't choke. But then I thought better he choke than get butchered any more. God, was I really giving in?

Blood was seeping out around the tape on Tooth's face and running down his chin. It reminded me of a movie I'd seen, *Force Ten From Navarone*, where Harrison Ford and Robert Shaw were trying to blow up a dam. When they blew the dynamite, little cracks zigzagged along the dam wall. The water trickled out slowly at first and they thought they'd failed the mission, but slowly the cracks widened until the whole dam broke apart and fell into the river. I almost expected Tooth's head to do that now, just crumble apart and spill his brains down his shoulders. But Skinny Man must have seen the same movie, because he took out a pocket knife and poked a hole through the tape into Tooth's mouth, letting the blood run out and pool on the floor.

Butch was on it like a fly on shit, licking it up as it fell. "Leave it." Skinny Man kicked at him and reluctantly the dog went back and lay near his dishes.

"Okay then," he said. "I think it's time to play another game. How about that, Butch, you wanna play some more?"

The dog looked up, tilted his head, gave a little wag of his stubby tail. He looked unsure whether he'd get a treat or a kick in the ribs.

"Who's feeling lucky? Will it be asshole number one, wearing the hat of a loser team made of midgets and immigrants? Or will it be asshole number two, who rubs his nub to pictures of Wonder Woman because he's too much of a nerd to get laid? Or perhaps," he smiled, licked his forefinger and stuck it in the air, "asshole number three. A sweet young hole if there ever was one."

I hated him talking about Jamie, but I forced myself to remain calm, to figure out what Tooth had hit on. It was difficult to ignore Skinny Man as he rolled the dice about and tossed them on the floor. I didn't look at the numbers, didn't look to see the expression on his face. I had to think. What had Tooth been doing when he tried to pull his hand through the cuffs? I tried to pull my hand through but my wrist wouldn't fit, and I ended up opening the cut that was there already a little more.

"Eleven. Boy, I am one lucky motherfucker, ain't I, Butch? Got to hand it to fate, I tell ya."

I let out a breath I hadn't even realized I'd been holding when I heard it wasn't my number.

Then the ritual began, the dancing, the fondling, the dog barking. I fought to control my mind, to focus on the chains, on escaping. But as he undulated in front of me, taking off his clothes, I found it harder and harder to concentrate until, inevitably, I started crying again. He danced right up to me, all the tattoos following his lead, his own little tribe of headhunters. When he was completely naked he went into the room with Jamie.

She started screaming when he opened the door, though her voice was muffled from the tape. It wasn't long before I heard a clink of metal and Skinny Man's heaving grunt as he lifted something heavy. Whatever it was smashed against the ground and reverberated off the walls, sent chills down my spine and stood my hairs on end. Jamie pierced my ears with an unholy wail that lasted until her breath gave out.

I started shaking like I was freezing, but it wasn't from any cold. I think I might have been going into shock, but I couldn't be sure. I wanted to tell Jamie to shut up. I just didn't want to deal with it anymore. I wanted to be in California, by the waves and smoking fresh dope.

She filled her lungs again and let loose with the same excruciating cry, and I couldn't take it. This wasn't happening. I was asleep, and any moment now I would wake up.

He came out of the room, blood smeared like war paint on his face and chest, carrying a large ax that looked like it had just been used to serve several pieces of cherry pie. Chunks of red flesh slid down the blade and plopped on the ground. Butch ran over, snorting like a wild boar, and sucked in the meat. Skinny Man rolled the largest piece of flesh up and down his stomach, then down to his erect prick where he rolled it up under his balls. I turned away, nauseated. I didn't want to know what it was, it didn't matter anymore. The daydream was safer, so I went back to the West Coast. But even then he wouldn't leave me alone, came out of nowhere and stood next to me on the beach.

So I took a walk toward a public park to watch the children playing. I saw Jamie and myself running away from our father who was busy chasing us, making his silly faces. My mother was sitting on a checkered blanket, laughing and taking pictures. Jamie tried to dodge my father and twisted her ankle, crashing to the grass with tears in her eyes. I stopped running and stood next to her, just looking at her puffy face as she cried. My father scooped her up and carried her to the blanket and kissed her on the forehead. My mother rubbed her ankle and made more funny faces until she laughed. Nobody seemed to know I existed at that moment so I sat in the dirt and played with some ants, wondering why this little girl had stolen my parents from me.

Why that particular memory resurfaced is beyond me, but it calmed me down. I think I was trying to tell myself something, find reason for being where I was. It was a peculiar memory to dwell on, watching myself give in to jealousy. But perhaps it was not the resentment that was the focus, but something else. The picture from that day hung on the wall in our family room, though it was taken in the field behind the elementary school near our home and not in California. And though I had never paid much attention to it growing up, it always reminded me of the blandness of my upbringing. We weren't a family of stature, or adventure, we were just your typical normal, no-flair unit. But we were a caring family, always there for each other when it mattered most, even if we couldn't stand to be in the same room with one another half the time.

No matter what happened now, we would never be a normal

family again.

I dared a look at the hell about me, and found Skinny Man on the ground petting Butch, who was in turn licking the stump of flesh that had just been placed in his bowl next to the mystery woman's arm bones. It played sort of like a movie, like I was in another dimension, trying to figure out how they lit the shot without drawing attention to the crew. If I wanted to, I could change channels by blinking my eyes and watch the California station instead.

Seemingly, the two worlds melted together like paint mixing, and soon I was watching Butch eat pieces of my sister on a beach in Malibu. Tooth stood next to me on the beach, his flat, sizzled crotch attracting seagulls.

Skinny Man walked up to the ice cream truck on the boardwalk and bought a molten red shovel, threw it over his shoulder and carried it back to a door that opened against physics in the breaking tide. He disappeared inside, fading into darkness and into a woman's screams. Out in the cloudy red sea, the dorsal fin of a dolphin broke the surface and then sank back into the depths.

CHAPTER 17

I don't know how much time went by before Skinny Man returned to our dungeon, but it was long enough for hunger pangs to make my stomach feel like it was tearing itself in half. Long enough for Butch to finish eating my sister's flesh and go back upstairs. Long enough for Tooth to wake up and cry and lean back against the wall and doze off again. Long enough for me to fall asleep myself without noticing because one minute I was happily engaged in coitus with Lucy Graves on a Malibu beach, and the next I was being slapped in the cheek.

I came to in a fog, blissfully ignorant of the fact I was being tortured in some crazy man's basement. The slapping, however, was lighting up my face so I instinctively lunged at whatever was causing my discomfort, only to snap back, crack my skull against the wall, and see stars. When my vision cleared, in front of me hovered the maniacal visage of Skinny Man, laughing at my surprise. He smacked me again for good measure and showed me the dice. I had forgotten about the game.

"Did you have a nice nap? Count any sheep? Can do lots with sheep, ya know. For instance, bet you never seen your sister get fucked by a big ol' billy goat, huh? Give me some time I can arrange it, perhaps throw in a flaming wasp nest while we're at it. Lock 'em all up in a big box and shake it up! Just shake it good! Man, that would be something to crow about. All in good time, I suppose."

I noticed for the first time he had fillings in his back teeth and wondered what doctor was crazy enough to get so close to this man that their hands were in his mouth. Even more distressing was the notion that Skinny Man took better care of his teeth than I did.

"Figure your number is due, boy," he said, and leaned in close toward Tooth, sniffing the collection of fluids around the tape. "You're friend here is starting to stink. Maybe I should put him out with the garbage."

"I'm thirsty," I said. Through the tape and gag it sounded like, "Mmm mmrrmmy."

"Thirsty?" he asked, deciphering my mumbles.

Jesus, how long had he been talking to gagged prisoners?

"You want a drink? Shit, you motherfuckers want everything. 'I want a drink, I want to go home.' Boo-fucking-hoo. You should have thought about that before you crashed my party. It ain't my fault you're down here parched like a sand trap. Shit, there's a whole frigging lake out there in that mountain. You should have gone there, done some swimming, drinked your fill. Drinked? Is that a word? Shit, I'm not so good with words, ya know? I said 'Ya know!'"

He grabbed my throat and squeezed—his old familiar tactic—and while he did it he grit his teeth like a child poking a dead bird. I frantically nodded yes, but he wouldn't let go, just kept squeezing. What did he want? Confirmation of his stupidity? Yes, you dumb fuck, you used the wrong word, because you're fucking insane and take orders from your dog!

"You must have the angels on your side, boy. Because something is telling me to play fair, roll the dice, even though I know I should snap your virgin neck right now."

I prayed he would do it, that's how far gone I was. But he didn't; he just let go of me in a huff.

"Shit," he said, seemingly annoyed at himself. "You want water? Okay, I'll get you some water."

What he got me was shit in a cup, a rancid smelling brownish-green fluid I could only have guessed came from some dead animal's ass. "The pipes are rusty," he said. "It looks bad but it tastes okay."

I shook my head no, closed my eyes. Naturally, that pissed him off, but that's what he was hoping for. "You ungrateful little shit! I didn't have to get you any water, you know. I could have left you down here to die of thirst. Now you drink this water."

He ripped the tape off my mouth, taking bits of facial hair with it. It burned like someone rubbing sandpaper on my skin. With one hand closing my nostrils, he forced my mouth open and poured the sludge down my throat. Instantly, I recognized the coppery taste of blood. But there was more than just blood. There was some sort of salty fat, and feces as well. Definitely shit from some animal or human, decayed flesh, bits of skin, something worse than bile. I felt it land in my hungry belly and fill up all the space, smelled it behind my eyes as I fought to exhale. Realizing I was drinking death, somehow, despite his vice-like grip, I coughed and spewed the rest of it onto his face.

Skinny Man snapped his fist back to hit me and that's when Tooth woke up.

"Mmmm."

At this, Skinny Man stopped short of dislocating my jaw and sneered.

"Well, I'll be a red-assed monkey in a banana factory, look who's awake."

Tooth was awake, and what was more, he was aware. Narrow slitted eyes, furrowed brow, hands balled into fists and flexing by his side. The sonofabitch was ready for a fight. And all this with his face so unrecognizable and his groin so hacked up you'd swear he'd just crawled out of the grave.

"I'm sorry to inform you," Skinny Man continued, "your angry stare doesn't do much to frighten me. Kind of hard to be intimidated by a man with no dick. Or does that make you a woman . . . technically speaking? Tell me, hot shot, how does it feel to lose both your guns?"

Tooth didn't waver.

"Okay, looks like the fun's about to begin. This here is more like it, sort of like the playoffs—who gets to advance to the next round and all that shit. C'mon, sing with me. Take me out to the ball game—hey, you still got those, that's gotta count for something."

He threw the cup over his shoulder and tossed the dice on the floor. I never prayed so hard it wouldn't be my number, and I didn't look at the result just in case. But when he looked back up, he looked right at me, a grin snaking across his bearded face. I knew he'd rolled one of my numbers, I knew this was going to hurt. I wanted to go back to my dream world but the rancid taste in my mouth kept me in the present.

"Oh God, please, no," I said.

"'Oh God, please no,'" he repeated, whining it like a baby.

"Please, you don't have to do this."

"Jesus, boy, you are a little sissy. It ain't even your number."

Looking down, I found the dice near my feet, two fives beaming back at me. I didn't know which was worse, that I was happy it wasn't me, or that Jamie was about to be hurt again. I was thanking God and at the same time cursing Him for putting me here.

The man did his song and dance, stripped bare and went into the back room. I was slowly beginning to realize how amazingly strong the human body is, how resilient and self-preserving it can be. But also how much pain it can suffer. I figured there was no way Jamie would even be conscious anymore, but her screams tore me in half, scratched my brain and I just cried and cried. Where the tears came from I had no idea; my body should have been empty of everything by now, including my will and concern.

Her screams brought the dog down the stairs, sniffing the air and looking for its master.

Tooth, in a subdued yet deductive mood, started pulling his hand through the cuff again, peeling back his skin like a banana. He groaned and pulled until the bone came through, a sickening pearl colored fragment scraping on the metal. I watched him in awe, both because the pain must have been unbearable, but also because he should have been dead, or at the very least, unconscious.

Through the concrete wall behind me the screams grew to a crescendo, but my mind started to focus on what Tooth was trying to do. It was that cosmic connection we had; I just knew what his twisted mind was playing at. He was trying to break his thumb, maybe even sever it off, get his arm free and use it on Skinny Man.

Pushing Jamie's cries out of my mind, I watched him like I was watching two girls kissing, trying to see it from different angles. If he got his arm free, he could grab the guy, pull him in. I could go for the keys in his pocket if he was close enough. The chains offered about two inches of slack, so he'd have to be practically on top of me. But then what? I wouldn't be able to unlock myself, would I? And wouldn't Skinny Man just push free and kill us? And did he even keep the cuff keys on that particular ring? And half the time he was running around naked playing with himself so he wouldn't have any clothes on anyway.

It was the start of a plan but it had no clear execution.

"Tooth," I yelled over the noise, "What . . ."

He lolled his head my way and stared at me, nodded toward the clothes on the floor, which pretty much told me I was right. Seeing my comprehension, he went back to sawing at his hand. The pain didn't seem to bother him; I guess he was just numb all over.

"But . . . but . . ." I didn't really know what else to say, and what was worse, I knew I should have tried to talk him out of his plan. But it was our only hope, pathetic as it was, because I couldn't bring myself to do it. "He's got to have his clothes on."

Swollen like a cherub, Tooth nodded in agreement. And that was that, we had our plan, our weak and feeble plan, which revolved around my friend's probable death. A death that would be a relief for him, and a lifetime of shame for me. I felt hollow, worthless, and yet . . . prepared.

The door beside Tooth flew open, rebounded against the wall, and shut itself. But Skinny Man was already through it and holding one of Jamie's feet.

She was still screaming.

Licking at the chopped bone, he came over and put it on my head, put the fucking foot on my head so that the blood ran down into my eyes. I shook it off and it fell to the floor between Tooth and me. Then the glowing shovel and the naked man went to play doctor on my sister's leg. That took a minute, which Tooth used to work his hand into the cuff, and then Skinny Man was back again and he had that fucking saw in his hand, the one he'd used on the mystery woman and no doubt on my sister, and he looked stoned to high hell, his eyes half closed and his thin lips content like he'd just swallowed some hot chocolate on a cold night.

He put the shovel back in the damn stove, picked up some wood from next to it and put it inside as well. Butch spotted Jamie's foot near my own and came over and sniffed it. But Skinny Man snatched it up and took the saw and cut one of the toes off. "Savor it," he said. The dog slowly took the toe from its master's hand, bit into it and chewed it up, dropped a half-painted red toenail back on the ground. Skinny Man cut off another toe, and another, and left them on the sticky red floor.

Then, sweet fucking Jesus, he rolled the dice again. No intermission, the game was on again. It was a three and a two, and that equaled Tooth.

Skinny Man snarled at me—actually bared his teeth like he wanted to eat me. "What's your deal, boy? Why are you so special?" He placed the saw on my neck and I felt the teeth bite in near my jugular. "Luck's gotta run out soon."

He ripped off Tooth's shirt and sawed his nipples off with four clean slices. I went dizzy, bombarded by the dual shrieking from Tooth and my sister. And to top it off the dog started howling, too, like we were all in some insane fuck-all butcher shop quartet.

The slabs of flesh fell on the ground near one of the severed toes, like two hamburgers next to a finger sausage. Naked, Skinny Man picked up the dice again, bounced them off my head and followed them as they rolled over to the dog dishes. "MOTHERFUCKER!" he yelled as he kicked the dishes against the wall. Butch ran up the stairs, apparently able to tell the difference between a psychotic fugue and a domestic tantrum.

He came at me again with the saw, stopped in front of me, fondled himself. "You must shit horseshoes." I watched him rub blood all over his erect cock, up under his balls, until I almost threw up again.

He went back in the room with Jamie, zing went the blade, out came an ear, arcing through the air. Zing went the blade again, and out came two fingers, followed by a wad of blood soaked hair. And the screams, so loud, so relentless. I was in space, I was out of my mind, even though I was still kind of in the moment. Like walking down an icy hill, knowing you're going to fall no matter what, I was just accepting it all, just going with it, like, yeah, man, cut us up, show me how bad it can be, bring it on and do your crazy dance with me. I could feel myself sliding into another world.

When he came out he flung a handful of bloody teeth—Jamie's teeth—against the wall.

He rolled the dice a third time, and again it came up with Tooth's numbers. It was funny, in a sick way. I began to go with it, thinking I was protected by Heaven, that maybe I did have some purpose for being here, here on earth, here in hell, here there everywhere.

He went and got his big ax once more, put it over his shoulder and undulated in front of us, a snake rising out of a basket. The ax cut through the air, a glint of chrome through a piss yellow light. The blade zinged into Tooth's soft flesh and crunched into his hip bone, and his body fell sideways, caught on the chains.

The ax fell to the ground and chimed off some stones on the dirt floor. Tooth passed out, or died, I couldn't be sure. I didn't really care. Jamie kept crying.

Skinny Man tossed the ax over near the door and left, the light went off, the door locked, I shut my eyes and dreamed of my mother.

CHAPTER 18

Scrape, *scrape, scrape.*
What the hell was that? I opened my eyes and saw a demon moving in the shadows beside me, sucking in a labored breath and choking on it. It took a moment to realize it was Tooth, awake again, and sawing at his hand. His vague shadow revealed bits and pieces of razor wire sticking out of his face. He was bent sideways at an awkward angle, like he'd been doing the YMCA dance and got stuck at C.

It became clear to me that the next time Skinny Man came down would probably be the last time; he was irate, if such an understatement could be imagined. The remaining seconds were ticking away slowly, counting down to an inevitable demise. It's hard to describe what I felt at that moment: sheer panic, absolute fear, anger at knowing I could do nothing about it. I wanted to say goodbye to Tooth and Jamie, figuring maybe I'd find some closure in it all, that maybe it would cleanse my soul. Who knows, really; it just felt right.

"Hey, guys . . ." I began. I stopped, searching for the words. If this was going to be my last time talking to them, I wanted to go out with dignity and meaning. It brought back a memory of when Jamie's hamster died, and how she'd made us all go out into the backyard while she said a eulogy in its honor. I'd hated that damn hamster because she used to let it run around the house and it nearly tripped me down the stairs a couple times. Sometimes I would torment her by pretending to step on it until she cried and hit me. In the backyard, she'd stood there with her shoebox coffin and said, "Nibbles is going to Hamster Heaven, where all hamsters have fun and play all day and there's lot of other hamsters for friends, and when I go to Heaven I can visit Nibbles, too." And she cried and put the box in the ground and I was annoyed because I was missing an episode of *Star Trek* or something. I didn't realize it then, but her idea of Heaven was pretty nice; for a ten-year-old, she'd put it pretty well.

Right now, I couldn't think of a thing to say, nothing even close to being poignant. So I said, "Tooth, I'm scared. Oh, Christ, I'm scared and I don't want to die. I'm so sorry for this and I know this sounds lame and stupid but, I just want you to know you were the best friend ever, and if we go to Heaven, I don't know, I hope there're a lot of naked women waiting for us."

I wanted to tell Tooth that Skinny Man was right—I was a virgin—but I didn't. Even in death I was embarrassed. Not only was I a virgin but I was also a geek, I mean a stereotypical nerd. Why had I cared so much about science fiction and comic books and horror movies? Lot of good it did me in life, and it sure didn't give me any insight into this hell we were in.

He didn't even look at me, just kept at his wrists.

"I guess I just want to say thanks, Tooth, for always having my back, for being cool to me when everyone else kind of ignored me. God knows you could have left me home most nights and hooked up with some girls. It means a lot to me that you didn't."

I was crying now, but not the frantic scared-shitless crying I'd been doing for the past—what was it?—couple days. I was crying from my heart, because I was feeling the beauty of life. I know that sounds like a crock of shit, but as I leaned there, the jingling chains supporting my tired bulk, I was able to understand why people hung posters of sunsets on their walls. Life really is amazing, and when you're about to lose it, you finally notice that you never really took it in before. And you realize the sheer magnitude of what it involves, from your first kiss to your hundredth slice of pizza. I guess that's why those tears drifted down my cheeks.

I also wanted to tell him I loved him, but it didn't feel right. I can't explain it, other than maybe it was too weak a thing to say. Plus I figured he knew in his own way. I just repeated that it had meant a lot.

Tooth, whether he heard me or not, was still moving about, albeit slower than before. Sonofabitch was strong, a real tough mother. Should have been dead already, considering the amount of blood he'd lost. I could see by the crack of light from under the door that he was still hunkered over to one side, his hip probably shattered into tiny shards. And though I couldn't see it, I figured he must be pumping out blood like a ruptured water main.

From above me, the ceiling shook with footsteps, a random pacing to and fro. Dust trickled down on my brow.

"Jamie," I shouted, not caring if Skinny Man heard me or not, "Jamie, I'm sorry we fought all the time. I'm sorry for this, it's all my fault. I'm sorry for not being nicer to you. I'm sorry. I'm sorry. I . . . love . . ."

And that was all I got out for Jamie, that I was sorry, because I felt the weight of the moment in my stomach and threw my head back and sobbed uncontrollably. I managed to say I love you, but she probably didn't hear it around the sobbing. For all I knew she was dead now anyway.

The footsteps came down the stairs, the key went into the lock, and the door opened. Silhouetted against the light from upstairs, the skinny maniac sauntered in, already naked with the damn dog behind him.

He didn't speak; he didn't come over and touch us either. There was a new look in his eyes, not so much fear but sobriety, as if he'd just received some sort of life-altering wake up call. He reached up and turned the bulb on, apathetic to my snivels, and bathed the room in the color of dead leaves; the once yellow bulb was spattered with blood.

I looked over at my best friend, who was beyond anything I would ever recognize as human. Naked. Burnt. Bound. Gagged. Split. Sliced. Drenched in blood with two round medallions of raw meat stuck to his chest where his nipples had been, his duct-taped face erupting with pus and blood and strands of razor wire that had wedged into his forehead and cheekbones. The hole in the tape sucked in and out of his mouth so faintly it might have only been the breeze coming down the stairs that made it move. His blackened groin was a mass of bubbles and blood-filled boils that oozed down his legs. He was in the process of dying, our plan not so much abandoned as improbable now.

Flies speckled the walls, lit on my body, on Tooth's body, in the dog dishes. The floor was brown with dried blood. A few toes, one with a silver ring, still lay about. The foot was gone, probably to wherever the mystery woman went. The pieces of Tooth's cell phone were sticking out of the gore like tiny sinking lifeboats.

Skinny Man was going through his instruments on the table, picking up little knives and trowels and axes, examining a handsaw and a long metal rod sharpened at one end. He spread them out on the floor and went through each one, picking it up, hefting it, looking at us, putting it down.

I was beginning to breath heavier and heavier, both because Tooth was about to die, and I was about to take his spot in the game. Skinny Man knew Tooth was on his last breath, which meant those instruments were for me. He was mad at me anyway, because he couldn't roll my number. Why I had been spared so far I didn't know. I didn't even want to begin to think about it. Not only did I not want to jinx it, but if I delved into it and sought for some religion, I would only attempt to find meaning in it. There was no meaning to this; this was just our bad luck. Nothing more. Purpose? Fate? Destiny? It was bullshit. We were in the wrong place at the wrong time, that was all.

And because I had my fucking driver's license on me, Jamie was in it with us. He had never gone back to get my parents, or to seek out Tooth's home. What were my parents doing now? They must have gotten back from Providence. But they wouldn't come looking for me, not if they knew I was with Tooth. They'd just assume we were off drunk and hanging out. But Jamie, she was another story. If she didn't check in they'd be concerned, they'd call her friends and ask if they knew where she was. She was supposed to have been at the damn mall flirting with boys. What happened? Cancelled plans? Bad luck again?

The wrong place at the wrong time.

Skinny Man chose a hammer and a spike about the size of a magic marker and stood up.

Tooth's body, up till now supported by both the wall and the chains, began to slide down. Small nerve spasms rocked it back and forth. He wasn't getting any air and his body was fighting for it.

"Tooth! Oh God, Tooth! No!"

Even though I knew it was my voice it still sounded far away. I'd read about how these moments appear as though you're watching a television show or movie. But that's only half right, because part of my brain knew it was happening right there, and so what I actually felt was split in half. I was two people, the mind and the body, looking at a picture of a cellar but feeling the wall and dirt floor within it. I wanted to be all mind, to see it all as a two-dimensional image. But it didn't go that way.

Skinny Man unwrapped the tape from Tooth's face. Underneath, the razor wire fell away to reveal branches of lacerations. His cheeks were shredded like tattered rags.

"I want to know why they call you Tooth," Skinny Man said. He smashed the hammer into tooth's jaw with the indifference of a man just doing his job and Tooth's bridge went flying against the wall in a splotch of blood. "Well I'll be, you ain't even got any teeth, Tooth." He pulled back his arm and swung again. Two molars shot out from the torn cheeks, blood spit out like black cherry sundae sauce. Tooth didn't make a sound; I think he was crawling toward the light.

I was still screaming, "You fucker! Stop it! Stop it! Tooth! No!"

Then he put the spike to Tooth's jaw and rammed it in with the hammer. Again and again he smashed the hammer into it. The jaw broke, actually came loose from the hinge. Skinny Man dropped the hammer and spike on the ground, grabbed the jaw with both hands and thrust downward on it, thrashing it, yanking, giving it all his weight.

My eyes were out of my skull.

Skinny Man pulled and pulled, picked up the hammer one more time and smashed it down on the front of the jaw. Then he yanked some more, ramming Tooth's head down into the neck collar, and finally there was a crack and then another crack and then the jaw separated from the skull. Skinny Man yanked it still until the skin peeled down and ripped around the neck and it tore off and he held it in his hands and just stared at it triumphantly.

Tooth was dead.

I went still. Before I closed my eyes I saw Tooth's skull, missing its jaw, the tongue hanging down like a necktie, blood flowing and some other goo, probably saliva or mucus, cascading out as well.

Under my lids, I went back to California and pretended I was watching Tooth pick up girls on the beach. He was wearing his Red Sox hat and had a beer in his hand, making lewd gestures that made the girls giggle. He waved me over but I was reading a *Spider-man* number one. I didn't want to ruin his chances and besides, he seemed happy.

CHAPTER 19

"Don't go anywhere," Skinny Man said, winded but grinning his stupid grin again.

I kept my eyes closed, watching the waves, trying desperately to make the dream real, but I heard him unchain Tooth's body and drag it up the stairs, the head smacking each step in succession, like Mark Trieger, and that washed away the vision. I waited a few minutes and then opened my eyes again, looked at the empty room, saw the jaw bone in Butch's dish though the dog wasn't around. He must have followed his master out.

I turned away from the jaw with its sheet of torn skin curled up under it. It was crawling with little black dots. The flies had phoned their friends, invited them to the cookout.

The reality of the moment hadn't sunk in, and even though I saw the empty chains, the notion that Tooth was dead was Greek to me. In fact, I couldn't feel much of anything. A heavy numbness started in my head and dripped like oil down to my feet. Numb from the insanity, numb from the shock, numb from the pain in my shin which had become more of an itching than anything else. I was a Novocain space ranger.

The little axes and knives still sat in the middle of the floor. The hammer and spike were near my feet, but they were just far enough out of reach I couldn't get them. If only the spike were a few inches closer, maybe I could shove it through my head and join Tooth.

There were no keys around, even though I'd heard them jingle when he unchained Tooth. That answered one of our earlier questions; he kept them all on the same key ring and he must have taken it with him.

From upstairs I heard, "I'll do it! You don't got to do everything yourself. Your way is not always the best way."

Canine domestic dispute. God was a funny motherfucker.

I heard him go outside, leaving me in total silence. Even the flies were hushed, contentedly sucking in the bits of carrion strewn about. I hadn't heard Jamie in a while, but I didn't want to think about that either so I just rolled my head side to side, apathetic that I could feel the cold cement against the back of it once more. I didn't care about anything; I just wanted to go to sleep.

But when my head hung forward and I found myself staring at the ground, I couldn't help but notice the spike again. It was so close yet worlds away. What if? I thought. How long would he be outside? What could I do with that spike?

As if I was being controlled by a puppeteer, I stuck my foot out as far as it would reach. The chain offered about two inches, but the spike was about three away. There had to be a way. I'd read so much about telekinesis, about moving objects with your mind, but no matter how hard I willed the spike to move it just lay still, happy where it was.

I looked over at the chains hanging empty beside me, the open cuffs stained red. Could I reach them, use them somehow? Did I really care?

But my musing was cut short when I heard the driveway door creak open real slow, like an old man with back pains afraid to fart too quick. It could have been the wind, but somehow I doubted it. I just had that feeling that something was amiss. Not hard considering my location. And sure enough, out of the shadows, came Butch down the stairs. Alone.

The fucking dog was a spawn of hell, had eaten flesh for a living of that I was sure. His oily black coat reflected the blood-stained bulb as he hungrily walked over to me. A cold, slimy tongue whipped out and licked the wound on my leg. I jerked my knee and he pounced backward.

"You like that," I said. "You want me to beat your face again, you fucking bitch?"

He cocked his head and studied me like I was abstract art.

"Yeah, you remember that, outside, when I punched you in the face. Hurt didn't it? Something broke, huh? What was it, a tooth, your jaw, a cheekbone? Come any closer and I'll do it again and I won't stop until you lie dead on the floor. C'mon!"

The black hellhound didn't move, just sat looking pensive. Then he sniffed the air a bit, like he was figuring out which part of me to bite first. Should have known he wouldn't run away. He probably grew up biting chained prisoners.

I jerked my knee again to entice him, and he jumped back and forth real quick, almost as if he was just playing. He gave a little bark and glanced at the stairs, like he was afraid the noise would bring his mentally handicapped owner and a smack to his ears. So I did it again, thinking at least that would be something.

Dogs are quick though, and you can't read them as well as humans, so when he charged me I yelped in terror. He jumped back, then snapped a few times and rushed me again. This time he went for my ankle but he bit the chain instead and shook it frantically. Growling and biting, he whipped the chain about. I spit a wad of phlegm at him and hit him in the eye and damn it felt good. Stunned, he took a few steps toward the stairs and licked his lips.

"Butch!" came from outside. "Butch, get out here now!" I heard Skinny Man getting closer to the house, yelling for his dog, until finally he stuck his head around the top of the stairs and said, "Butch, you know better than to go down without me. Get yer ass up here right now." I could see from his torso he was still naked, his garish gray tattoos looking like spots of decomposition. Didn't anybody live nearby enough to notice a naked man with a corpse in his backyard?

Butch looked at me, looked at his owner, and trotted up the stairs a defeated animal. As the two of them drifted out into the yard again I heard Skinny Man say, "Don't worry, we're gonna play with him in a few minutes."

It was a small victory but it was mine and it was all I had so I took it. The flies were landing on me like early arrivals to a concert looking for the best seats. It was all very telling of what was about to come. And I knew I couldn't win, not really, so I put my head down again and tried to find that spot on the beach once more.

And damn if I didn't notice something lying by my feet.

The fucking spike.

How the—? It was right next to my left foot, practically touching it. A few half-smudged paw prints decorated the dirt next to it. Butch must have kicked it when he lunged at me. My heart started to race and my body broke a sweat. I almost fought the feeling off, because I didn't want hope to fuck with me, but I also realized I didn't really want to die.

I lifted the toe of my sneaker and got the spike under my foot. I would have to do this very carefully, I thought, and I'd probably only get one shot. I drew it back and placed it perpendicular to the wall so that it stuck out like a nail. Using my heel, I pushed back on the tip of it and lifted it slowly until it was upright. Quickly, before it could fall, I slammed my foot flat against it and trapped it under my sole. The leg iron bent outward and cut my ankle open, slicing in deep enough I could feel it in my head. I gnashed my teeth against the pain, telling myself if this worked a lifelong limp would be worth it.

I reached down with my hand as far as I could, about two feet away from the spike. At this point I cursed myself for having never played sports because I was going to need more than luck on my side. I needed some fancy footwork and some serious skill. With the spike facing up like a rocket nearing takeoff, I flicked my foot up as much as the chain would allow and shot the spike up the wall.

Into my hand.

My heart was a salsa beat trying to rip through my rib cage. I couldn't believe it. I was so stunned I just leaned back against the wall and sighed, a big exhalation of tutti frutti emotion: rage, determination, fear, sadness, but mostly rage. I flipped the spike around so that the point was out and twisted my wrist to see what I could do with it. You ever see monkeys pick up a toy at the zoo and not quite understand how it works, try to eat a soccer ball or stick a comb up their nose? That's how I felt. And forget what I'd seen in films. I sure as fuck wasn't about to pick a lock with it, not only because I had never done so before, but also because the tip was too big to fit in the keyholes of the cuffs.

But I had it, so now what?

I thought maybe I could pry the cuff open, but thought better of it. The handcuffs were too strong to be broken and I'd probably break the spike or sever my wrist. I could see if Skinny Man would get close enough to jab it in his belly, but that would be a waste, he'd just take it away. I had to use it to get free somehow.

"Jumping Jesus, that fucker was starting to stink like my Aunt Gretchen's ass sores." It was Skinny Man, bounding down the stairs with Butch in tow. His limp prick swished back and forth like a broken watch hand. He was dirty, like he'd been digging, and the sonofabitch was wearing Tooth's Red Sox hat. I put the spike behind my lower back and pressed my body against the wall to hold it there.

"I put him next to Sundance, so the dog can get his revenge," he said. "Better late than never, you know. And Sundance, he don't like people that mess with him. He's a mean mother when he gets mad. Like this one time, delivery man comes to the door, and Sundance he's all barking and fixing to bite the guy's nuts off. But the guy figures he's safe because Sundance is behind the screen door and all, so he yells, 'Shut up, you smelly mutt!' And Sundance, you know what he did? He goes around the back and opens the back door and runs around to the front and bites the fucker in the ass. Tore a chunk right out. The guy's screaming and hollering for me to get the dog off him. But at that point it was out of my hands. Butch comes tearing through the house right behind Sundance, sees his brother having so much fun, and goes right for the neck. BAM! Just like that. Boy, we had fun with the fella, didn't we, Butch? Say, you ever seen one of these?"

He held up a short, slick, tube-like object. It was grayish-white where it wasn't covered in blood, and ringed with ridges.

"It's called a trachea. Interesting, I think. It's Butch's favorite. Here, boy, here ya go."

The dog took it and went over to his dish and put it on the floor. This seemed pretty amusing to Skinny Man, whose cackle filled the room. "What's the matter with you? You look like you got a pole up yer ass." He walked over to the dice, shooed away some flies and picked them up.

"I suppose you know what that looks like." I cursed myself for replying. What if he grabbed me and I dropped the spike? I wasn't thinking worth a shit.

"Actually I don't, but we got time enough to find out. Where's that duct tape?"

"Who was she?" I asked.

He looked at me funny, then hit on what I was talking about. "That bitch? She was probably someone's girlfriend or wife or mother. I don't really know, I didn't ask."

"Why did you kill her?"

"What is this, a Barbra Walters special? What do you care?"

"I just want to know what she did to you, what *we* did to you, why you're doing this."

"You're just stalling. But it won't help you because I'm in the mood for walking, not talking."

"I want to know." I really did want to know, but I was also stalling.

Skinny Man got kind of sullen and put his nose to mine and breathed into my mouth. "Because if I don't they get mad at me, hurt me. Even right now they're listening and if they hear what I'm telling you they're gonna be pissed. And if they get pissed nothing I do to you is gonna satisfy them. They'll just make me go on and on. Oh, son, I really wish you hadn't come here, but what can I do about it now?"

Who was *they*? The dogs? The flies? Ghosts? But then he chuckled and I couldn't tell if he was serious or not. Did he ever stop laughing? Psychiatrists might classify it as a nervous tic, but somehow, I knew he was truly finding pleasure in all this pain. That, on some deep level, scared me more than anything.

"My odds are looking good this time," he said as he played with the dice. "Fifty-fifty chance I roll your number. You want odds or evens?"

"I want you to die." I didn't know where that came from, it just burst out before I could stop it. I figured he'd slug me for it and I'd drop the spike and then all would be lost, but he didn't seem to mind. I'm sure he'd heard it all before.

"You're kind of an oddball, so I'll make you evens."

In his own head, he was the funniest thing since the whoopie cushion, and that last remark must have been his coup de grâce because he doubled over and snorted a bunch. "Get it?" he asked, still choking on his laughter, "'cause you're odd . . . see . . . and I said even. Get it? Shit, boy, don't you ever laugh? They say it's good for the soul, ya know. Aw, forget it, you're no fun."

He tossed the dice at my chest and they bounced across the floor like two kids playing tag. I couldn't see the numbers where they landed, but Skinny Man looked really pissed when he looked at them.

"Fine," he said, coming over and looking at me. "Fine. I'm a patient man, I am. Good things come to those who wait, I tell ya. And when she's gone you ain't gonna have no easy out. You fucking freak!"

He bent down and scooped up all his torture toys and started wiggling. He had to catch a couple small knives as they escaped his grasp, but he held them tightly and went over into Jamie's room. Within seconds she was crying. My chest went tight and breathing came hard. She was alive, and I thanked God for that, but was it worth it, was this really living?

I dropped the spike back into my hand and thought frantically about what to do. The links in the chains might be breakable, though my only experience in handcuffs before this told me not to get my hopes up. Still, without another choice, I jammed the tip of the spike into one of the links and tried to bend it. But it was no use. I needed a fulcrum point, some way to pry at the link without moving the chain. The wall, I thought, use the wall. I put the spike against the wall and leaned back against it, and held it still with my hand. It was a tricky position to maintain, but the wall provided reinforcement, and when I thrust my body backward, the spike drove in the link. The cuff ripped into my wrist and it felt like my bones were mashing. Ever so little, I could see the link warping, but at this rate I'd either break my wrist or die an old man before I got free.

"What you got there?"

I jumped at the voice, dropped the spike to the floor.

"When did you get that?" Skinny Man asked, holding a small knife in his hand that was covered in Jamie's hair and dripping blood. "You're a real sneaky Pete, ain't ya. But I believe that belongs to me."

He snatched it up and hit me on the head with it. The blow rang through my skull and lodged behind my eyes.

"I forgot something upstairs. If I come back and find you doing anything funny I'm gonna cut your ears off and sew them into your sister."

He took off up the stairs, leaving me alone with Jamie's screeching pleas for death. Well, not entirely alone—Butch was sniffing at the door to Jamie's room, riled up by the noise and jonesing for flesh.

CHAPTER 20

While Jamie cried, Butch whined and shot me a sad face as if to ask whether I could open the door for him. The dog had no manners. He gave up after a minute and went and lay near his dishes again, eyes glued to the door, his collar jingling against a piece of bone as he stretched out.

Dog collar.

Like a slap across the face something hit me. Something out of left field I had never noticed before. Butch was wearing a dog collar. I mean, I had noticed it all along, but it hadn't meant anything before. It never registered. But dog collars had buckles, and one part of a buckle was the small arm. Small enough, say, to fit into a cuff lock?

I was still pretty sure I'd never pick the lock. Fuck, I was so drained I probably couldn't do it with the key. But hope was still squatting in my brain, like a shit-faced drunk in an empty Beverly Hills estate, stretched out on the wraparound couch drinking fine aged bourbon, feet up on the wall, scratching his ass with a priceless antique rapier. In control is what I'm getting at. Making it impossible to sit still.

From above me I heard Skinny Man banging pots and pans, stomping across the floor and then back again. Slowly, Butch looked up too, like he'd seen this movie before but couldn't find anything better to watch.

"C'mere, Butch," I said. He turned his attention to me, tilted his head. "C'mere, I won't hurt you." Not now anyway, I wouldn't, but like Skinny Man said, good things come to those who wait.

"C'mon, you stupid fucking mutt, c'mere so I can pet you. C'mon."

I whistled a bit to entice him, but I think he had learned not to approach me carefree. Still, he looked interested, and if I could only lure him over. Perhaps what was needed was incentive. My leg was still coated in flaky blood, the wound was itchy and red and a couple of the tooth marks were moist with puss. I shook it like an elderly stripper auditioning for a Vegas review, and Butch finally stood up. He padded over and sniffed the leg and I reached for his neck, but he was out of range. Shit. The leg idea was working against me. I'd only get bit, and Butch would get a free meal.

I had to get him near my hand. So I rubbed my wrist against the cuff, opening the cut I had inflicted earlier. The pain shot up my arm like electricity and burned my insides. My teeth felt like they were being scratched with a file. It was so bad I almost stopped before I drew blood, but I forged on thinking of the larger picture. I needed to save Jamie, I needed to get free and call the police. I missed my parents. Tooth was dead. Jamie was butchered. So much blood.

No, I thought, don't ride that train. Stay focused.

As hard as I fought though, that train began running away, the images filling my head like too many people cramming into an elevator. Jamie tortured, Tooth's jaw on the floor. Oh God, no, don't lose it, don't think about it. There is no Jamie, no Tooth, nothing other than the chains on your wrists and the collar on the dog. Rub the wrist. Harder. Pain equals freedom.

The first drop of red hit the floor with a light plop and was eaten by the dirt. But Butch could smell it. Immediately he came over and put his nose against the cut, sniffed enthusiastically, and started licking the blood as it came out. To keep him where I wanted him I smeared some of the blood on my hip. He licked it off my shorts, and maybe decided it must be coming from there because he kept on licking until I could feel his saliva against my skin. With my hand on his head, I moved him closer with my fingers until I could grab the collar. The buckle was under his head, so I spun it up onto the back of his neck and got a good grip on it. Frantically, I worked my fingers to unclasp it. It wasn't easy. My thumb pushed the flap backward into the buckle, but it would only go so far before the eyelets stopped it and it bunched up. The difficult process was further compounded by the dog's inability to keep its head still as it licked.

"Stay still, will ya."

Dust was falling from the ceiling. Above me, the man walked toward the stairs. The collar was bunched up again. The footsteps got closer, they were coming fast. Butch moved his head but I grabbed the collar and yanked him back.

"You move again I will kill you so slowly you'll think the world's rewinding. Now stay still!"

I worked the flap backwards once again and slipped a finger under the loop that formed. Triumphantly, the arm came out of the eyelet. No sooner had it freed than Skinny Man was back at the top of the stairs. I ripped at the collar and the whole thing came loose. Skinny Man came down the steps, yelling something. I almost took the collar but knew he'd see me so I left it dangling around Butch's neck.

"Knew I'd find it sooner or later," he said. He held up a jug of bleach, unscrewed the cap. "Gotta be careful with this stuff, it can burn something awful." He shook the jug at me and a stream of bleach leapt out and hit the dirt in front of me. I pressed back into the wall. When it hit the floor it smoked a bit, and I thought, bleach doesn't smoke. Whatever he's got in there it ain't bleach, it's something much worse.

"Shit," he said, and flung his fingers about. He'd spilled some on himself and I smiled watching him try and wipe it off. "What are you laughing at? You still thirsty, Roger? How's about a drink."

"No thanks." Not that drink anyway. Real water, yes. Absolutely. Thirsty did not begin to describe the anguish my body was experiencing from the lack of food and water.

"Oh, now you don't want my hospitality. You sure are ungrateful, aren't ya? Snooping around people's yards, asking for favors and then showing no appreciation, stealing my tools."

He came over and ran his hands around my pockets, behind my back. I thanked God I had left the collar on Butch. The dog stepped aside quietly and sat near the boiler. His collar hung down on the sides of his neck, but Skinny Man didn't notice.

Still bare-assed, Skinny Man went over to the door to the back room. "I'm gonna have fun with you real soon, teach you some manners. But first there's a sweet little girl needs my attention."

He put his ear against the door and listened. Jamie had never stopped crying completely, alternating between moans and sobs. He looked like he was going to push the door open, his hand on the knob, but instead he backed up and returned to me.

With a skeptic look he said, "I gotta know."

Bending over so that his backbone poked through his skin, he scooped up the dice, looked at me like I had a small animal sticking out of my ear and then dropped them straight down toward his feet. They bounced a few times and came up nine. He didn't say anything, just glared and worked his jaw on some imaginary cud. It wasn't just anger; I could see fear in his eye as well. He was afraid of me, or rather, what he thought I might be. And I was afraid too. It hadn't been lost on me one bit the fact that my number had never come up, not once. Earlier, when I thought about the dice, I thought maybe there was a reason behind it, like maybe I had a purpose for being here. But even then deep down I feared it was luck or coincidence.

Now I was starting to believe it was something else. Why hadn't my number come up yet? What was expected of me? How much credibility was there to an old drunk's preachings? Destiny, purpose, fate. Who was I to the world? Just a stoned comic book lover who couldn't get his dick wet. But the dice . . . . Wrong place, wrong time? Or was I supposed to be here?

It scared the shit out of me.

Skinny Man stormed off into the other room without so much as a grunt and slammed the door shut. I heard him yell at Jamie with renewed vigor. Jamie shrieked and called for God but then the shriek became a gurgling, choking soundtrack of hell. Oh Christ, I felt it once more, the terror of the moment. I got the shaking feeling, the loss of breath. I fought it harder than ever before because I now had this crazy idea that I was being chosen for something. I concentrated on me, on the collar I needed.

"Butch, come over here, boy."

Jamie was gurgling, screaming, the repeated thumps most likely her body flailing from acid burns.

I rubbed my wrist again, drew more blood, and that got Butch real interested in me again. As soon as he got close enough I snatched the collar and looked at the small arm of the buckle and compared it to the keyhole.

They looked close.

Remembering Butch's distaste for my spit, I coughed up a chunk of innard and spewed it at him. It hit him in the back, completely off target, but enough to send him away for a moment. Twisting my hand around I barely was able to get the buckle arm near the hole. My wrist bent forward like a cripple and the cuff threatened to rip it open further, but the "key" was getting closer. I wiggled the buckle until it poked into the hole.

It was too big.

I went flaccid, sort of hung by the chain around my neck and felt all hope ooze out of my body. It was over, I would never escape—I would die here. I would watch my friend and sister die bit by agonizing bit, then I would die too. Fate meant nothing; it was all a sick joke.

Skinny Man kicked open the door and hurled the empty jug at me. It hit my shoulder and rebounded toward the stove where it came to stay. My muscles locked as I waited for the burning liquid to eat through my skin, but it never came—the jug was completely empty. As I flinched, I put the collar behind me like I had done the spike, expecting him to come take it and go for my ears. But he didn't see me hide it. Luck again, or fate?

From the open door, an inhuman wheeze meandered into the room. It was the sound of someone's last breaths.

Skinny Man still looked afraid. There was no satisfaction on his face like before. Why didn't he just have at me, forget this whole game he was playing with the dice? Clearly his mind was working overtime, he wasn't in control anymore. What was the old saying? Making monsters out of shadows? His imagination was becoming his worst enemy; he was believing the lie. Motioning for Butch to follow, he turned off the bulb and went up the stairs without a word. A minute later he came back with his keys and locked the basement door. Once that was done, he returned to his home above, but not before he locked the door at the top of the stairs as well. He was afraid of something.

Alone in the pitch-black of my cell, while the flies gorged themselves on the littered remains of my late friend, I listened to the wet wheezes coming from the room behind me. He left that door open.

On purpose.

CHAPTER 21

The wheezes became more labored and further apart. Jamie was dying. I wanted to get the collar from behind me, get down to business, get the flying fuck out of here, but I stopped myself. Somehow I knew I only had a few minutes before she gave in, and no amount of struggling was going to get me out of the cuffs in time to save her. Either I made my peace with it or I'd go mad.

"Jamie," I said into the void, "I'm right here. I'm right beside you. Listen to my voice."

I didn't know what to say, nothing in my past came close to anything of this magnitude. All I knew was I couldn't let her die thinking she was alone. She had to know I was here. My last attempt to say goodbye was only a notch above sniveling. I wanted so much to take her place, to take her pain for her, and it was killing me both mentally and physically. My insides were a knotted mess of brambles, ripping apart and twisting about. I couldn't let her die alone. I wanted her to know she was special.

"Jamie, oh God, Jamie. Do you remember the Christmas you gave me the Darth Vader model kit?" What a dumb thing to focus on, but I found myself unable to stop. "I thought Mom bought it and put your name on it, like always. Then a few weeks later I heard Mom and Dad talking in the kitchen and Dad was upset because I'd watched a horror film and had nightmares the night before, and he said he wished you hadn't bought me the model because it looked so menacing in the dark, and he thought it was giving me bad dreams. But, Jamie, I had no idea you spent your own money on that. I never said it, but it was the perfect gift. I'm sorry I never told you."

I wanted to tell her I still had the model, but the memory was too painful. Somewhere, probably in some dumb comic, I had read that a person's last thoughts followed them into the after life, and true or not, I wanted Jamie to be happy wherever she was going so I said the first thing I could think of.

"Jamie, we're at the park near home," I said, "and there're kids playing catch. Mom and Dad are sitting on a towel nearby, drinking iced tea. There's a good-looking guy over there checking you out. He looks just like Brad Pitt. You're gonna get a burger with him later, and then someday he'll marry you and you'll be wealthy and happy. Do you see the kids? Watch them, Jamie. Look at them run."

Suddenly, I was crying so hard the words were almost gibberish.

Though I'd been on a roller coaster ride of fear and exhaustion since my capture, it was the first time I realized—really realized—I was going to die, and die alone. Tooth had been my courage and Jamie my urgency, but now it was just me. And while I'd had moments of strength, it wasn't until Jamie's breath stopped a minute later that it really hit me no one was coming to save me.

No one knew where I was.

And perhaps that's why it was easier to tell myself to be a man for once and fight, say fuck you to fear. I knew if I had any chance of escape, it was now, it was up to me, and it was going to take every ounce of muscle I had. Not just physical, but mental as well.

So I swallowed my sobs, said goodbye to Jamie, grabbed the dog collar and twisted it in my hand to locate the buckle. Unfortunately, in the darkness I couldn't see the keyhole of the cuff, couldn't get my fingers on it. I already knew the buckle arm was too big, but if it was thinner, then what? Could I really pick a lock?

The answer came from somewhere, maybe my mind, maybe an angel whispering in my ear—yes.

It wouldn't be easy, though. I didn't know how to do it; I had never seen anyone do it. But I'd read my share of stories and comics and thought that maybe, just maybe, I knew the mechanics of it. Same way I knew that if these were the newest police standard cuffs I was probably screwed. A new set of police handcuffs would never unlock without the actual key, improvements in the last decade had made them virtually failsafe. But I didn't think these were regulation, they looked out of date, ovoid in appearance. They must have come from the Internet or an army navy surplus store. At least I hoped.

Jamie is *dead*. The thought punched me in the brain, an unpleasant reminder of what just happened. No, I thought, don't give in to it. Not yet. Get back to the cuffs.

And so I thought hard about everything I'd ever read that related to handcuffs or escapism.

Thanks to some brilliant comic book authors who had done their research, I knew that handcuffs had a bit on the inside that needed to be pressed back to trigger the release. I knew they had another pin on the outside that locked the cuffs in place so they wouldn't tighten themselves. And I knew they could be picked, somehow, with a small thin object provided it was shaped properly.

A small sharp object. That's what I needed. And it's exactly what I didn't have. What I had was a fat buckle on a dog collar.

With tears drying on my cheeks, I rested my head against the wall and racked my brain for a solution. *Jamie is dead* assaulted me again. I shook my head, slammed it back and let the physical pain push out the mental. The cold cement felt oddly refreshing on my scalp, like a compress. I was suddenly sleepy, sapped of energy, on the edge of forfeit. This was it, my last chance. How to make the buckle arm thinner? How to make it skinnier?

I played the mantra over and over in my mind, until it felt like it was eroding my skull. And that's when it dawned on me—I needed to erode the buckle.

With a prayer, I placed the buckle arm against the concrete wall . . . and rubbed.

It scraped over the concrete, flaking off bits of cement like dandruff. I did it a few times and then touched the tip. It was hot. It hadn't gotten any skinnier, but I felt certain it would.

With black all around me, and silence filling my ears, I rubbed and rubbed and rubbed. I don't know how much time passed. I don't know how loud it actually was, though to me it sounded like a car engine. I just scraped that little piece of metal against the concrete until my biceps flared up, until I was gnashing my teeth like a child waiting for a tetanus shot. Little cold specks of cement tickled the backs of my legs as they flew up then drifted to the floor.

After a long time, I stopped to check my progress and felt an incredible heat radiating off the metal. It had thinned ever so slightly, not enough, but it was enough to know this plan might work.

So I went back to work, and I rubbed and rubbed some more. My eyelids grew heavy; I had probably been up over forty hours by now. But sleep meant nothing to me; I had to keep rubbing.

Time was kept in relation to sounds from above. The television, a laugh track, Skinny Man talking, someone walking around, a voice I recognized, David Letterman, Skinny Man again. After awhile the television went silent. Maybe he was retiring for the night; maybe he was listening to *them*. Movies claimed the night was witching hour, and if so, shouldn't he be on his way down? Maybe he thought the night was too quiet for screams, maybe he worked, maybe he was just tired. Who knew?

I didn't stop again until my shoulder felt swollen, until the passing hours became a blur. Then I touched the small piece of metal and smiled. As I'd hoped, it had thinned into a pin. I couldn't believe it, it had worked! Now all I had to do was pick the lock using the exact hand that was bound. Why, I thought vexingly, was every jumped hurdle met with an even larger one beyond it?

It was an issue of *Chaos Legion*, number twenty-one or twenty-two, if I remember correctly, where Stanley Horner—aka Greymatter, so named because he could steal your mind and leave you babbling like a vegetable—had to get out of handcuffs before a bomb turned him into what would be considered a delicacy in my present whereabouts. As a mental mutant with no elevated physical strength, he'd saved himself by pulling a nail out of a floorboard and using it as a key.

I sifted through the debris in my mind trying to remember the context of the comic. Bits and pieces started to come back to me like roaches to an open trash can, and soon I could visualize the page, the words, and the illustrations. Inside a handcuff was a sloped lever that allowed the cuff teeth to slide forward but not backward, so that the cuff tightened and wouldn't slide open. Additionally, a tiny pin on the outside of the cuff, when pushed in, slid in over the sloped lever and blocked the cuff from sliding forward anymore, preventing the cuff from tightening itself further. But this pin could very easily be pushed out from the other side with something thin.

I decided to attack that challenge first. It took a few attempts, what with my hands all gimped up by the cuff, but by using my leg and the wall, I pushed the pin on the right cuff back out with the sharpened buckle. After I had done that, I swung the collar to my other hand and did the same thing over there. Now I had to be very careful; I could easily tighten the cuffs and snap my wrists.

Back inside my head, I reread *Chaos Legion*. What was Stanley telling me? Handcuff keys end in a small flag, like a P, which is turned to flatten the sloped lever and allow the cuff to slide back without the teeth hitting it. The flag is essential. Stanley had used the leg of his chair to bend the nail.

Using the wall and the cuff itself, I began bending the tip of the buckle arm at a ninety-degree angle. Despite still being hot and thin, the metal was as strong as the Hulk's erection and I had to strain to get it shaped into a small hook. It wasn't a flag but it was probably close enough, or so I hoped.

I put the buckle in my belt loop, the collar strap hanging down near my leg, leaving the buckle arm sticking straight out. Slowly, with grandma speed, I slid the cuff's keyhole onto the "key" and pushed it in as a far as it could go. Then, using my wrist, I rotated the cuff.

The buckle arm fell out of the keyhole.

Shit, I mumbled, welcome to Dexterity 101. This wasn't going to be easy.

CHAPTER 22

I repeated the process ad nauseam. Sticking the "key" out, pushing the cuff on it, turning my wrist. Hour after hour I kept at it, until I could faintly hear birds singing the ain't-it-great-to-be-alive song in the trees outside. And then, as my eyes were sliding shut . . . the key flattened the lever, and the cuff opened just enough for me to slide my hand out.

And that was that. No fireworks, no dancing bears, no parade. Just me holding my hand in front of my face, straining to see it in the dark, and feeling my lips spread wide in an involuntary smile. I stood like that for who knows how long, motionless, sweat dripping down the nape of my neck, not believing what I'd just done. How long before I was able to get my head straight? It felt like it had been in a blender, shot into space and time-warped back.

I went to work on the other cuff, which was much easier to manipulate with my one hand free. Working furiously, I picked it the same as the last one, but for some reason it wouldn't come open, the "key" felt wrong, like maybe I had bent it out of shape somehow. I tried to pull it out to check on it, but it was stuck inside the lock. FUCK! I nearly screamed. Instead, I jimmied it and prayed it would find the lever. My desperation to escape was now beyond need, like a drug, an impulse I couldn't fight.

The whole while the voice in my head kept saying, *Calm down, you can do it, don't give up*. And I'd be lying if I didn't say that voice sounded as if it came from somewhere else in the room as well. But I didn't think on that too long. Besides, I was tired like a man forced to listen to a congressman's speech, so I couldn't be quite sure of what I was seeing or hearing. I just hoped it wasn't a dream, because if I woke up and found myself still bound, well, I didn't want to think on that either.

Maybe a half-hour passed, the faintest glow of light now seeping in under the door, when the cuff snapped back and the "key" dislodged.

I was free.

Soon as I rubbed my wrist to ease the pain I heard the voice again. *Don't stop, get free now.*

Wasting no time, I went straight for the neck iron. Skinny Man was smarter than he let on, because the clamps around my neck prevented me from just leaning forward and stretching out for one of the tools against the far wall. Skinny Man was also a sly man.

I felt for the keyhole and plunged the sharpened buckle inside and rooted around. The lock was a different type than the cuffs, bigger and older. It probably used a skeleton key with several teeth. Of course, I couldn't be sure in the dark, but I had seen the one used on Tooth so I figured it was the same.

Out of nowhere a cool breeze ran across my face. It smelled like the trees in the mountains outside. It smelled like freedom. Where it came from I didn't care, under the door, a crack in the foundation, it didn't matter; it spurred me on despite my heavy fatigue. A fatigue that had me feeling like I was walking in a dream.

The makeshift lock pick was having about as much effect on this lock as a finger would have on a woman with ten kids. It was just too small for the hole. I ran the dog collar through my belt loops so it wouldn't fall to the ground, and with both hands, grabbed the chain that connected the collar to the metal plate in the wall. It was stuck fast. Yanking only hurt my arms and back, and the metal plate had obviously been built into the wall somehow and wasn't budging.

Spinning myself around, my legs in a painful X, I faced the wall and got my first real look at what was holding me. The chain from the collar was welded into a link in the wall plate. No way it was going to come loose no matter how hard I pulled. The back of the collar had a hinge, and unlike the front which was locked with a padlock, it was held tight by a long screw. The screw allowed the collar to open and close, but true to Skinny Man's precautions, it had no crevice for a screwdriver; it was smooth and solid and held tight by a nut on the bottom. Years of rust had fused the nut to the screw and the top of the screw to the collar, and no matter how hard I twisted it wouldn't come undone.

With a wrench I could make a go at it, but with nothing but a dog collar I was back to square one. At this point I was a firm believer in making do with what I had. If a wrench was what I needed, a wrench I would have to make. So taking my new wonder tool from my belt loop, I turned it over in the wan sunlight, thought about how to modify it. I stuck the flat end of the buckle under an exposed lip in the wall plate and bent it upwards. You'd be surprised how strong the metal of a dog collar buckle is. Small and thick, it damn near refused to give. I was forced to bend down and use both my legs and shoulders, thrusting my body up before it started folding. The pain this caused the palms of my hands was excruciating.

I kept at it till I had folded it at about a sixty degree angle, forming a V. Once bent, no amount of prying by my bare hands would open it, which hopefully meant it was strong enough to counter the screw's resistance. The nut, to my surprise, fit snuggly in the V. There was no time to ponder the convenience of it all—I just gave the collar a hard turn. With the screw rusted to the hinge, the nut began to give. My heart was beating fast, my tongue hanging out in some stupefied expression of determination. I twisted harder, till my back cracked like a brick of firecrackers, until the nut spun free. I grabbed it and twisted it, spun it faster and faster until it fell to the floor. Then ramming my palm against the bottom of the screw, I shoved it up and out of the top of the hinge. I pulled the clamp apart and let it swing back against the wall.

Rubbing my neck, I felt the cheese grater scars the collar had inflicted. Terrified as I'd been, I hadn't even noticed how it had eaten away my skin.

Clomp, clomp, clomp.

Footsteps echoed above me and before long dust was trickling down from the beams overhead. My heart did zero to sixty in one second, slamming against my ribs, trying to escape my body. My stomach was doing somersaults. If Skinny Man came down right now I was a goner, my legs still shackled as they were. I thought about slipping the collar back on and putting the handcuffs back, but loose enough that I could pull free if I needed to, but I knew he'd never be fooled. The footsteps stopped at the top of the stairs. He took out his keys and unlocked the door. I froze.

The door didn't open.

"Butch," he said, "get yer ass out here and stop trying

to get in the garbage. Sometimes you piss me right off. Always cleaning up after you. C'mon, get out here now. Now sit and listen up. We got a lot to do today and I'm gonna need your help so stop messing around. First thing we gotta do—what the? Where's your collar?"

My heartbeat went from sixty to one hundred. He knew! Trying desperately to be quiet, I put my arms over my head and slid down out of the waist chain and stood back up a free man but for my feet. Quickly, I sprawled out across the floor, and reached for the big ax that lay in the light spilling in under the door. It was close, my fingertips brushing against it, but I couldn't get a good grip on it.

"Did you leave it downstairs?"

The door at the top of the stairs opened. Stretch, I told myself, stretch!

"It better not be festering in your food." His footfalls bumped down the wooden steps.

Stretch! Just a little more!

Footsteps halfway down the stairs now. My fingers touching the handle but not enough to grab it. More steps, closer, near the door. Another couple steps and he'd be here. My fingers, walking on the handle, inching it into my grasp. There!

I worked it backwards with my fingers, grabbed the hilt like Babe Ruth and stood ready to swing. My heart was beyond miles per hour; it was doing warp speed. My palms filled with so much sweat the ax kept sliding around. Then Skinny Man stopped.

"Wait a minute," he said. "Did you bury it? Jesus Christ you did, didn't ya? That's the millionth collar I've bought you this year. If you buried this one too, I'm gonna make you regret it. No, I don't want to hear your excuses. Do you think I'm made of money or something? Shut up and let me talk for once, you don't always need to interrupt. I'm not gonna buy you another so I suggest you go out and dig it up. Whatdya mean, 'Help you?' Why should I help you, you did it? Do you see me in the backyard digging up the dirt with my hands, dropping my shit in it and covering it up? When was the last time you saw me do that? Yeah, okay, Mr. Wiseguy, but aside from that, you're the only one who buries shit out back. I swear it's like you got the O-C-D. I couldn't find the butter last night, did you bury that, too? What happened to the butter? Probably resting in a shallow grave out back, I bet. God, you make me so mad. No, I will not help you go look for it. Why should I, give me one good reason?"

There was a pause. I stood waiting, my sweat dripping down the ax handle.

"You better hope I don't find anything else I been looking for out there. I swear, why you gotta bury everything is beyond me."

He went back up and closed the door. Then the driveway door opened and he and his maniacal mutt drifted away. Thank God for insanity, I thought. With those two out of the house, I figured I had a couple minutes to improve my situation. I glanced at the ax. From the dim light I could see it was still covered in blood, most likely my sister's, but I forced the image out of my head. What was important was that it was sharp and it was heavy.

Enough adrenaline was coursing through my body I felt I could jump to the moon. But it was also making me shake and I needed steady hands if I was going to get out of this alive. So I took a couple deep breaths until my ability to focus returned.

I raised the ax over my head and brought it down on the chain connected to the leg irons.

CHUNK!

Metal and dirt resounded off the walls as the weapon struck. *Weapon*, I thought. Was it wrong I saw the tool as a weapon? I guess I always saw tools as weapons because of the horror movies I'd seen, but this was different; I honestly could not find another use for the instrument in my hands other than chopping someone up.

CHUNK!

I hit the chain again, tiny bits of dirt spitting up at my face. I hit it a third time and a fourth time and a fifth, fearing that each bang would bring Skinny Man running down the stairs with a knife in one hand and butter in the other.

CHUNK! CHUNK! CHUNK!

The chain broke, just a little, but I was able to slip the broken link off the rest of it. The leg iron was still attached to my ankle, but I was mobile. I hit the other chain that connected the other leg iron as hard as I could. Two times. Three times. Then the blade bit through one of the links and I separated the cuff, still on my leg, from the chain.

I was free. Totally free.

First thing I did was listen for signs of Skinny Man outside. I could barely hear him, so next thing I did was go to the basement door and check the knob, which I already knew was locked. Using the ax, I slipped the blade into the door jamb and worked it like a crowbar. The cheap wood buckled easily with a loud crunch and the knob cracked out and fell to the floor. Again, I listened to see if the noise would bring Skinny Man but I could still hear his voice coming from outside.

Like a man playing with dynamite, I cautiously opened the door and placed a foot on the first step. The wood groaned under my weight, my leg iron chain jingled. Sunlight came through under the door at the top of the stairs, a bright blue that caught the dust motes and swirled them about like an enchanting spell. I took another step, listening to my heart pump a tribal drumbeat, squinting into the sunlight. How long had it actually been since I'd seen this much natural light? Two days? Three? More? Before I could take another step I heard something that nearly caused me to drop the ax.

I heard a moan. And it came from Jamie's room.

My gut felt like lead, my knees buckled, I spun around and fell to my ass. It couldn't be. She was dead, I had listened to her die. Oh God, my sister was alive, and I was suddenly so terrified I couldn't bring myself to go back down the few steps I'd ascended. She moaned again, a guttural, confused tone that reminded me of a cat I'd once seen crawl into the woods and die after getting hit by a car. Then she coughed and went silent.

I sat for a few seconds, slowly going out of my mind once more, losing any sense of control I had maintained to this point. I felt my shoulders shaking and my head bobbing a bit. I saw the waves in California come back like a tsunami, rolling over me with oblivion. At some point, I could feel myself rising and walking over to the door that hid my sister, though my mind was beginning to drift away somewhere else, erecting defense barriers to deal with what I was about to see.

Oh God, oh please God, oh please don't let it be bad. Oh, Jamie, I'm sorry, please don't let it be bad.

I stepped into the room. Everything was black, cast in shadows. The windows had been covered with spray paint or marker or something. A putrid smell hit me full on and would have caused me to vomit had I not already been breathing death for so many days. Still, it was stronger in here than where I'd been. If you painted the walls with a thousand years of decayed flesh, that's the smell I was experiencing.

Through the distant noises from the backyard and the wind blowing by the windows, I could hear the shallow, labored breathing of my sister from somewhere not far away.

"Jamie?" I called. "Please, Jamie, if you can hear me, just make a small noise."

There was no reply other than her raspy breath. Feeling around the door jamb, I located a switch and flicked it on, but it did nothing. I walked through the room, sweeping the ax handle in front of me in case there were any traps or sharp objects. I cleared a path through a collection of metal objects that littered the floor, some little, some big, all indistinct.

As I got closer to one of the blackened windows, I could hear Jamie's breathing getting louder. The stench grew more caustic. Paint was flaking off one of the nearest windows, and some light drizzled through enough that I could see her silhouette. Unlike me, she wasn't chained to a wall but rather lying on the ground. I stopped a few feet away, afraid to see her up close.

For one thing, from where I stood the shape on the ground looked too small to be Jamie.

I took another step.

Candles had been placed on the floor in a circle around her, most of them now burned down into puddles of wax—like Mystery Woman, I thought.

Another step.

My foot nudged something and I caught a flash of reflected sunlight from a small blade. Assuming it was a knife, I reached down to pick it up and felt many more sharp blades resting near my feet. Knives, handsaws, nails, barbed wire, a hammer, a circular saw blade, several blunt objects that were sticky, lots of rags. I also picked up something smooth and light, and held it up into the thin ray of sun falling through the window.

It was a human bone. And that's exactly when Jamie's body lurched.

I jumped back and landed on something sharp, cutting open my hand. In front of me, Jamie's body bounced up and down like a fish out of water, arcing into the sunlight and slamming back down into shadow. Up and down, up and down, and breathing as if a small rodent was trying to run down her throat. Chains jingled and hit the floor while she thrashed, held tight to what looked like stakes driven into the ground. I caught strobing glimpses of her body in the light. It wasn't human. It wasn't anything—a creature that had crawled out of hell, asphyxiating on earth's atmosphere.

With my hands walking over all the blades, I crawled backwards to the door, my breath caught, the whole while thinking there was no way that thing was my sister. Still clutching the ax, I found my way out the door back into the room I had called home for too long, stood up and took it in. The stove, its small door open with the shovel still sticking out, the fire long since dead. The hedge cutters leaning against the wall. The various devices Skinny Man had left on the table. The bloodstained chains dangling from the wall. The pile of gore in the dog dishes at my feet, with Tooth's jaw sitting like a crown on top. The sticky puddle of skin from Mystery Woman, who had been so close to freeing us, if only she'd had a few minutes more.

The dice. On the floor near the door, sitting in the sunlight. Two red cubes of terror that had saved my life.

I picked them up, held them in my hand. My number had never come up. Was it luck that had spared me? Or something else? Tooth's father's words ran around my mind once more: Got to have a purpose in life.

I put the dice in my pocket. I don't know why, it just felt right, like I was acknowledging something higher than myself, something ethereal. I think maybe I figured they'd protected me this far, it might be good to have them around.

I saw California again. It came in bursts like that now. One minute I'd be staring at so much blood and horror, the next I was watching the Pacific. I couldn't control it anymore, something more instinctual was taking over. The sensation of sand between my toes, the smell of salty air in my nose, the susurration of waves in my ears—it was all too real. Part of me wanted to sit down and enjoy it, but instead I headed up the stairs. The thing that used to be Jamie was still alive.

I needed to call for help.

CHAPTER 23

At the top of the stairs, I pushed the door open into the tiny alcove we'd first spied from the trees, and threw my hand over my eyes to block out the daylight. Overcast as it was, the natural light threatened to burst my pupils. The fresh air was like a plumbing snake unclogging my lungs. The smell of evergreen trees and mountain wildflowers made me want to rush out the door at full speed and kiss the ground. It was the best smell I had ever smelled, light and fresh, with hints of pine and sap, juniper and wild lilac. It smelled so safe. Briefly, I believed I could open my eyes and find myself back at home, this whole nightmare having been just that: a nightmare.

It took a few seconds for the ache in my pupils to subside before I could see what was around me. To my right I noticed the door to the driveway, and to my left was the opening to the kitchen.

From outside came Skinny Man's voice: "I'm sick of this shit, we ain't gonna find it and quite frankly I don't care anymore. Just don't expect any more gifts from me, you ungrateful mutt. Get away from that mound! That ain't for you, you already had your fill of that one."

The driveway door wasn't a viable option or I'd be seen. Plus I needed to find a phone, dial 911, and get some authorities out here pronto. Maybe I could call O'Conners' bar and tell the skinheads a bunch of eggplants were raping white women here? Knowing the police as intimately as I did, the skinheads would most likely get here quicker. Then again, knowing their kind, they'd probably see

Skinny Man and join him in a beer.

Stepping slowly into the kitchen, I scanned the walls and table for a phone but didn't see one. The blinds on the windows, coupled with the drab slate-colored clouds outside, bathed the room in a dark and gloomy grayness. The walls were covered in wallpaper from the disco era, a faded collision of orange and yellow and brown that reminded me of the puddle of filth on the floor downstairs. The counters were buried under flotsam and jetsam of all sorts: books, papers, dirty dishes, silverware, clothing, toys, bottles, and lots of tools like hammers and screwdrivers. A table sat pushed up against the wall, some dirty plates on it and a fruit bowl with a mostly brown banana in it that matched the walls. A puke green refrigerator hummed in the corner with pictures of Butch and the late Sundance stuck to it with magnets. Next to it sat a stove that looked like it had lost a fight with a jar of Ragu. Flies buzzed at the windows looking for a way out.

Being in the kitchen sent my stomach ablaze. The last thing I'd eaten were some eggs at my house before we set out for Bobtail. The refrigerator was sure to have food, I thought, but I didn't open it. I didn't trust any of the food in this house. I wouldn't put it past Skinny Man to poison it somehow.

Ignoring the cramping in my stomach, I ducked low and moved across the kitchen until I was in front of the sink. Over it was a window that looked out into the backyard, and Skinny Man's voice was coming through it loud and clear. "You bury that back up 'fore someone sees it. And don't touch that one neither." There was a pause. "Poor fella, he didn't deserve to get shot like that. We were probably too quick with that fucking kid, felt like it was over before it began. Unsatisfactory, I tell ya."

Butch's black teeth marks in my shin were opening up once again and dripping blood down my ankle. The pain was sensational, making my head throb, but I ignored it and rose up slowly and moved aside the edge of the curtain. Outside, Butch was sitting on the ground under the swing set watching Skinny Man tamp down dirt on a freshly-dug hole. As usual, he had his shirt off, his tattoos like thick veins on his skin. The shovel he carried was different than the one in the stove downstairs. This one was newer, the handle still shiny yellow. On his hip, dangling through a leather loop that fastened to his belt, he wore the hand ax he had so recently removed from Mystery Woman's skull.

The man was like a walking advertisement for the Tool of the Month Club.

Turning on the sink, I bent down and lapped up some tap water. There were hints of chemicals in it, possibly chlorine and other bacteria-killing agents poured into the reservoir by the city, but I didn't mind. My throat was dry and sore and it was hard to swallow, but it was the greatest feeling in the world. I filled my empty stomach, gasped for breath, and did it again. Not for too much longer though, a few seconds tops, and then I turned it off. My body demanded more but the house was old, and I feared the pipes might knock and give me away.

Just to be safe I checked the window once more and found Skinny Man was still preoccupied. He hadn't heard me. I let the curtain fall back and slid down to the floor again. My adrenaline was wearing off, my leg was aching badly, and the grimy tile floor suddenly felt very comfortable, beckoning me to put my head down and sleep. Each time I blinked I saw something different before me: my parents eating dinner, the waves of the Pacific, Jesus playing basketball. Then, like sap down a tree, my back began to drift toward the floor. I was falling asleep and couldn't stop it. It felt so good.

No, you'll die, I told myself, and Jamie will die too. Get up!

I slapped myself in the face and when that didn't work I stuck a finger in the dog bite.

Sweet Jesus the pain was intense, like someone peeling back a giant hangnail on my lower body. But it served its purpose. I woke up in a flash and crawled out of the kitchen, trembling as I held the blade of the ax in my hand to avoid any noise. It was damn near pointless since the leg irons jingled so loudly you could hear them in Vermont.

I crawled into a musty, wood-paneled living room that was likewise buried in shadow from drawn curtains. Standing up, fighting the pain in my shin, I saw a couch that looked as if it had been made out of hand-me-down clothes. A collection of notebooks and Polaroid photographs were strewn about on the cushions. I picked one up and immediately threw it down when I saw what it was a picture of. No amount of shaking my head would clear away the image of two little boys on a floor, naked. One had a rottweiler's prick in his mouth, against his will. The other boy was mutilated, diced, and the second dog was feasting on the remains. Don't think about it, I told myself. Think about Jamie, think about Jamie and about California and find a fucking phone. Just don't, whatever you do, think about it.

A water ring-stained coffee table sat in the middle of the floor, covered with dirty dishes and a bowl full of keys. Car keys by the looks of them. Maybe ten different pairs. Quickly, I ran my hand through it, hoping to find Tooth's Camaro keys, but came up empty. As I was turning away to continue my search for a phone, I noticed something else on the coffee table that made my heart leap.

Under an upturned magazine, poking out like a turtle's head, was the black muzzle of a gun. I snatched it up and looked at it, and sure enough, it was a 9mm—Tooth's gun. Shaking so badly I almost dropped the damned thing, I rested the ax against my legs, ejected the gun's clip like Tooth had shown me and checked for bullets. It was empty. I rummaged about the coffee table in the hopes of finding ammunition but all I found was junk. With a sigh, I slammed the clip back in and tucked the gun in my waistband in case I came across any bullets later.

There was no phone in here either.

Next to a black pipe that ran from a hole in the floor up through the ceiling—no doubt from the stove in the dungeon—was a staircase leading upstairs. I grabbed the banister and hauled myself up. The guy had to have a phone somewhere, didn't he?

At the top of the stairs I stopped and listened. Skinny Man was still out back talking to Butch and I figured if there wasn't a phone up here my best bet was to run out the front door into the woods across the street and make for Bobtail. Once he noticed I was gone, he'd be all over the road looking for me, probably send Butch out through the woods just to cover all the trails. The ax would help me, but I was very tired, and its weight was hurting my shoulders. My eyes were stinging from lack of sleep, and fatigue was creeping back up on me.

The stairs ended at the start of a hallway with three rooms— what appeared to be two bedrooms on either side and a bathroom at the end. I went into the bedroom to my right, which turned out to be filled with various boxes of clothes and other belongings. Pocketbooks, backpacks, sleeping bags. There were even a couple bicycles leaning up against one wall. Again, the drawn shades cast the room in a thick darkness, and from what I could see it was phoneless. Cursing under my breath, I turned back toward the hallway and noticed a small knife lying on top of the dresser near the door. It wouldn't hurt to have as many weapons as possible, I thought. I picked it up and held it flush with the ax handle, so that if I had to I could drop the ax and still be holding the knife.

That's when I noticed the photo.

It was lying flat on the dresser as well, and behind its cracked glass was a family of three: a mother, father and daughter, all standing next to the swing set that Skinny Man was standing next to right now. The little girl was maybe six or seven, blonde, with a front tooth missing, and she looked happy holding her father's hand. The mother's smile looked forced, and dark circles under her eyes spoke of extreme stress. The father was . . . well, the father was Skinny Man. The smile that stretched across his face was longer then the Rio Grande. Was this his family? Where were they now? Did they leave him, or did he butcher them as well?

Truth was, I didn't really care. I put the photo back on the dresser and left.

Skinny Man's voice carried up to me as I went across the hall and peeked into what was arguably his bedroom. "Soon as I finish this up you're gonna help me take care of that troublemaker down there, make him wish he was his friend, and I want you to help me out and not give me any lip. What do you mean do him fast? I don't want to do it fast. We been too hasty with these fuckers. We gonna take our time and do him right."

I had to find a phone or get out now. In the bedroom, a large four poster bed sat among heaps of more clothing, magazines, notebooks, photographs, and a broken acoustic guitar. On the nightstand beside the bed was a glass of water and some crumpled up pieces of paper. Hanging on the post of the bed was a beat up Red Sox cap. I walked over and took it off, looked at it and knew instantly it was Tooth's. Holding it brought back the recent events I was trying so hard to block out. The torture, the pain, the way he'd fought till the very end. The way I'd cried and cried through it all, praying the dice would ignore me. We had set out to shoot beer cans and smoke weed, just two friends trying to hold onto a childhood that was slowly disintegrating with age. And then . . .

I rolled up the hat and put it in my back pocket. Given a choice, Tooth would have taken this hat to the grave with him, and I figured I could do that much for him.

Something crunched under my foot as I moved back to the door. I looked down and saw a collection of plastic prescription pill bottles, maybe twelve in all, scattered on the ground. A few were empty, were missing their lids, some lone pills resting nearby, but most were full. I picked one up and read the label: Clozapine. Never heard of it. I didn't know what the drug did, or what it was for, but it sure as shit wouldn't surprise me if it had something to do with psychosis. The date on the label was over a year old. I picked up another, also still full, and saw the date on it was also a year old.

I dropped it back down to the floor, next to a child's doll with wiry blond hair.

I gave the room a final once over and didn't see a phone anywhere. Okay, I decided, the fucker doesn't own a phone, time to leave by the front door and run as fast as possible on my rotting leg to Bobtail.

In the hallway again, I took a breath and steeled myself for the journey. I was moving toward the stairs when it hit me that the backyard was suddenly quiet, too quiet, the kind of quiet that scares the shit out of new parents. Rushing into the bathroom, I slid up next to the window that looked out over the backyard and, barely breathing, pulled back the corner of the blind. I looked out toward the swing set.

Skinny Man was staring right back at me.

The curtain fell out of my hand as I plastered myself against the wall, my heart slamming against my ribcage. At the same time, Skinny Man let out a bloodcurdling wail that sent squawking birds flying from the trees, a wail that raced from the swing set to the driveway door.

And then he was inside the house and rushing though the kitchen, knocking pans to the ground. I heard him in the living room, screaming, a clatter of falling objects bouncing in his wake.

A shadow exploded up the stairs, followed by a body that was swinging a shovel like a crack addict frantically looking for a piñata full of drugs. Then he saw me, and in his wide ape-shit eyes, though I was at least fifteen feet away, I swear I saw the trembling reflection of a man with nothing more to lose: myself.

He stopped at the landing, maybe stunned, maybe collecting his strength, maybe hearing voices, who knows. My body was shaking, both in fear and anticipation, and I thought of Jamie downstairs, and what I had to do for her. I thought of Tooth and the way he died. I thought of myself and how unfair it all was. A silence passed between us, him staring at me, me staring back, like two gladiators in ancient Rome. There was no noise but our eager breathing. He was pissed, outraged that I had escaped, outraged at himself most likely. With a spit-drenched roar, he raised his shovel and rushed at me.

"Ahhhhh!"

Without thinking, I charged him with the ax, holding it high like a reaper taking souls, screaming unholy nonsense and simply beyond concern of catching a shovel to the skull. And that's when I saw something that nearly made me stumble, something behind Skinny Man that I knew couldn't be real, something that gave me a renewed burst of speed.

I swung the ax.

With an explosive clang, the two weapons collided in mid air, accompanied by angry screams and cracking handles. Then, either because the ax was heavier, or because of what I knew couldn't possibly be in the hall with us, Skinny Man fell backwards and toppled down the stairs, the shovel arcing through the air with him. My momentum carried me forward and I fell down on top of him, losing the ax as I tumbled.

Still holding the knife, I rolled past him and into the wall at the bottom, spilling into the living room like dirty laundry. Pain erupted throughout my back, my vision blurred. My shoulders seemed to swell up before my eyes, and I was pretty sure my spine was sticking out the top of my head. The dog bite on my shin was gushing like a geyser. I looked up and found Skinny Man lying on the stairs, upside down, with his leg caught in the railing. Above him, the ax peeked out over the top stair, out of my reach. He swung the shovel at me but he was a couple feet too far away to hit me. I braced myself for it to come flying at me next, but he held on to it instead. Watching him watching me, I noticed one of the railing spokes had stabbed through his calf muscle, pinning him there like a fish on a hook.

He yelled, "You are in a heap of shit now. Only people who leave here are the ones marked paid in full, and I don't see a receipt on your toe, now do I?"

And with that he punched through the spoke and broke it off from the railing. Standing up with the thin piece of wood impaling him, he reached down and took hold of the shortest end and proceeded to pull it all the way through and out the other side of his leg, grinning the whole while. Once the spoke was out, blood began to pool on the stairs and run down toward me. He took a step and winced, sweat flowing from his brow, and his face twisted in surprise. I guess he didn't think his little trick would hurt that much, but from the way he was breathing through his clenched teeth, and the way he was now afraid to walk, he had obviously misjudged his own threshold for pain. Still, I was in no shape to make for the ax above him so I turned and limped toward the front door.

"Where you going, mama's boy? You still have to atone for your crime. Hey, Butch!"

A loud bark came from behind me and I spun with my fists raised and ready. Butch came charging through the living room like a runaway train and slammed me into the door. Sharp teeth bit down on my hip and sank into my flesh, thrusting me into the door repeatedly. In excruciating pain, I wrapped my arm around his head and tried to shove the knife in his throat.

From the stairs, Skinny Man yelled, "No! Don't you hurt him! I'll kill you!"

But Butch was thrashing, and the knife missed its target and sank into his shoulder instead. With a yelp he burst back into the kitchen and disappeared, the knife still protruding from his body. My hip was filled with red hot gravel. Blood was seeping down my groin. Realizing I had to get out now, I reached up to undo the latch on the front door. From behind me I heard the Frankenstein clomp of Skinny Man shuffling down the steps, and a second later a shovel swooped over my head and took a chunk out of the lintel. I grabbed the handle before he could pull it back and wrenched it from his hands, swung it back at him with all my might. But I was hurt and beyond fatigued, and I misjudged the swing and hit the banister instead. The reverberation sent a shock wave up my arm and I dropped it on the floor. In an instant Skinny Man was on top of me.

"I'm gonna cut you up nice and fine," he whispered in my ear as we struggled. I saw him go for the ax on his belt. "Hell, I didn't ask you to come here, you did that on yer own. So many people always trying to come through my property, hike through my hills, drive through my woods. Nobody ever learns, do they?"

My shoulders felt like cornmeal and my punches had little effect. Getting a thumb up to his eye, I jabbed it in but it was a weak attempt. He pulled his head away and put me in a headlock and squeezed, still trying to undo the ax. Spots jumped before me; I was losing my breath. In a way, it felt good, like I would soon be asleep and in a better place. Again, I could see random images before me, the ever-present image of California that had lodged into my subconscious, a quick flash of Jamie when she was younger, holding her teddy bear, my father yelling at me for watching too many horror films. Then I saw another vision: Tooth, standing in the corner of the room. He was saying something to me. "Go for the leg, he's hurt in the leg."

Kicking back, I hit the gaping wound on Skinny Man's calf, rubbed the heel of my shoe down it and ripped it open wider. At the same time I scratched at his face and tore open the flesh under his eye. He lost his grip on me and I dropped straight to the floor, out of his hands. Groggy and gasping for breath, I lifted myself up as quickly as I could manage and kicked him in the chest, sent him into the bottom stair, which he tripped backwards on. Before he even hit the ground, he was pulling the hand ax free from its loop.

Knowing I was outnumbered two to one at that point, I unfastened the latch on the door and threw myself into the sunlight. I burst through the overgrown front lawn and made for the trees across the street.

CHAPTER 24

I was halfway across the lawn when I looked back and saw Skinny Man coming at me with the hand ax. With the wound in my leg I wasn't able to run as fast as I needed to and he was gaining on me, either used to the pain in his leg or so afraid of what would happen if I got away he didn't care. By the time I reached the street he was nearly on top of me, swinging the bloodstained blade at my head. I fell to the cement and rolled out of the way, rolling myself back onto my feet and swinging my fists at him. Again, he tried to play whack-a-mole with my brain, but I managed to get my arms up under his and deflect the blow, our forearms smashing into each other. I kicked at him and he jumped back, putting his weight on his bad leg, which stopped him for a second.

"Stop that crying," he told me. "If you're going to act like some fucking superhero least you could do is play the part."

I hadn't even realized I was crying; I was too intent on not dying to notice what was going on physically. But as soon as he said it I realized my face was awash in tears. My body was shaking and my legs felt deflated. In front of me, the shirtless, bloodied madman was smiling like he'd released the frightened child inside of me.

Frightened yes, child no.

"Where you gonna go?" he asked. "Nowhere you can run I can't find you. Butch is a good tracker; he'll find you in a heartbeat. Best if you just came back over here and took your medicine like a man. In case you forgot, I know where you live, mama's boy."

I had forgotten that he still had my driver's license, that he knew where I lived. Could I make it to Bobtail before he drove to my parent's house and killed them? Or would he pack up and disappear for a long time, only to resurface ten years from now on my front porch, his little ax in his belt, a new pair of dogs at his heels?

It was driving me mad. He had all his angles covered, knew all the ways to defeat his victim even when he wasn't around.

"You gonna kill my family like you killed yours!" I screamed.

He stayed back and replied, "Wasn't me, mama's boy, I just follow directions, and besides, they were bad. Always snooping in my stuff, nosing around where they shouldn't be, trying to steal things. That little bitch was trying to steal my soul, sell it to the highest bidder. Kids are the devil's minions, ya know. But she learned right from wrong when I dragged her behind my truck till her face came off. Yeah, she knew not to do bad things then, with her eyes smeared on the road."

"You're fucking crazy!"

"Get back here! Don't make me drive and pick up yer mama, 'cause I will. I'll fuck her rotten on top of yer corpse. I'll fuck her with yer severed limbs. You want that? Either one works for me, as long as somebody is keeping them happy."

Again with the *them* and *they* talk, psychotic babble that would land him in an institution instead of the electric chair. Somewhere deep down I knew that I could never live with that. I couldn't let him go free, not now, not ever. Murder was the only option. I knew that. In a way I'd known it since waking up in the cellar; I'd been kidding myself it would never come to it. I wasn't afraid of it anymore, I knew something was owed to Tooth and Jamie . . . and myself, too.

As I reached the trees across the street, Skinny Man followed with the ax at the ready. Behind him loomed his house where I could only guess how many hikers and travelers had met their untimely ends in ungodly painful ways. It was almost as if I could look through the walls and see the ghosts of the unfortunate, Jamie's dismembered torso on the ground in the dark, the empty chains where Tooth had suffered unthinkable pain.

"What's it gonna be, superhero?"

Suddenly, I stopped. With an early afternoon breeze kissing my blood-streaked, tear-covered face, I watched him come at me a little slower, as if he was wondering what my plan was. There was no plan though, just that I knew I had to kill him. I knew once and for all I couldn't just run away; I had to seize the opportunity that had been given to me. Given to me by the dice, given to me by years of reading comics, given to me by something higher than my understanding allowed. Given to me by what I had seen in the hallway upstairs.

Do it now, I told myself. Do it while he thinks you're too weak and scared to attack. For Tooth, for Jamie. Don't think about it, just do it. Do it for what he took from you, from this world.

And so I did.

From every ounce of my being, hatred welled up like an angry sea, and I rushed him head on. I heard myself scream, "NOOOOO!" but it sounded very far away. Remembering my trick on the boy at the liquor store, I pulled out the gun from my waistband as I charged, and tossed it to him. Reflexively, he went to catch it. But before he could our bodies collided and flew to the ground and I cracked my forehead into his nose, felt his blood erupt into my eyes.

Without thinking, my hand went to the ax he was swinging and stopped its descent toward my neck. My other fist pounded his eyes, pounded his mouth, pounded his broken nose. His punches landed square on my face, though I barely took notice of them. In the melee, my teeth sank into his neck and tore out a chunk of flesh which I spit back into his face. Blinded and choking on his own blood, he flailed like an overturned beetle in a puddle, punching me and trying to get the ax free of my grip, trying to reach with his other hand for the gun which had slid to the curb. Another headbutt dazed him and I wrenched the ax free from his hand. He put both arms over his head to protect himself, and I saw that he was no longer laughing—he was terrified.

Our roles had reversed.

I got off of him and took a step back and just watched him for a few seconds. He took his hands away from his face and looked up at me, the gaping wound in his neck wet and wide like a second mouth.

"What are you gonna do, boy?" he said as blood bubbled out from the hole near his Adam's apple. He forced a smile I knew was wreaking havoc with his nose, the same stupid grin he sported in the photo upstairs. Upstairs where something else had been with us. "You gonna kill me, here, in the middle of the road?"

I looked around at the surrounding forests. The odds of anyone coming through here were slim. People were already at work, summer school buses had come and gone. We were alone.

"You fucking mama's boy. You fucking loser. What do you think you can do to me?"

I didn't even care enough to listen to him; I just kept seeing Tooth and Jamie lying in pools of blood. Those images would be with me forever, ruining my life until the day I died. Would I ever sleep again? Would I ever be happy? No matter what happened in the next few seconds, I would never be the same. I knew I was about to go somewhere I had never dreamed possible. All because of this man, and his sickness, his twisted insanity that had turned me inside out.

Let's go to California.

Tooth's one and only goal in life: to get away from the shitty hand he'd been dealt and start fresh. Now he wasn't in California; he was in a shallow grave in some lunatic's backyard. I had to do this for him.

"Look at you, crying like a pansy. Shit, you can't hurt me, you're coming back to my place whether you like it or not."

True, I was still crying, but it wasn't out of fear anymore—it was for what I had lost, what I would never regain. What I had been made into, like so many comic book heroes I had hung on my walls growing up. I was crying because I was now a monster.

Roger Huntington was dead.

With tears dripping into my bleeding lips, I reached into my pockets and pulled out the dice that Skinny Man had been so fond of.

"We gonna play a game? That's good, I like games," he said.

I held them in my hand, two red dice that seemed at home in the smears of blood in my palm. Skinny Man was on his feet now, one hand over the hole in his neck, the other a fist by his side. He turned and saw the gun he'd been reaching for and began to hobble over to it. It was empty, but I didn't care. I squeezed the dice against the ax handle and cleared my mind of anything and everything. Except California—I would go there one way or another.

I limped over to Skinny Man and waited while he bent down to pick up the gun. With a triumphant, "Ah," he grabbed it, spun around and pointed it at me. And that's when I swung the ax.

With a crunch, it wedged into the right side of his face, splitting open his cheek, lodging in his jawbone and exploding his teeth out toward the lawn. The thick blade locked his upper and lower jaws together so that the gurgle of surprise came straight from his throat. Both his body and the gun fell to the ground, bounced on the cement. I put my foot on his face and yanked out the ax, which came loose with a squeak. A fountain of blood spit up around the white, exposed bone. He reached up for me, but I grabbed his hand, placed it on the road, and swung the ax at it. The blade went straight through with one clean cut. I tossed the hand out toward the middle of the road. The only sounds he seemed able to make were grunts and blood-filled coughs. I grabbed his other hand and swung the ax down on it, taking it off in two chops. He was looking at me with more fear than I had ever seen a man convey before, and I wanted to end him right there, but I owed something to Tooth and Jamie. So I swung the ax at his bare chest and it sank into his breastplate with a thud. His body lurched, and he tried to grab me but his stumps couldn't get a hold. I pulled the ax out and watched blood ooze from the fissure in the bestiality tattoo covering his chest

"You did this!" I screamed. "Why! Why did you do this!" I was crying so hard it was like looking through saran wrap.

Something over my shoulder caught his attention, and I spun around as a brown station wagon drove down the street. It came at us slowly, as if it was concerned about hitting us. Maybe it thought we were a couple kids wrestling or something. But then I saw recognition in the driver's eyes, a small old lady with pearl white hair. She slammed on the gas and sped away.

I looked around me and saw the forest and the street, but at the same time I was having those flashes of California—the beach, the palm trees, so free, so warm, beckoning for me to stay, to never go back to New Hampshire. But I wasn't finished.

Skinny Man sat up waving his arms like two snakes, his half-butchered head tilted to the side. My tears were stinging my eyes now, I could hear myself crying. I swung the ax again, swung it into his shoulder and began to take his arm off of his body. I had to pull it out and repeat it several times before I got through the bone, before the arm actually came off, after which I tossed it out into the street near the hands. His eyes glazed over and I knew he was near death, so I swung the ax at his head and sank it into his forehead over his right eye. The skull split wide open, the eye fell out. He fell back to the ground with the ax still protruding. His legs kicked a little, and he blinked at me with his left eye while his mouth tried to form words. I dropped the dice onto his chest and screamed. At first no sound came out, as if I'd forgotten how to use vocal cords. Then, in one giant rush of air, my scream erupted into the heavens above. I screamed so loud it hurt my own ears. I screamed until my muscles burned with exertion. I screamed with everything I had in me, purging myself of every ounce of sanity. I screamed for so long I tasted blood. I was still screaming, my head thrown toward God, when the police car pulled to a stop several feet down the road.

CHAPTER 25

"**Get** on the ground right now!"

I kept screaming, my tears dripping on the cement like rain. The cop was ducked behind his car door, arms outstretched, with his gun aimed at me. He reached up one arm, clicked the radio receiver on his shoulder and spoke quickly, "Officer needs assistance, now! I've got a ten-fifty . . . uh . . . a ten-thirty-seven . . . Jesus Christ I don't know what I got! Goddammit somebody just get to Highridge Way right now!"

"Teddy? That you?" came a static-laden reply. "Hold on, I'm on my way."

"I said lay down, motherfucker!" he yelled, turning his attention back to me. "Don't make me fucking shoot you. Get on the ground and kiss the fucking dirt or I will empty your brains onto the road. NOW!"

He could have started firing for all I cared. I was somewhere else. I was in California eating ice cream and drawing superheroes.

Again he called over his radio. "I need an ambulance out here right now. And somebody tell the chief." Slowly, he came around the door with his gun still trained on my head. Probably he wanted to shoot me, get a medal for his bravery, win a trip to the capital to meet the governor. "Stop fucking screaming and lay down, I will not tell you again!"

Did he really think I was listening to him? Hell, did I even care if he shot me at this point? Yeah, I guess I did. Truth was, part of me was just tired, both physically and mentally, to the point I'd been seeing things for a while, but the other part of me knew that Tooth and Jamie would want me to live. I didn't want to die; I was just too messed up to do anything about it.

He stopped a few feet away from me, leaned forward and took a long hard look at my handiwork. "Oh, sweet Jesus. What have you done? What the flying fuck is that? You sick fucking maniac. I ought to shoot you right now. Oh, my God, what did you do? Where's his arm? Where are—Oh, Jesus." He had finally noticed the body parts in the street. He clicked on his radio again. "Hurry up, goddammit!"

Finally, all my voice ran out, and I sat with my mouth gaping open, saliva dribbling down my chin, not making a peep. The officer could see that his threats were useless; he could tell I wasn't right. For a moment he just stared at me muttering "Sweet Jesus," and I stared back, and he didn't know what to make of me. I think he was starting to put something together though, like he could see the difference in age between me and Skinny Man, could see the disgusting tattoos on his torso, could see the piss stains on my shorts, the dried blood on my body and the leg irons on my ankles. His angry expression turned to confusion and caution. I think he was adding it up.

Suddenly, Skinny Man's body jumped. I don't know if it was nerves or if he was still alive or what, but the officer screamed, "Holy shit!" and sprinted back to his car. His hands shaking, the gun trembling, he hid behind his door once more. But Skinny Man didn't move after that. Maybe it was his soul trying to escape toward heaven, and the movement had been the devil yanking it back through his ass toward hell.

"Sir?" Officer Teddy called. "Sir, are you alive? If you can hear me, make a movement, anything to let me know you're alive."

My savior, the cavalry, trying to save the corpse of the bad guy.

"Sir? Sir?" he kept goading the cadaver. Then he looked at me and asked, "Is he dead? Did you kill him?"

I don't know why I responded, but I nodded my head. Maybe I was trying to sin as little as possible at that point, not make it any worse than it was. Maybe I was proud.

"Do you have any weapons on you?" he asked me.

I pointed to the ax sticking out of Skinny Man's head.

"Are you hurt?"

I nodded.

"Okay, I want you to lie down on the ground. I'm going to come over and put these cuffs on you—"

I lost it. I slammed my fist against my head, punched myself in the chest, swearing that if he came near me I would kill him. I would never wear handcuffs again.

"Okay, okay," he said, in some lame effort to calm me down, "but you gotta lay down for me, you gotta give me that. Otherwise I can't check and see if he's alive. Can you do that for me?"

Before I knew it, I was sprawling out on the ground on my stomach. My chin plopped into the puddle of blood running out of Skinny Man's body.

"Now don't move. Do you hear me, don't move. I'll still shoot you if I have to."

He came back, full of trepidation, and went to place his hand on Skinny Man's neck but stopped before he touched him. Then he mumbled something soft, put a hand over his mouth and backed away, disgusted.

"Is anyone in the house?"

I nodded.

"Are they hurt? Did you hurt them? Are they dead?"

I kept nodding, though I was only answering his first question. Once I remembered Jamie was downstairs I just wanted him to go in and save her.

"Don't move, you hear me, I will shoot you dead on the spot if you so much as lift a finger."

He walked up the grass to the front door, his gun at the ready, his head swiveling side to side in case anything surprising came at him. When he reached the door, he glanced back at me and saw me still on the ground. Satisfied, he grabbed the doorknob and opened the door.

Butch exploded out like a cannonball and caught Officer Teddy by the throat. His gun went flying into the bushes beside the door as the dog hauled him to the grass and tried desperately to rip open his neck.

I thought, no, this can't be happening. Butch is dead, I stabbed him. Why is this still happening?

For a long time after, I wouldn't remember what happened that day. I spent several years not thinking of anything much. No matter how many treatment wards I stayed in, or how many psychiatrists tried to open me up, I pretty much shut that day up in the back of my mind and threw away the key. I spent a long time in California, without ever going there. My dad, strong as he was to take care of me and my mother for the next several years, even went so far as to buy me a surfboard and put it in my hospital room in the hopes I would answer the doctor's questions. Still, no matter what anyone did to unlock the door I had sealed in my mind, I more or less refused to remember it.

But one thing about that day I never forgot, through all of my self-induced fugue, was what I had seen in the hallway upstairs when I had rushed Skinny Man.

I had seen Tooth.

Now I know I was tired, and losing my mind, but there was something odd about that vision, something that told me I wasn't just seeing things. I'm not sure when I worked it out exactly, but eventually it hit me, and it kept me carrying on through life.

He wasn't wearing his Red Sox hat.

I know that might sound stupid, but whenever I had thought of Tooth up to that point, it was the Tooth I had always known, the Tooth never to be caught dead without his Red Sox hat. And it wasn't like he was just standing in the hallway with us—he was down on all fours. When Skinny Man fell backwards, I could have sworn he had done so over Tooth's body. I had seen Tooth again in the living room, telling me to kick Skinny Man in his leg wound, and it had freed me. Again, he wasn't wearing his hat.

And as Butch hauled officer Teddy to the grass with the knife still sticking out of his furry, red shoulder, I could have sworn I felt hot breath in my ear as Tooth's voice whispered, "Roger, I told you, always check the chamber first."

I lay motionless for what seemed like an eternity, though it was probably a very short blink-of-an-eye second, until I understood what I had just heard. I rolled over in time to see a shimmering blur that kind of resembled Tooth, and yet kind of resembled heat wave. But it was gone so quickly I couldn't be sure I hadn't imagined it.

For some reason I reached for the hat in my back pocket and it was gone, which didn't mean a whole lot since I'd been rolling about with Skinny Man. Probably it was on the stairs inside or on the living room floor. It didn't matter anyway. What mattered was I had never checked the chamber of the gun.

I flung myself toward the 9mm resting against the curb and picked it up just as Butch tore the radio handset off Officer Teddy's shoulder. The man was screaming, bleeding profusely, probably pissing himself. I had seen it all before, and I hated that dog for continuing it. When I slid back the chamber of the gun, a small bronze bullet stared back at me.

"Tooth." I looked for the heat wave again. It was gone.

Quickly realizing his mistake, Butch dropped the radio on the ground, freeing the cop from his bite. Not wasting any time, the cop began crawling to me. When he saw me pointing the gun his way he opened his mouth in disbelief, threw his hands in front of his face. He thought I was going to shoot him. Butch, seeing his meal scuttling down the lawn, gave chase, saliva whipping out behind him like a kite tail. I had one bullet, and I wanted it to count. I remembered shooting beer cans with this gun, how it shot slightly to the left, how if you could compensate correctly the shot was pretty accurate.

Out of the corner of my eye, I saw the second police car come screeching to a halt, the door flying open, a cop shouting, "No!" Butch was running at Officer Teddy, eyes mad and hungry. Officer Teddy was screaming.

There were two gunshots.

The first went in between Butch's eyes and exploded bits of brain out the back of his head, throwing his body into a gyrating heap of black fur that crashed full on into Officer Teddy. The second went whizzing under my chin and took a nick out of my throat. Searing hot pain spread across my Adam's apple, and I fell backward and dropped the gun.

With a sudden rush of realization, Officer Teddy pushed Butch's heap of dying flesh off of him and ran over to me. "Whoa! Don't shoot! Don't shoot!"

"Get out of the way, Teddy!" screamed the other officer.

"No, put the gun down! It wasn't him, it was the dog! He shot the dog. Look, he shot the dog. It was attacking me."

"You're bleeding! Get out of the way!"

"The dog! He shot the dog! Put the fucking gun away!"

The second officer lowered his weapon and looked at the dead dog on the grass. Utter confusion spread across his face, and he looked back at Officer Teddy a couple of times and tried to speak but couldn't think of what to say. He walked over to us as Officer Teddy put a hand on my throat and asked, "Where did the bullet go?"

I pointed to my neck, to the scratch the bullet made. He sat back on his ass and wiped his brow. The dog bite in his shoulder looked like roast beef. "Thanks," he said. "Don't know if you deserve it yet, a thanks that is, but I got a feeling there's more going on here than meets the eye."

Cop number two was standing over Skinny Man's corpse, waving flies away. "Teddy," he said, nice and calm like he was trying to rationalize what he was seeing, "what the hell happened here?"

CHAPTER 26

Two ambulances arrived shortly after, and the paramedics put both me and Officer Teddy on gurneys and ran around like beheaded chickens trying to figure out the best way to stop our bleeding. As they laid me down, the second cop suggested cuffing me but Teddy talked him out of it, relaying his already failed attempt to do the same thing. A third, fourth and fifth cop arrived on the scene, then a county medical examiner and a meat wagon. Finally came the chief, who went about waving orders to his men and making sure more ambulances were on the way.

First thing they did was close off the street and cover Skinny Man's body with a sheet, after which they covered up the body parts I had tossed about. Together, with guns raised, they entered the house and searched for persons unknown that Teddy had told them I said were inside.

A couple of minutes after they went in, bitching about the ghastly smell in the living room, one of the officers came running out and threw up on the lawn. He started screaming, "Oh my God, oh my God." Then the other cop, the one who'd shot me, came running out behind him with his shirt over his face and his eyes shut, and sprinted to the EMTs.

"Forget them, forget them," he said, pointing at me and Officer Teddy. "We need you down there right now! She's still alive. She's still alive. Hurry!"

The EMTs grabbed their toolboxes full of needles and bandages and took off like they were on the front line. The puking cop walked over to me slowly, and with chunks of half digested food on his chin grabbed my chest and said, "Who is she?"

"Jamie."

He squeezed my shirt in his fist so hard I could see his arm shaking from the strain. "Why?" he said, his face red from throwing up. He was crying, tears running down his cheeks, though it could have been from losing his breakfast and not the sight of the butchered girl in the basement. "Why?"

I didn't know why. Because everyone has a purpose, right? Because we're all part of God's master plan, a master plan that lets evil men take away the lives of innocent people, that lets some of us live while our friends and loved ones die before our eyes. Or maybe because God's just up there rolling some dice, using us as tokens in a universal board game. Or maybe it's bad luck, or maybe it's good luck, or maybe shit just happens and you deal with it. Or maybe the dice are loaded so your number never comes up, or maybe the game is fixed. Who knows?

Jamie was cut to pieces, chained up in a basement, and I had no answer.

The cop let go of me and walked back toward the house to do what he could. The chief came back and questioned Teddy for a few minutes. I heard them talking about gunshots and bullets and who did what. Teddy pointed to me a lot and pointed to Skinny Man and the dog corpse on the lawn. Then the chief came over to me.

"What's your name, son?"

"Roger."

"Roger what?"

"Roger Huntington."

"You want to tell me what the hell is going on here?"

I told him as much as I could, as I much as I would allow myself to remember, which didn't amount to a whole bunch. I was mostly non-responsive, my mind still wandering around the West Coast. Teddy finally asked the chief to call it quits and get me to the hospital. But first the EMTs came out with something on a stretcher, something that resembled a giant cooked marshmallow wearing a Jamie mask, all done up with oxygen tubes and IV drips. One of them was carrying a medical cooler, and out of the top of it flopped a hand with painted fingernails. They were moving that stretcher as fast as they could, lifted it up into the other ambulance and sped away with screeching tires.

The medical examiner came out with the other EMTs, the ones who'd been busy bandaging me up, with the kind of stares you see on men who've just walked away from a six-car pile up. He came over to the chief and said, "We're going to need forensics down here, and tell them to bring some shovels."

Jamie would die two days later in the hospital with my parents at her side, both of them weeping and cursing God. I stayed in the same hospital, but didn't see them as much, or so I felt. Eventually the story came out about what really happened. Skinny Man's backyard was dug up and nine bodies were uncovered, though it took several days to match some of the bones to the correct bodies. They found his wife and daughter among them, as well as Mystery Woman, two in hiking gear, some others. They found bones: adult bones, kid bones, lots of bones they couldn't match up to any bodies. They also found Tooth.

They showed me photos of all the corpses and asked me to identify whoever I could, though aside from Mystery Woman the only one I said I knew was Tooth. I told them how Mystery Woman died and they confirmed the story with the M.E. Then they too left me alone. The only time I left the hospital was for Jamie's and Tooth's funerals, which were closed casket. Then I had to come back to the psych ward for more "counseling."

My dreams were filled with the ghosts of the dead, and I had a lot of trouble sleeping without jumping every time I heard a nurse walk by jingling keys. Many nights I would just lay awake and try not to remember the carnage I had seen, try not to think about Tooth and Jamie. How far away my parents' bed seemed, or any safe haven for that matter.

I guess to believe everybody has a purpose in life, you've got to believe that there's even a cosmic plan to begin with. Which means you've got to believe in God, or some other higher power, something that is working toward an ultimate goal, or at least working toward the continuation of life. And if each person does have a purpose—like those people buried behind the house, like Skinny Man himself—to what end does it serve? I lived, unharmed save for a couple of bruises and some dog bites and cuts, though my mental state was the stuff of comic books. But if my whole purpose in life was to kill the man who murdered my sister and friend, what was left? Was the rest of my life meaningless? Or had I yet to fulfill my true reason for living? Of course, like I said, all this introspection only mattered if you believed in something higher.

This is what I thought about as I lay in that hospital bed, day after day after day. This is what I still think about, as I fight to stay awake most nights, as I try to avoid the nightmares of that summer, pinching myself to ward off sleep. My purpose. All of our purposes. The afterlife. God. Why I am still alive, and why the dice never rolled my number, and why I had even taken them to begin with. I think about superheroes and villains, about good and evil, about strong and weak, always wondering what it means for me. And I think about that other thing, which makes it all the more confusing and urgent. And yet, makes it all make sense, somehow.

When they dug up Tooth's body, he was wearing his Red Sox cap.

About the Author

Ryan C. Thomas works as an editor in San Diego, California. You can usually find him in the bars on the weekends playing with his band. When he is not writing or rocking out, he is at home with his wife and two dogs watching really bad B-movies. Visit him online at www.ryancthomas.com

Other books by Ryan C. Thomas:

Born To Bleed (Aka The Summer I Died part 2)
Ratings Game
Hissers
Hissers II: Death March
Salticidae
The Undead World of Oz
Scraps & Chum
The Bugboy
Monstrous (as editor)
With a Face of Golden Pleasure
Enemy Unseen
Malcontents

EXCLUSIVE PREVIEW OF BOOK 2 IN THE ROGER HUNTINGTON SAGA:

Born to Bleed

CHAPTER 1

Do you know what a two-headed camel fucking a rocking chair looks like? I do. It looks like the shitty abstract painting that hangs over my therapist's desk. It's really just a blotch of colors, a glorified Rorschach, but I defy you to see anything else in it. I'd always wanted to tell her what I thought of that painting but found more humor in letting her believe it was a good purchase. If I told her I saw freaky animals and furniture engaged in coital struggles, it would just be overanalyzed and end up in my file. There's already enough weird shit in my file as it is.

The last time I was there, watching that two-headed camel go to town on that chair, it almost made me horny. But mostly it made me angry. I dunno, I was feeling fed up that day and bad art kills me; and bad art that sells makes me want to cry. I should know. I do it for a living. And that certainly doesn't help my depression any.

Dr. Marsh leaned forward on her couch. "Your birthday was yesterday?"

She knew full well when my birthday was; she was just trying to open up a new line of questioning. I don't know what she thought she'd get from talking about my age. Maybe she thought I'd gained some maturity points in the last few days. Maybe she wanted to test my age-to-wisdom ratio. I had no idea how old she was, but I doubted it was more than five years more than me. Whatever, I obliged her. "Yeah. Thirty years old."

"Feel any different?"

"No."

"Feel more adult?"

Depends. Do adults get jealous of things that fuck rocking

chairs? I shook my head. She kept staring at me, her eyes almost sad, as if she were looking at a puppy. If I didn't say something she'd keep pestering. "Not really. When my mom turned thirty, she seemed a lot . . . older. I don't feel old. Kind of feel like a kid, still. Is that weird?"

"Oh, I don't think so. Times have changed. Thirty is the new twenty. Plus your mom had children so her mindset was different. She was responsible for you and your sister's lives. That makes people grow up pretty quick."

The mention of my sister cut through me, made me look at the ground. It was an involuntary response, as if I might be able to remove myself from the room by staring down through the carpet. I didn't like talking about Jamie and Dr. Marsh knew that. I couldn't tell if she did it on purpose or if she'd forgotten. Part of me wanted to yell at her, but I wasn't about to lose my cool here.

"Do you want kids?" she asked.

Oh, for the love of . . . . We'd been over this before. She was like a broken record. "Someday. Maybe. I dunno."

She scribbled something on her legal pad. She was always taking notes during our conversations. I can't imagine what they amounted to. Roger Huntington, thirty years old, might want kids, has the personality of a sock, seems way too interested in that painting over my desk . . .

She put the pen in her mouth and sucked on its end for a minute. Freud would have been proud of where my mind went. "What have you been doing with your free time? Any dates recently?" Only with porn sites and an Xbox console.

My life was pretty boring, but Dr. Marsh and I had discussed my tendency to be negative so I decided not to get into it. Maybe that's weird. I guess you're supposed to tell your shrink about your pathetic nights alone looking at HotCollegeChicksInHeat.com, but I wasn't up for the spelunking she'd do inside my brain if I did. "No. Don't meet many girls."

"What about that one at the gallery? What was her name?"

I hesitated. "Victoria."

"Yes . . . Victoria. Do you talk to her?"

I nodded. "She works there. I sell there. See her sometimes."

"You like her?"

"I guess."

"Roger, you'll never know if you don't take a chance. Are you afraid of the rejection?"

I shrugged. Who isn't afraid of rejection?

"I mean, if that's what's holding you back, then you're going to go through life alone and miserable. You've got to stop hiding in this shell you've created and start talking to people. That's when the healing will really start."

Then what am I paying you for, I thought, to test steno pads? "Doesn't matter. She has a boyfriend. Gabe something."

Dr. Marsh set her pad and pen down on the couch cushion next to her. Unlike some shrinks, Dr. Marsh preferred to use two couches—one for her and one for her patients. I think she felt it leveled the playing field. All it really did was make the whole process look unprofessional. I mean, you go to a shrink, you expect to lie on a couch while some twat in tortoise shell glasses analyzes your dreams from a leather chair. You don't expect to sit across from each other like it's a frickin' tea party. Times have changed. Except for the part about dissecting my dreams. She was always asking about my nightmares. But, you know, since they were a big part of my issues, I guess I couldn't blame her for practicing some archaic therapy.

"Roger, don't tell anyone I told you this, but unless a girl is married--and even then sometimes, but that's not the point--she can be swayed. I think you should give it a shot. Who knows? Maybe she hates the guy but is too codependent to end it."

She was analyzing people she didn't even know. Brilliant. She might as well have her own talk show and commune with people's dead grandparents.

"Maybe."

"Do you want her?"

In the worst way. But I didn't say this; I just nodded. I'd become a professional nodder these last few years. You'd be amazed at how much easier it is than talking, and most people prefer it. Saves them the trouble of having to politely probe for conversation. You nod, they nod back, you each move on.

She picked up her pad again and scribbled something, maybe her grocery list for all I knew. "How have the nightmares been?"

Ah, now we were getting into that twat zone. My dreams. My nightmares. The only thing I could count on these days. Last night's dream had been bad, waking me up in a sweat, but still not the worst I've had. Some nights I wake up screaming. Some nights I find myself in the kitchen, disoriented and shaking. Sometimes I'm holding a knife and crying. My left thumb has a nice scar on it from one of my somnambulistic episodes. I almost severed it off into my fish tank.

If you want to know what my dreams really consist of--the blood, the rituals, the screams and pleas for help--you'll have to read Dr. Marsh's notes. I tend to forget them after I relay them to her. Sort of like a purging function. Once they're out, they're out. The stronger ones that linger are overwritten by the next terrible nightmare anyway so . . . I almost didn't want to get into last night's with her, but I knew she'd keep pushing if I resisted.

"Did you dream last night?" she said.

"Yes," I replied.

"About the man?"

Yeah, about the man. She didn't need to say his name, didn't need to describe him. We both knew who the man was.

"If you don't tell me we can't put it behind us," she said. "Come on, spill it. We need to do this."

We? Right. She liked to think she and I were some team going through this together. She might have known my past, but she knew absolutely nothing about the reality of that summer ten years ago. She and I were not a team; she was not ever going to empathize with me no matter how hard she tried. If I could take her back to those few days in the mountains and put her in that freak's cellar, chain her to the wall next to Tooth and me, she wouldn't be patronizing me now. She'd be drooling in a corner begging for death. And yet, she'd come highly recommended by my old counselor in New Hampshire. She was an expert with trauma victims, or so he'd said. If Tooth was here he'd just say she had nice tits and wasn't too old for a late night fuck.

I could hear his voice now: Dude, you don't have to talk to her, just stick it in her mouth, gag her with your sack, and then let's go grab a brew.

"Yeah," I replied. "He was sitting in my car with me, the man.

We were smoking weed and he asked me to go to a party with him and I said okay."

"And you feel regret for saying okay?"

"I guess."

"Then what happened?"

I reached up and adjusted the Red Sox cap on my head. My finger brushed the ripped cloth of the brim and I reminded myself I'd have to sew it up soon before it fell to tattered ribbons.

"He lit a cigarette. We just looked out the windshield at this empty street. There was a girl walking across it. Young, in jeans and a tank top. He laughed, got out of the car and started walking toward her and . . ." I hung my head. It was pointless to relive that dream. They were all some iteration of a fucked up bloodbath anyway, so I'm sure Dr. Marsh knew how it would end. They always ended the same way. I looked at the floor again.

"He killed her," she said.

I continued to study the carpet. Of course he killed her. She knew that.

"Okay. You can stop if you want," she said. "Do you want to?"

"Yeah."

"Okay. Well, our time is almost up anyway. It's just a dream. It's your subconscious dealing with stress. You know that. We've talked about it. You spend all day every day thinking about this stuff and it builds up in your brain. Try this for the next week. Think about that girl Victoria. I bet you'll have better dreams." She smiled in a weird sexually suggestive way. A shudder ran down my back. "And try to let go of your cynicism. I feel you getting a bit more pessimistic these days. You seem more down than the last time we met."

I'd been tortured, chained up, brutalized, and forced to watch my sister and best friend die under a maniac's ax blade. How do you get it across to some people that you simply have little belief in the benevolence of humankind? Being angry was all I had these days, because how else could I deal with ten years of regret and night-terrors? It was the only feeling I'd developed in the last decade that felt comfortable.

But I knew she was right, even if I didn't want to admit it. "I'll try."

I got up and put my zippered hoodie on while Dr. Marsh rattled on about needing to meet a half hour later next week. I wanted to tell her that in fact I wouldn't be back next week, but I didn't want to get into it in person. I had decided on the drive over this would be my last session. The nightmares would never end, and this was costing too much money as it was. I'd lived with the bad dreams for this long, I could go another twenty years, I guessed. I was content being messed up and cynical.

I stopped as I opened the door to the common room, turned around and looked at her. She was rifling through papers on her desk. "I'm not afraid of him," I said.

She studied me for a second, then reached for her pad again. But I shouted, "No!"

She tensed up, kind of froze. It was the first time I'd seen Dr. Marsh scared. Scared of me. Mind you, my intent was not to scare her; I just didn't want to watch her write as I talked. It's fucking annoying. I wanted to see her eyes. She glanced quickly at the telephone on her desk, maybe gauging how fast she could call security. How's that for gratitude. She pretends to be my friend for a year, but at the end of the day, I'm just another freak with a potential anger management problem that may or may not do someone real harm one day.

"I'm not afraid of him," I said more firmly. "I let him kill the girl in my dream, then I killed him. That's what I hate. That I let him kill the people in my dreams first. I could get him before he does, but I don't. I wait. I always wait. I don't know why, because I'm not afraid of him anymore. I stopped being afraid a long time ago I just…wait."

Dr. Marsh was still on edge. I could tell she wanted me to leave. "We'll discuss it next week, Roger. I have another patient to deal with."

I liked the way she let that slip: "deal with." Just proof that we meant nothing to her, just part of a job that paid her rent. She could deal with my absence from now on.

I pointed to the wall above her desk. "That painting sucks."

I left, and drove to the Robertos near my apartment to get some lunch, had a carne asada burrito but only ate half of it. The first time I had Mexican food in California was a real surprise to me. I mean an eye-opening experience of cosmic proportions. Back home on the east coast Mexican food consists of Taco Bell and frozen burritos you buy at the supermarket. But that's not real Mexican food. Real Mexican food is found at places like Robertos, Aibertos, Titos, etcetera. Little stands on Southern California street corners that serve up made-to-order taquitos, rancheros, chimichangas, burritos, all authentic and covered in fresh guacamole. The taste is from another world. Taco Bell is a travesty by comparison.

I took the remainder of my burrito home to my small studio apartment and put it in the fridge. It would provide good company for the half-empty bottle of ketchup and the two cans of beer that made up the rest of my dietary needs.

My cell phone vibrated in my back pocket. I took it out and looked at the number. It was the gallery. I prayed it was Victoria. "Hello?"

"Roger. What the fuck!" It was Barry Goldstein, gallery owner and pain-in-my-ass extraordinaire. "I thought you said you'd have the paintings to me today. We've got two days before the show. Where are they?"

In the background I could hear Victoria talking to someone. It sounded like she was on her own cell phone. She was giggling and I had a momentary image of me kissing her someday. Yeah, right, as if that would ever happen. I tried to will Barry to put her on the phone, but apparently I don't have the Force.

"They're not done," I said.

"Are you . . . are you fucking with me? Not done? Roger, they need to be framed and lit and hung up! It takes time. How not done are we talking? Half done? Three quarters? What?"

"Not started."

There was silence on the other end of the phone. Then, through forcibly calm breathing, "Roger, if you don't get me those last two paintings by tomorrow morning this show is off and I'll make sure all the other galleries in town know how unreliable you are. Got me?"

I took a nickel out of my pocket and dropped it in the coffee can on my counter. The label on it read Barry's Empty Threats. Trying to scare me was his MO. The guy needed therapy more than I did. He hadn't fired me yet and he never really would because I sold well.

"Roger," he continued, "these are important people who buy this stuff. They're collectors, and they rely on me to get them the product. Some of these people pay very well for what I solicit. And you're not the only artist in town. Understand?"

"So you can get me more money?"

"That's not what I'm saying. What I'm saying is . . . these people . . . they've got the money to pay for whatever they want. They could get it elsewhere but they stay with me because I deliver. That's what I do. Right now they want your work, so I'm giving you my built-in customer base. But if you waste my time, I can make it so they don't want your stuff anymore. I can break an artist as easily as I can make him. I will not deal with your lazy attitude anymore."

"But this is California. Everyone's lazy."

"Stuff your New England east coast bullshit up your ass. If you don't like it here, then go home and piss in the snow. If you're staying and you want to get paid, deliver me two fucking paintings by tomorrow morning!" He hung up.

I put the phone down and leaned against the counter. The comment I'd made about Californians made me smile. I never used to talk back to people like that. At times it didn't even feel like me; it felt more like Tooth. Tooth who'd never had a serious thing to say in his life . . . until that stuff in the basement happened.

I knew I'd gone batshit the first time I caught myself having a conversation with Tooth in a bookstore at the mall. He kept telling me books were stupid and I finally told him, "Maybe you should try reading one instead of using them to kill bugs? You might be enlightened, you ignorant jackhole."

Everyone in the bookstore had stared. Some even moved away from me. Of course they had good reason to, since Tooth was not in the store with me. He'd been dead for years at that point. I just couldn't get him out of my head. I still can't.

I feel him sometimes. I don't know how to explain it. It's like a haze inside my brain, like I've swallowed his aura. When I'm alone and I talk to him, his answers don't feel like they come from me. They're always unpredictable and snarky, which was Tooth's natural way of corresponding, unique only to him. Dr. Marsh says it's a coping system of mine, which makes sense clinically, but sometimes I'm not so sure.

I stared at my living room walls where I'd framed and hanged two paintings I'd done since moving to California last year. One was of a female assassin, Lena 12, fighting a red-fanged alien with a sword. I'd painted her in a thong and metal bikini top, her mouth in a tight sneer. The other one was the inside of some industrial machine shop that was an exercise at playing with shadows. In the foreground loomed a giant lathe with a big green button on it that read PRESS TO STOP. I often thought about pressing it, just putting my finger through the painting and seeing what would happen. Would the world go black, would it all just end? It's an enticing thought.

They were good paintings and I was proud of them. Proud that I'd proved my father wrong--I could make money being an artist-- and proud because I'd sold the image rights to an independent comic book publisher for enough money to buy a six pack of beer and a beta fish. Independent publishing doesn't pay, my friends. But then, pride is worth more in the long run so it evens out.

I tell myself that, anyway.

Thing is . . . these types of paintings were not my bread and butter. Californians don't want dark, sci-fi geekery; they want schlock culled from tropical paradigms, images from films like Endless Summer and Cocktail. So that's what I paint for money. They call it Plein Air, which stands for open air, meaning you paint outdoors. Really it's just a fancy way of saying "boring landscapes that get old women's panties wet." Long stretches of beach with palm trees blowing in the breeze, waterfalls and rock formations, the occasional woody with a surfboard on top. Collectors hang them up in their game rooms or over their kitchen tables. Hell, you can buy a thousand just like them at Bed Bath & Beyond, but collectors want one-of-a-kind stuff. They want to brag to their guests about how it's an original from a famous local artist and they got it at a gallery show and blah blah blah look at me I'm so important. Little do they know I live in a crappy box of an apartment because what little money I make off those paintings goes toward my shrink bills and car payments on my vintage '82 Camaro. Hey, I'm entitled to a little bit of luxury, right?

The other reason these collectors want originals is because they like to go to the exact spot in the painting and take a photograph. Then they hang the photo next to the painting to prove the scene wasn't just made up. Plein Air collectors are weird, but don't look at me . . . I have aliens on my wall. A quick look outside the window told me I still had the brunt of the day to get the paintings done. My process is simple: scout a location that hasn't been painted before (I'm not the only plein air artist in So Cal), set up my easel so I can get it right, and paint until I'm drunk. The natural lighting really does make a big difference when mixing colors for the final product. And the alcohol makes me not care that I'm painting stuff that would make even Bob Ross groan, were he still alive.

I figured I could get one done this afternoon, albeit sloppily, and take a photo for the next one to do at home tonight. Burn the midnight oil and all that. The lighting would be off but Barry probably wouldn't notice. Only color he really cared about was green, which I don't say to sound like some anti-Semitic jerk. It's got nothing to do with him being Jewish, just with him being an asshole.

I grabbed two canvases, my paints, and those two beers from the fridge and made my way down to the parking lot.

It was almost one in the afternoon. The Clash was on the radio belting out "The Magnificent Seven." I checked my rearview mirror to back out, saw my Red Sox hat looked worse than I'd thought. It was faded and ripped and the red B was starting to unthread. This hat had been through a lot, and it meant a whole bunch to me. Tooth's father gave it to me a few months after the funeral. If Tooth had ever written a will, I'm sure it would have specified he be buried with it (and maybe a beer and some Traci Lords videos, too). It needed a major overhaul. I took it off, mussed my hair, and put it back on, checked the rearview mirror and froze.

The man from my dreams was looking at me from the backseat, his gaunt, unshaven face stained in blood. He held up a bloody fishing gaff and said, "Bet you didn't know I raped Jamie with this for a whole hour. She weren't no virgin when I was done with her. I covered it in Butch's dog shit first. Oh yeah. And when I yanked it out all sorts of good stuff spit out at me. That fucking bitch came, I swear." He laughed that high-pitched witch's cackle, the same laugh that haunted my dreams every night.

I closed my eyes and gripped the steering wheel so hard my knuckles popped. You might be thinking I said something like "I know you're not real," like some lame movie cliché, but I didn't. Because I'm not afraid anymore. I said, "When I open my eyes, if you're really there, I'm going to rip your fucking head off, reach down your throat and tear your lungs out."

I opened my eyes. He was gone. Another hallucination. I'd been off my meds for a month now and Dr. Marsh said some old symptoms might reoccur. It's classic post traumatic stress disorder, or so she said. Same as the war veterans get. It's no fun, let me assure you. Dr. Marsh advised me not to stop taking the pills, but I wanted to try, just to see if I could move past them. Not to mention they were expensive.

I started the car and left, the two cans of beer tapping together on the passenger seat. One for me, and one for Tooth. Only I'd have to drink Tooth's for him. I knew he'd want me to.

CHAPTER 2

I needed to stop by Murray's Art Depot on Franklin Ave. to restock a few oil paints. It's a small mom-and-pop business with tons of brushes and paints and canvases and anything else a true starving artist could want. Unlike the big chain stores like Michaels, they really know their shit. I mean, real artists do not shop for supplies in places where the majority of aisles are dedicated to scrapbooking. The way those sagging, old women cluck for that stuff you'd think they were pigs in a feed store. "Oh my gosh, Hazel, did you see the cute little bunny stickers they have! I'm going to do a whole new scrapbook of just bunny pictures! Wee!"

The third World War will start over who gets the last bunny stickers for a scrapbook . . . mark my word.

When I got to Murray's, Cameron Plimpton (Murray's kid) was working the counter. He looked up from whatever he was reading when the bell over the door jingled.

"Hey, Roger. Hail to the King, baby."

"Klatu, Verata, Nikto," I replied, our own little joke that drove his father nuts. Cam was in high school, but he was a pretty cool kid. He reminded me of me ten years ago, swept up in comics, always on the lookout for the next great horror film or anything starring the amazing Bruce Campbell. (Thank God the Academy finally recognized him.)

"You need some paints to do another lame palm tree picture?"

"You know it."

"You should paint big ol' buttholes on them so your clients can screw them. Ha!"

"Cam!" Murray came out of the small room behind the counter where he kept a small fridge and a TV. "What did I say about that kind of talk when you're working. Hi, Roger."

"Hi, Murray."

Murray grabbed his son by the back of the neck in a loving fatherly way that meant he was two seconds away from grounding the kid for his own good. "I hear you spout anymore homophobic bullshit in this store you're gonna work for free. I'm not gonna lose customers because of your ignorance."

"I'm just joking, Dad. Don't go all Palpatine on me."

"I don't know what that means. Is he mocking me, Roger?"

I laughed. "Not really. Well, maybe. Emperor Palpatine was the ruler of the galaxy in the *Star Wars* films."

Murray cocked an eyebrow. "I'm gonna bet the guy was bad. What happened to kids respecting their parents?"

"Shit, Dad, it's just a joke."

"And no more swearing!"

"But you said 'bullshit.'"

"I said enough. What do you need, Roger?"

"Just need some oils. I know where they are."

"Hold up," Cam said, "I'll come with you. I wanna show you my new stuff." He picked up a sketchpad from next to the register and hopped over the top of the counter. Murray rolled his eyes and went back to watching TV.

Cam and I walked to the paints and I started looking through the various tubes for the colors I needed. I noticed the prices had gone up since I had been here last, but I kept my disappointment to myself.

"Hey, you get the new Batman/Green Lantern mash-up?" Cam asked, flipping through his pad.

"Of course. Got the limited edition foil cover ones as well."

"That was badass when they fought. I thought Batman would kick Jordan's butt, but man oh man he got served."

"All a misunderstanding, anyway. You knew it had to be. They'll never really have two superheroes be enemies for long. Heroes have to stay heroes."

"Oh, here's what I'm looking for. Check this one out," Cam said, offering the sketchpad to me. He was a pretty good artist, dare

I say better than I was at his age. On the page was a charcoal sketch of a naked girl with some kind of space gun riding a giant dick and fighting off what looked like more giant dick monsters. As a testament to his skill it was good stuff. As a testament to his hormonal urges, it was scary.

"See, each cock monster shoots sperm grenades and their balls have afterburners in them. She's gotta shoot them in the big vein running down the center to kill them."

"You've got issues," I said.

"Okay okay, that one's just a joke. Seriously, what about this one?" He flipped the page. This new drawing was better, done in colored pencil. A woman in a red bodysuit riding on top of a giant alligator. In the sky, spaceships dueled with lasers. A large red planet shimmered behind the distant clouds. Some kind of sci-fi-fantasy hybrid. It reminded me of a Borris Vallejo book cover.

"That's not bad. Have you tried to enter it anywhere? There are websites you could put it up on and maybe make a sale."

"Not yet. I want to mess with the colors a bit more." He flipped through some more pages and I caught the Lena 12 comic book in between them. That's the one I did the cover for, the same painting of the female assassin that's hanging in my apartment. I'd signed the copy for Cam a few months ago. It made me feel good to know someone appreciated my geek art. He kept flipping.

"This one here," he said, "I just started yesterday. I'm going to do a big whole ocean battle scene over here. Add some hot mermaids and stuff. But what do you think so far?"

"I like the woman riding the shark. Do you ever have animals that aren't mounted by half-naked women?"

"Well, sometimes they're fully naked. Tits, ass, and big fucking guns, right? Just like you draw."

"Like me? My young padawan, all I do is palm trees."

"Yeah, but you drew Lena 12. She's hot. And deadly. But mostly hot. Really hot. I mean, damn, if I could fuck that--"

The bell over the front door jingled. "Shit," Cam said, "frigging customers."

"It's cool. I'm done. I'll just get these four here." I held up the tubes of paint.

"C'mon, I'll ring you up."

I followed Cameron back to the counter and glanced at the door to see who'd come in. It was a tall brunette girl, maybe in her mid-twenties. She was cute, had a beret on. Cameron was eyeing her as well. He puffed out his chest a bit like a rooster.

For a moment I debated taking Dr. Marsh's advice and trying to talk to her, maybe even use my upcoming gallery show as a way to impress her, but I decided not to. I have no real understanding of how girls work. I had one girlfriend right before I left New Hampshire. The sex was great--I wish Tooth had been around to celebrate with me--but ultimately she couldn't deal with my past.

No one really can. At first they say, "I'm here for you. I understand." But they never do. Then, when I wake up screaming and punching the air with all my might, yelling for someone to leave Jamie alone . . . then they realize they've underestimated how broken I am.

Too bad; this girl was a looker.

"Yo, Iron Man, you doing cash or debit?"

I handed Cam my debit card and he ran it through the reader. The girl made her way up to the counter next to me, stood to my right and smiled. I smiled back. "Hi," she said.

"Hi."

Good so far. Then my palms got sweaty. I dug down deep for something witty to say. "Hi," I repeated, like a moron.

She nodded. And I knew what that meant. She thought I was a dumbass.

I had nowhere to go from hello. I tried again to think of something clever to say but all I got out was, "Like art?"

Fucking moron. Real smooth. She's in an art store, of course she likes art.

"Sure," she said.

Cameron was trying to hide his embarrassed smile by looking down. The bastard was amused by the way I was crashing and burning. Then what did he do? He cock-blocked me!

"I draw, and you're a hottie. I could draw you on, like, a giant frog or something, in a bikini waving a battle ax."

She actually laughed. This kid had much better game than me. "Thank you," she replied, "I've always wanted to ride on a frog, but I don't really want warts."

Cameron handed me my bag of paints. "Just an urban legend, the warts thing," I said, hoping for another laugh. She just stared at me. Someone kill me.

"Roger here is the real artist," Cameron said, finally coming to my rescue. "Look." He took out the Lena 12 comic and showed her the cover. "He painted that. Fucking cool, huh?"

"Cam!" This from Murray in the back room.

"It's good," she said, politely, though I could tell she was one of those girls that thought comics were for kids. "But I'm not here to model. My husband and I just bought a condo and we want to stencil the trim. Do you have stencils here?"

I glanced down and saw the ring on her finger. Shit. They were all taken. Just as well. I'd have scared her off soon enough anyway.

"Yeah, over here." Cameron hopped over the counter again.

"Cam! Go around the counter!" Murray again.

I said bye to Cam and left him to woo his married frog-riding warrior princess.

Parking on Franklin Ave. is a real bitch. You have to be lucky enough to find a meter on the road, which is nigh impossible on a Saturday afternoon, so I'd parked up a residential side street earlier. The air was pretty warm so the walk back didn't bother me. Not like in New Hampshire. February in So Cal gets as cold as sixty degrees during the day. In New Hampshire it's almost negative sixty. I wasn't missing it much.

There was a dog near my car. A German Sheppard. It wasn't wearing a collar.

I stopped a few yards away and watched it sniff around my tires. My muscles tensed and images of a bloodied Rottweiler flashed through my mind. "What do you want, boy?" I whispered to no one. Dogs and me do not get along for reasons you'll have to talk to Dr. Marsh about. That summer long ago left a pretty dry taste in my mouth for most animals that eat meat.

The dog took a whiz on my back tire and turned around to find me watching. Tentatively, it lowered its head and took a step toward me. The bag fell from my hand as I balled up both fists. The dog took another step, sizing me up.

"If you're gonna do it just do it, fucker." My biceps flexed, my eyes locked on the approaching animal. "Just know it'll be the last thing you ever do."

It was close now, a few feet away, head still down. A debate rang out in my mind whether to rush it or wait for it to rush me. Instead, I stood still, fists at my side. My knuckles cracked.

The dog took four more steps, right up to me, sniffed my shoe. I felt like a slingshot pulled all the way back, waiting to snap. A second passed. Then another. Then, it looked up, kind of smiled the way dogs do, and licked my tight, white knuckles. Must be the sweat, I thought. It likes the taste of my sweat.

Dr. Marsh's words echoed through my head. Bad dogs are made by humans, they're not born that way. Either that or they're afraid for some reason.

Was Skinny Man made bad, I'd wanted to ask back? Was he afraid of something? No, that sick fuck had been born bad. And there were more of his kind in the world, I knew. Some things are just born evil.

The dog's tongue began to tickle the back of my hand. Slowly, I relaxed, knelt down and got face-to-face with it. I didn't know if it would suddenly turn on me and bite, but I didn't care. Why I test myself in these situations is beyond me, but I have to do it. I have to know I'm truly not afraid, not just spouting off tough words.

The dog licked my face. Its hot breath swam up my nose.

"You're a good boy," I said, and ran my arms around its neck, gave it a playful hug. "A good boy."

"Bogart! Bogart! Leave him alone."

Over the dog's head I could see a man in shorts and sandals heading my way. He jogged over and grabbed the dog by the scruff of the neck and yanked it away from me like he was starting a lawn mower. The poor dog let out a terrified squeak as it was briefly lifted off its front paws. Instinctively, I balled my fists again. This guy's roughness was setting me off.

"Sorry," he said, "he gets out of the yard sometimes. He's harmless though."

Can't imagine why he runs away, I thought. But I said nothing. Just nodded.

"C'mon, Bogart, stupid dog, c'mon." He began dragging the dog back down the street, its paws fighting to get a footing. "Bad dog." He gave Bogart a smack on the ass that elicited another yelp.

They disappeared into one of the nearby houses.

"Good boy," I whispered, as if Bogart might hear me on the wind and get some encouragement from it.

My fists uncurled, and now I could hear the plastic bag with my paints whip-snapping in the breeze. Despite wanting to go have a talk with Mr. Animal Lover, it reminded me I had to get a move on or I'd be painting in the dark. And despite the warm weather during the day, the temperature does drop at night in So Cal and all I had on was my sweatshirt.

When I got back in the car, I checked the rearview mirror for my boogey man, but all I saw was the car parked behind me.

Continue reading when you purchase BORN TO BLEED, available at all major online retailers.

ALSO FROM GRAND MAL PRESS

The Roger Huntington Saga
by Ryan C. Thomas

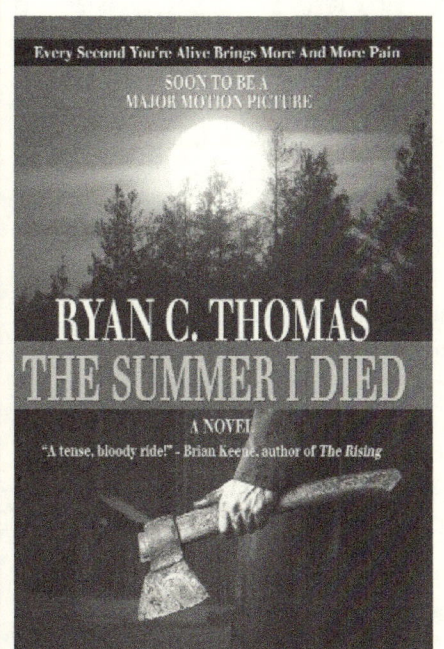

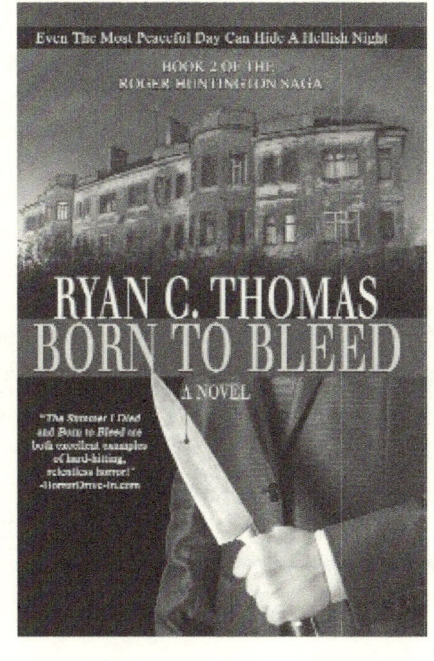

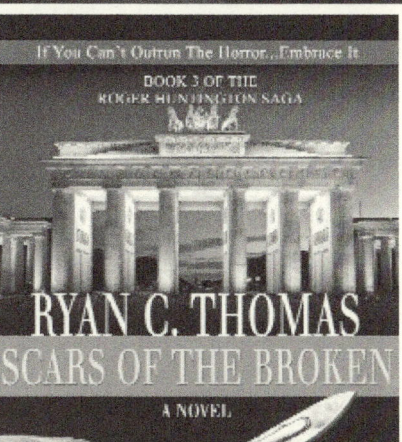

"*The Summer I Died* is a tense bloody ride!" - Brian Keene, author of *Pressure*

"*The Summer I Died* will leave a mark on you! This is not a tale you will forget!"
- Scream Magazine

"*The Summer I Died* is an endurance test. If you want to freak yourself out on your next camping trip, you can't really do any better." - BloodyDisgusting.com

"*Born to Bleed* is an excellent example of hard-hitting, relentless horror!"
- HorrorDrive-in.com

"Ryan C. Thomas absolutely delivers! *Scars of the Broken* is an expertly-crafted mixture of suspense, gore, and humor!"
- BMoviesandEbooks.com

ALSO FROM GRAND MAL PRESS

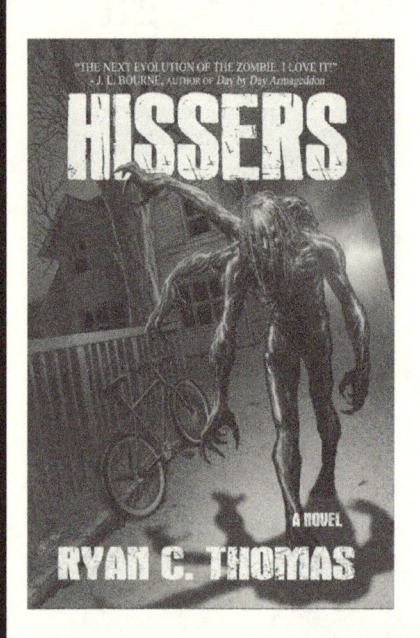

HISSERS
BY RYAN C. THOMAS

In the small town of Castor, it's the last weekend of summer break. In just two days four teenage friends will begin their high school careers. Dating, who to sit with at the lunch table, and what to wear seem to be the most important decisions facing them. But as Connor, Seth, Amanita and Nicole venture to the most popular end-of-summer high school party in town, they soon discover there are even more important decisions to be made. Namely, how to outrun the massive wave of mutated undead that have suddenly crashed the party.

WALKING SHADOW
by Clifford Royal Johns

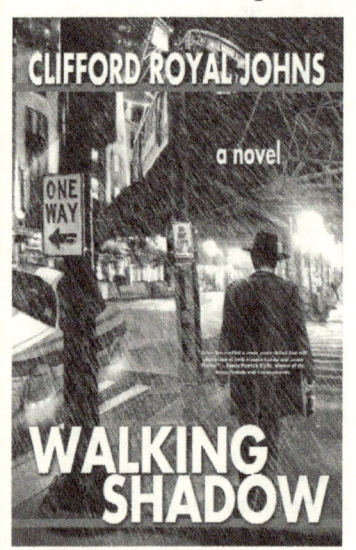

Benny tries to ignore the payment-overdue messages he keeps getting from "Forget What?," a memory removal company. Benny's a slacker, after all, and couldn't pay them even if he wanted to. Then people start trying to kill him, and his life suddenly depends on finding out what memories he has forgotten. Benny relies on his wits, latent skills, and new friends as he investigates his own past; delving deeper and deeper into the underworld of criminals, bad cops, and shady news organizations, all with their own reasons for wanting him to remain ignorant or die.

Walking Shadow is a future-noir science fiction mystery novel with action, humor, suspense, smart dialogue, and a driving first person narrative.

ISBN: 9781937727253

ALSO FROM GRAND MAL PRESS

Ratings Game
by Ryan C. Thomas

ASIN: B005O545IO

With their news stations neck to neck in the ratings, and the threat of hipper, younger anchors waiting to take their places, Roland Stone and Doug Hardwood know they must each come up with a juicy story to save their jobs. When a horrific murder rocks the airwaves, Roland Stone has the inside story. But great minds think alike, and it's just mere hours before Doug Hardwood has the inside scoop on a different serial killer. Two desperate news anchors. One city. A whole lot of bloodshed. Story at eleven.

PLENTIFUL POISON
BY KYLE LYBECK

Denver was ground zero. At the time, nobody knew what they truly had. It was too late once they had a grasp. A killing machine unlike any other: fast, adaptive, and brutally bloodthirsty.

A quiet morning starts for the Baker family, until the news stories start to flood in. The complete absurdity of them seems impossible. That is, until they meet their first rager.

Nobody is safe. Everyone is at risk. All you can do is avoid the poison.

ALSO FROM GRAND MAL PRESS

HAFTMANN'S RULES
BY ROBERT WHITE

The first full-length novel to feature White's recurring private investigator, Thomas Haftmann! Out of jail and back on the streets, Haftmann is hired to find a missing young girl in Boston. But what he uncovers goes beyond just murder, into a world of secret societies, bloodshed, and betrayal beyond anything he has experienced before. HAFTMANN'S RULES is an exhilarating read into one man's maddening journey for truth, justice, and self destruction.

ISBN: 9780982945971

MALCONTENTS

Four thrilling, disturbing novellas by Randy Chandler, Gregory L. Norris, Ryan C. Thomas, and David T. Wilbanks. An unfortunate prostitute joins a freak show to get away from her sordid past only to find that death follows her everywhere. A cooking show host is targeted by a jealous chef who wields a sharp blade and a supernatural grudge. A family man is given a choice by a deadly stranger to decide between love or survival. A former lover enlists the help of a shaman to find his kidnapped girlfriend in a land of mystical demons and gods.

ISBN: 9780982945940

ALSO FROM GRAND MAL PRESS

DEAD THINGS
by Matt Darst

Nearly two decades have passed since the fall of the United States. And the rise of the church to fill the void. Nearly twenty years since Ian Sumner lost his father. And the dead took to the streets to dine on the living. Now Ian and a lost band of survivors are trapped in the wilderness, miles from safety. Pursued by madmen and monsters, they unravel the secrets of the plague...and walk the line of heresy. Ian and this troop need to do more than just survive. More than ever, they must learn to live.

Dead Things has been called "an amalgam of Clerks and everything Crichton and Zombieland."

ISBN: 978-1-937727-10-9

HOBBOMOCK
BY RYAN C. THOMAS

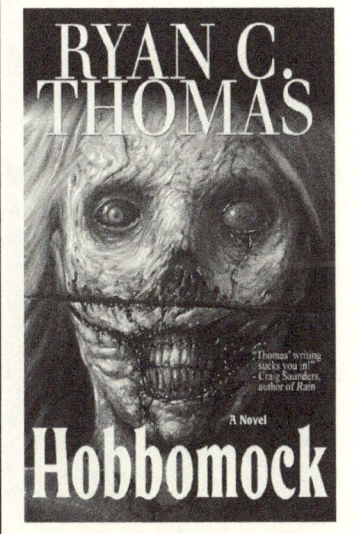

In the late 1800s, deep in the woods of a small New England town, something is called forth for the purposes of revenge and death. Something evil, something blodthirsty, something unstoppable. Now, what has lain dormant for over a century has been released on four unsuspecting teens trying to enjoy a quiet weekend alone. All they want to do is watch some movies and play some games. But their fun is cut short, and what starts as a series of strange and unsuspecting events soon turns into a bloodbath in which no one is safe. Hunter, Josh, Gemma and Kailyn have only hours to figure out how to survive, because the Hobbomock is getting closer, and if it feeds, the world will never be the same.

ALSO FROM GRAND MAL PRESS

Zombie Bitches From Hell
by Zoot Campbell

A plague has turned all the world's women into brain-eating zombies. Join reporter Kent Zimmer as he takes a hot air balloon from Colorado to Massachusetts in search of both his girlfriend and a cure. Along the way he encounters hungry undead, psychotic doctors, evil nuns, racist militias, zombie pregnancy farms, drag queens with machine guns, and neurotic stock brokers. And that's just the tip of the iceberg.

ISBN: 978-0-9829459-0-2

Dust Of The Devil's Land
By Bryan Killian

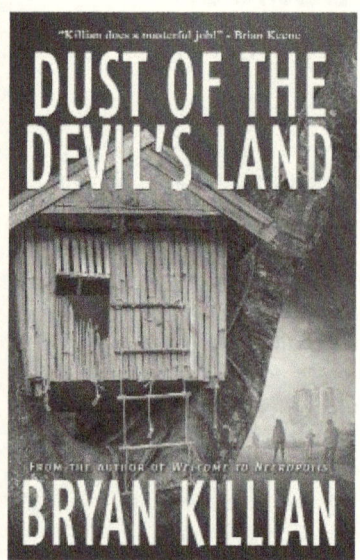

It only took a matter of days for the zombies to overrun Redding, California. Those unlucky enough to survive prayed for salvation at the hands of the military only to find new horrors awaiting them. Two boys, riding out the end of the world in a tree house, are now faced with eventual starvation unless they venture beyond streets of their once idyllic neighborhood. Not an easy situation to be in when you can't trust adults. Pockets of survivors huddle together to form what's left of humanity, not knowing a new threat is clawing its way near. Even the strongest survivors can fall to the teeth and claws of the dead. *Dust of the Devil's Land*, Bryan Killian's follow up to Welcome to Necropolis, explores the agony of loss, the will to survive, and the fight to reclaim humanity. Take a wild ride to the final minutes of all we know.

For more Grand Mal Press titles
please visit us online at
www.grandmalpress.com

Made in the USA
Coppell, TX
20 June 2025

50955642R00132